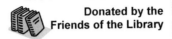
Still**Black**Remains

Kevin Michaels

Literary Wanderlust LLC | Denver

Still Black Remains is a work of fiction. Names, characters, places, and incidents are the products of the author's imagination and have been used fictitiously. Any resemblance to actual events, locales, or persons, living or dead, is entirely coincidental.

Published in the United States by Literary Wanderlust LLC, Denver, Colorado.

www.LiteraryWanderlust.com

ISBN print 978-1-942856-14-6
ISBN digital 978-1-942856-15-3

Cover design: Ruth M'Gonigle
Layout design: Meghan McLean

Printed in the United States of America

AUTHOR'S NOTE

Thanks to a really great team at Literary Wanderlust who helped make this happen, especially my editor Sharon Salonen and my publisher Susan Brooks. Your advice, work, and tireless efforts have been invaluable. I've been fortunate to have been taught by some great teachers and surrounded by a community of writers and editors who gave my stories a platform where readers could find them while helping me find my voice. Thanks to my children, family, and friends for their love (usually) and support (sometimes) and criticism (more often than I would have preferred). None of this could have happened without you.

Most importantly, a special thank you to my wife Helen for her love, constant support, and belief, especially those times when she continued believing in me and my dreams while I was filled with doubt. Your are truly the love of my life and I am thankful every day that we get to take this journey together.

To everyone else who expected to see your names here, it doesn't mean I'm not thinking of you—I just ran out of room.

PROLOGUE

In the morning right before the sun comes up, the neighborhood is still. There is a quiet that rolls up and down the streets, and with it, a calm but uneasy peacefulness that hangs on everything. The low din of cars on the New Jersey Turnpike blends softly with the sharp clatter of PATH trains pulling out of Penn Station before both sounds fade into the distance. There is nothing else at this hour—it is too early for the day to have meaning. It is still hours before anger and pain are born into the streets, and at least for a little while the day holds promise and potential.

Hope.

The morning is about hope and what the day might bring.

Twist is sitting with his back pressed to the bedroom wall, his gray Celtics T-shirt soaked with sweat and clinging to his body, and when he leans forward the wet impression made by his shoulders stretches across the yellowed enamel paint. Twist takes the last drag on a Camel and crushes the butt into the top of a Pepsi can, blinking away the tears created by the curls of smoke. He has been awake for hours—he's not sure if he had ever truly slept, and he is so far into that point where night has turned into morning he's lost track of time. He squeezes his eyes shut for a minute and takes slow deep breaths before letting his head roll backward onto the wall.

He is six feet tall, thin and black, and his whole life has been spent in New Jersey except for six months in Alabama with an aunt when he was ten years old and his mama got sent away for a couple of months. All he remembers about that is the inside of the Greyhound bus and the long hours it took to go south—hours filled with nothing to do but stare out windows, watch the states roll past, and lose himself in thought. Sometimes it seems that all he does now is live from one long, dull stretch of time to another with nothing in between but his thoughts. Here and there he can find moments filled with purpose, but those minutes never mean much when measured against the rest of his time.

Twist opens his eyes and stares again at his reflection in the bedroom window. He doesn't look twenty-five anymore; probably never did. The years have passed by too quickly to ever be meaningful the same way they are for other people. His expression is hard and tired and his eyes drawn, but at least the face looks familiar. Same haircut high on top and shaved close on the sides, the diamond stud in one ear and two silver hoops in the other, with that jagged scar jutting out from the corner of his right eye and down toward his mouth. Nothing that's changed much from every other morning he can remember.

At least that much is good.

It's the other times—the times when he can't recognize the reflection—that make it difficult to know who he is or where he's come from.

Sometimes he'll look in a mirror and see a stranger's face. That face is different and unfamiliar; like it belongs to somebody he's never met and doesn't know—a face filled with hurt and pain. Maybe a face he's passed on the street or seen on the basketball courts while going one-on-one for twenty bucks a point. The kind of nameless, unrecognizable face that could belong to anyone from the neighborhood. Nobody who meant anything to him. Just somebody you pass without thought—the kind of person you look at but never really see.

Twist stares at his own reflection and wonders what that's supposed to mean; if that stranger in the mirror has a life any better than his own.

CHAPTER ONE

They find their target as he is coming out of a Baskin-Robbins with a woman half his age, and everyone in the SUV knows he's the one. Twist figures it will go down so fast the guy won't have time to react.

As long as nothing goes wrong and they get it right.

There are no second chances.

The 9mm is pressed hard against the small of his back but it doesn't hurt, and Twist can barely feel the gun barrel on his skin. It's there but nothing that matters. It's no different than the feeling he gets when the silver cross around his neck rubs against his chest or catches in the buttons of his shirt and the edge cuts into his skin. It's just something that is. His stare is edgy and straight ahead, his eyes focused on the cars pulling into the intersection in front of him and the others jockeying for parking slots along the curb in the Belleville, New Jersey neighborhood. The gun creates a small measure of comfort, even when he doesn't feel or think about it. The nine takes the edge off his nervousness. Twist likes the reassurance it gives.

He presses his back against the seat and keeps his hands tight around the steering wheel.

He can feel the nine digging sharply into his skin.

It's a comfortable kind of hurt.

A block ahead the police cruiser he's been trailing slows to let a young mother push a stroller through the crosswalk, then turns the corner. There's risk doing this mid-afternoon; cops are everywhere. A black-and-white can pop out of a side street or pull up behind you with flashing rooftop lights and everything can change in ways that are never expected. It takes patience to wait for the right moment.

Waiting is something Twist has learned to do very well.

He can do it forever, if he has to.

It is a hot August afternoon. Without a breeze the air is stale and heavy. Even when something blows down the street it carries the same kind of heat and offers nothing in return. At least nothing that changes anything.

The guy is easy to spot. There is nobody around him and the younger woman, and hardly anyone else on the sidewalk; the two of them are so absorbed in each other and their own conversation it's like they're the only people who matter. From the view of the Expedition the guy looks about six feet tall, average weight, in his late forties or early fifties, with long dark hair turning gray and pulled back in a ponytail. He is wearing a navy suit, white shirt, and red tie, with one hand in his pocket and the other holding an ice cream cone, shaking his head and laughing at something the woman said. She is shorter, with dark hair that is almost as long as the guy's and a small, compact body.

She turns to toss a napkin in a trash can and Twist can see that her face is young and pretty—she's not more than nineteen or twenty. He also sees the outline of her belly straining against a floral sun dress as she moves.

"Looks like his woman is pregnant," he says. "Didn't notice that before. Did you?"

"Guess the Guinea still be cuttin' his bitch, huh?" Rasheed says from the backseat.

"She don't matter," Cuba says as he rolls down the window and flicks his cigarette butt out. "She ain't a part of this."

Cuba sits in the passenger seat next to Twist wearing a red Cardinals jersey with a silver and black Raiders baseball cap turned backward, wiping away the sweat trickling down his forehead and cheek. He is taller than Twist, shaved head and gold caps on his teeth, with a harder edge to his stare. There is anger and hurt in everything about him. The two kids in the back seat are wearing black Nike warm-ups, T-shirts, and the same kind of Raiders hats Cuba wears.

Cuba holds a .45 in his lap, rechecking the clip one last time before jamming it inside the waistband of his pants and pulling the black bandanna around his face. He wears a weird smile on his face before it disappears behind the bandanna. "I like this, you know? How it feels doing this," he says. "Kind of thing I understand best."

It probably wouldn't bother Cuba too much if he has to shoot the guy with the pony tail, or even take out the pregnant woman if she gets too close or becomes a distraction. Things like that never get in the way of his decisions, and never seem to linger with him afterwards.

He doesn't carry around scars like Twist does.

The guy stops at the corner, licking his ice cream cone and sharing a smile while waiting for the traffic light to change. For him there's nothing different about this day. He can't see the dangers that are a minute into his future, and any nightmares he has ever had have nothing to do with Twist or Cuba or the other kids in the car.

He doesn't know anything yet about Twist's world or the fears it can create.

"Let's roll," Cuba says in a quiet voice.

"Hold up," Twist says.

Another black-and-white inches down the street from the opposite direction. Twist folds back in his seat, easing out of sight until the cruiser finally passes and disappears in his rearview mirror.

"Cops everywhere," Cuba says.

"Do this fast," Twist says. "Ain't time to waste."

"Been out of time ever since this whole situation started," Cuba says.

Twist is watching the traffic signals, counting the number of DO NOT WALK blinks. Establishing a pattern and getting into a comfortable rhythm as the two kids in the backseat slip out each side of the SUV.

Rasheed eases between two cars at the curb and onto the sidewalk, moving quickly, but not fast enough to draw attention. Little Joe, nicknamed LJ for short, goes the other way, dodging cars as he hurries across Passaic then ducks into the shadows and corners of buildings along that side of the street. Twist loses sight of him but knows LJ is hurrying to get to the intersection before their ponytailed target gets there. Doing it without turning heads.

He taps the gas pedal when he sees LJ start across the street. He moves fast but is not yet running, and gently pulls the black bandanna over his mouth and nose. Rasheed comes up behind the couple, his own bandanna masking his face with his Raiders cap pulled down low to hide the remaining features. He's close now. Space and distance are key. The timing has to click, the same way it's supposed to be perfect when you hit a guy with a cross court pass or catch an outlet throw on a fast break, running past the last guard with the ball bouncing inches ahead of you. A second too early or too late and nothing comes together. When that happens there aren't many ways left to pull everything back together.

Twist times it so he's cutting the wheel and pulling into the intersection when the light turns green, slamming on the brakes, and blocking the crosswalk as LJ hits the guy from one direction and Rasheed cuts his legs out from behind him.

It goes down exactly as planned.

The guy has no time to react.

He turns his head for just a second, and in that moment Twist sees something in the Guinea's face. It could be surprise or shock—maybe confusion. He's not sure if its fear. Whatever is there doesn't last.

The guy can't even manage to spit out much of a protest.

"What—the fuck!" he cries out.

He drops to the ground, his ice cream cone landing in the street as he flips over Rasheed and lands hard on his back and shoulder before rolling onto his stomach. LJ is on top of him with a forearm pushed hard against his throat. He buries a fist in the Guinea's side then pumps another shot to the same spot to keep him down.

Cuba is out of the Expedition with the .45 in his hand, crossing the pavement in three quick steps. "You a dead man, motherfucker!"

The guy scrambles for balance and position on all fours on the sidewalk with LJ riding his back. The gun doesn't scare him and he doesn't give up the fight. At least not easily.

For a moment the woman watches in stunned silence, then lets out a hysterical scream.

The guy kicks left and right, then gets a hand free and tries reaching inside his coat. LJ takes a handful of the guy's hair and has his other arm wrapped underneath the Guinea's chin, struggling to hold him down while Rasheed wrestles his hands to his sides.

"I'll fucking kill you," the guy spits between clenched teeth. "All you bastards"

The woman reaches for him but is afraid to get close, and stands planted on the sidewalk. "Please!" she cries.

"Shut up, bitch!" Cuba snarls, leveling his gun at her.

In that moment Twist thinks he's going to pull the trigger.

Cuba shoves away the woman, grabs the guy by his jacket, and pulls him off the sidewalk.

It feels like every eye on the street is watching them; like it's happening in slow motion while the rest of the world cruises past at regular speed. Twist sits behind the wheel, watching the struggle, checking for more cops and signs of other Guinea suits but sees nobody. It doesn't mean they aren't there; just that he can't see them or they haven't shown up yet. An old couple coming from the First Union Bank watches from the other side of the street but they have no idea what's going on. Cars slow in the intersection as drivers try for a better view but nobody stops and nobody offers help.

They are all too scared to take a risk for something that doesn't involve them.

The Guinea flails, trying desperately to get free or connect with a punch, but Rasheed has him locked in a bear hug with his arms pinned against his body. Cuba has his hand wrapped in the guy's jacket. The three of them drag him toward the car but the struggle is so hard and furious they can't move him more than a couple of feet at a time. Every couple of steps they have to stop to tighten their grips. Cuba whacks him once across the face with the butt of the .45 but it doesn't take away any of his fight.

"Hey!" a voice yells out. "What's going on?"

A tall guy, bald and in his late forties, in a suit and tie drops his briefcase and comes toward them. He says something else but Cuba wheels around and cracks the .45 across his face so hard that it drops him to the sidewalk before he can become a hero. Blood sprays from his nose and mouth as he hits the ground, and his words are lost before he can spit out the rest of the sentence.

Cuba buries a foot into his ribs.

The man curls up on the sidewalk and doesn't move again.

There are suddenly more voices. Words and noises and reactions as people see what is going on, and Twist watches the crowd on the street grow.

"Oh my God!" somebody cries.

"What the fuck is going on?"

The woman finds her voice again. "Call the cops! Please!"

"Stop!" somebody else yells but nobody moves.

The image of the bald guy on the sidewalk in a pool of his own blood and broken teeth holds everyone in their place. There are more cries for help but the crowd shrinks backward at the sight of Cuba's .45 leveled in their direction. Nobody else is willing to get involved.

At least not without the cops there to take away the danger and their own fears.

It's not worth that kind of trouble.

"You're all fucking dead," the ponytail is roaring as he works a hand free and tries reaching inside his coat again. "You don't know who I am."

Cuba gets a hand around the guy's tie. "Don't fucking care a shit about who you are. Know what you did—"

"You're dead men! All of you—"

"So are you, motherfucker."

Twist is edgy in the Expedition, certain they've wasted too much time and that it's taking too long. They should be in the car by now, racing back to Newark instead of struggling with him on the pavement. A black-and-white can show up while they're dragging him to the SUV. Everything can change in a heartbeat. With each passing second the chances of getting nailed grow and the risks increase.

He has to make it happen faster.

Twist comes out of the Ford with the nine in his hand. He grabs the woman by the arm and yanks her into the street where the Guinea can see her.

Twist aims at her belly.

"You see this?" he yells. "See where we are! You out of time."

The guy's head snaps up.

"No!' he wails. "Angelina!"

"You don't want her and everything inside her dead you get your ass in the car now, motherfucker," Twist yells. "No more fucking around!"

The guy lifts his head high enough to see his woman reaching out for him. Tears streak her face; her eyes are wide open and scared at the end of Twist's nine, but the guy is helpless. He stops struggling and hangs his head, weighing the choices offered and the consequences of giving up. There's nothing else to do.

They drag him into the SUV, headfirst to the back seat with Rasheed riding him down to the floor in a headlock while LJ bounces across the seat. He fishes between the cushions for one of the .22s, jabbing it under his chin. Twist bangs his head on the door jam as he slides inside and gets behind the wheel. Cuba is already in the front seat, ripping the bandanna from his face and throwing the Raiders cap through the open window. It drops to the sidewalk by the woman's feet.

"Calling card," he sneers. "Let the Guineas know who was here."

Twist slips the car into drive and roars down the street, letting the speed of the car slam the doors on its own.

"You'll all be dead," the guy says in a muffled voice face down on the floor. "All you motherfuckers. I'm talking to a car full of dead men."

Cuba just smiles and shakes his head.

"Shut the fuck up," LJ tells him.

"You our bitch now," Rasheed says.

Twist looks back in the rear view mirror. The woman is in the intersection, chasing the Expedition as it races away. He thinks he can hear her voice above the engine but the sounds of the street blend together and Twist can't be sure what it is he hears. She doesn't get far before giving up the chase. Same way her old man did. A crowd of people rushes to her, although the last thing Twist sees before he turns his head are the people who stay riveted to the sidewalk and don't move, and the other ones who walk away quickly like it's none of their business. The old couple from the bank have already turned away from the scene.

He's sure somebody is scribbling down the license plate number but it's a waste of time. Within an hour the plates will be at the bottom of the Passaic River and the car abandoned somewhere along a dead stretch of road between Elizabeth and Linden near the Turnpike oil refineries. With any luck it'll never be found.

They drag the guy hard into the back seat. They pull out a .45 from inside the Guinea's coat and toss it to the front. They take his cell phone and throw it out a window. LJ has the gun aimed at the guy's head as Rasheed leans hard on him, using his body to pin him against the seat so he can't move. The front of the guy's shirt is ripped, buttons are missing, and a flap of material hangs loose from the chest where a pocket had once been attached. His coat is pulled over his arms and shoulders and his tie hangs loose, dangling at an odd angle from his neck. There is blood on his face and a large purple welt under one eye but he still fights, trying hard to break free. This time he refuses to give up so easily.

LJ buries a fist in his stomach that sucks air from his lungs and slows his fight.

"Ease up."

He shows a big smile. "Should have killed the bitch when you had the chance," he says to Twist, cocky and full of himself now.

"Yeah, put a bullet in her belly and see if the little Guinea bastard inside comes out shitting lead," Rasheed laughs.

"Motherfuckers!" the guy says, thrashing again. "You're all dead!"

They just laugh at him.

"You ain't got nothing else to say?"

"I'm gonna kill you. All of you," he cries, straining hard to get free. "I'm gonna hunt you down like fucking dogs. Cut out your fucking tongues and wipe my ass with them—

"Fuck you—then fuck your families."

LJ grabs his hair and yanks hard, opening his face enough for Cuba to reach back and slap his cheek with the butt of the .45.

Twist sees the smile that comes over Cuba's face. It's the kind of smile that says Cuba likes the feel of his hand and the metal against the other guy's flesh.

The skin reddens and a small, thin line suddenly streaks across the cheek. A moment passes before the blood explodes from the cut, streaming down his face and smearing his white collar.

"Ain't gonna be you doing no killing, white man," Cuba says. "Not no more."

Twist watches in the rear view mirror. There is a defiant look in the guy's eye that doesn't go away, even though he can't move, while the guys in the back seat laugh at the blood streaming down his face and mock the cries his woman made. It's a penetrating stare—a stare that cuts a hole in his chest when he hits him with it.

A stare that slices its edge into Twist and gives him a shudder.

Rasheed jerks a canvas hood down over the guy's head before he can train that stare on Twist much longer.

Just as well. There are enough fears haunting his sleep; Twist doesn't need any more to keep him awake.

Their Ford Expedition slows behind a line of cars approaching the traffic light at Passaic Avenue. A few heads on the street turn but there's nothing of interest and nothing out of the ordinary, and the stares are the kind that don't hold too long.

Twist grips the wheel tighter; the faces he sees are no different than the line of cars in the street; all of them stuck in one place and going nowhere.

Like everything else he knows.

Making him edgy and tense.

Twist keeps looking in the rearview, expecting to see the flashing lights of local patrol cars coming up behind them. Hearing their sirens. Then seeing uniforms coming at them with their guns drawn.

The Expedition is a bulky four door with New Jersey plates, a few months old and showroom clean except for scratches in the driver's side door and a dented quarter panel behind the rear door. Nothing that makes it different from any other car on the street. The .22s and .45s are stuffed under seats or stashed in a hole torn out beneath the dashboard, and the empty beer cans that had rolled around the floor were tossed once they turned off the highway. Nothing to draw suspicion. Conversation fades. The heavy bass had been thumping from the speakers and through open windows when Twist left Newark and steered up Route 21, but the sound is so low now it can barely be heard above the noises on the street, the sounds of the air conditioning blowing through the vents, and the hard idle of the engine as the Expedition inches forward another foot and stops again.

"Never could handle waiting for answers," Cuba says. "I like making something happen, you know?"

"Doing this takes it to a new level. Makes me feel like we taking care of business for Ice and Spider."

"And Malik," Twist adds.

The two kids in the back nod their agreement. They are soldiers— along for the ride because they provide muscle—sixteen, maybe seventeen but no older; razor cuts in their hair with the kind of tough cool and cocky attitudes that come at that age. Jumpy and hungry to do somebody, they grab Cuba's words like junkies reaching for a needle.

"Know he was one of them," Rasheed says. "Let's take him out now."

LJ nods. He's a kid with nothing but attitude and balls. LJ's not even his real name although nobody can remember what it is. He had a brother named Joe six or seven-years older than him, and when he was just a kid trying to hook into the gang he got tagged as Little Joe because he was always a step behind his brother, no matter where his brother went or what he did. The name stuck, even after his brother got shanked in the showers in the Essex County lockup. "Got to be something else we can do now besides driving back home in this four door big body."

Twist shoots back a stare.

"You got something better you need to be doing?"

"Ain't that," Rasheed says. "Just all this driving ain't getting nothing done. Got me lunchin', know what I'm saying? We should be on this motherfucker."

"Taking a lot of time," the other kid says, "and we ain't getting no answers."

"Don't matter how much time it takes," Twist says as he eases his foot off the brake and inches the car forward. "What matters is we get this right and don't fuck it up. Think I need to learn you how it works. Learn the game."

There is something in his voice that holds their attention. A firmness that brings back the silence and turns all eyes to the street again. Twist has them, at least for the moment. "Ain't got no second chances," he says.

Their silence doesn't mean much. The voice Twist carries has everything to do with longevity and nothing to do with respect or authority.

When the light turn green Twist turns right on Passaic and the conversation fades away.

◆ ◆ ◆

Twist jams his foot down harder on the gas pedal and cuts back across Main Street.

He can take Passaic south to Franklin Street, follow it back to Route 21, and with no traffic or cops be in downtown Newark inside ten minutes like they planned. Or follow it north around Belleville and Nutley to Route 3, then drive east a few miles to the Meadowlands before taking the Turnpike south to Newark. Once in grade school, Twist had gone there to see the Nets play the Bulls— back when the Bulls still had Jordan and Pippen, and before the Nets meant anything. Back then it was easy to get tickets because nobody went to the arena, even when it was the Bulls or the Lakers or the Celtics and they had all those championships between them. That was when the Newark Recreation Department did things like that for city kids, sponsoring days to the beach, trips to ball games, and outings to parks in white suburbs outside the city where the kids were never welcomed, only tolerated, and none of them ever felt comfortable. Those were the days when things like basketball were all that mattered to kids like Twist.

Before everything changed.

Before even basketball stopped mattering.

Twist keeps the SUV at least two car lengths behind the one in front, his eyes darting from side to side, taking in everything as he drives. The other guys are watching the street, eyeing every car that approaches the same way they would check out a new girl in the neighborhood or one passing the courts while they played one-on-one. Looking for signs of trouble or any kind of clues beyond the obvious body language and expressions.

It will go like that until they get back to Newark.

He maintains the same speed, never running yellow lights and always keeping an open eye for a cop in the wrong place who could fuck up their plans too easily.

Success comes from being ready for things like that.

Twist drives the Expedition cautiously along Passaic, his eyes moving from storefront to storefront and from person to person, watching the street the same way he would sometimes stare at that stranger's reflection in the mirror. The neighborhood feels motionless and unreal, and he feels disconnected from his surroundings.

He thinks about that middle-aged white couple coming out of the First Union. They were late fifties, overweight, and looked like the kind of blue collar couple that live a lifetime in a place like Belleville. Oblivious to danger. Probably the kind of people who aren't happy but can't do anything about it. Change has never been an option or a consideration. The two of them weren't more than fifteen feet away when everything went down and until minutes ago they didn't even know the guys in the Expedition existed. They didn't know anything about Twist or who he is or where he was going, and if Twist had kept driving he never would have existed to them in any way—never be that nightmare that will creep into their thoughts in the quiet times of the night when there is nothing left to worry about or fear.

Their world has nothing to do with his—if he had kept going the two never would have collided.

That guy crumpled on the sidewalk will never forget them for the rest of his life. No matter how much time passes or where he goes, he's lost something he'll never get back—all because he tried getting involved. Fifteen seconds worth of involvement that will haunt his sleep for years.

For the rest of his life he will never be the same.

Things like that make Twist think about fate and destiny, and wonder about the power he has to change people's worlds unintentionally.

The way his own world has been changed by things out of his control.

Cuba is on the cell. "It's all good," he says.

"Be glad to get out of this fucking town," Cuba says in a low voice when he hangs up. He starts again but something catches him and freezes the words in his throat, and nothing more comes out.

He turns his head and stares back out the window.

In the back seat the Guinea starts kicking at the seat. Rasheed buries another fist in the guy's stomach that sucks more air from his longs.

"Step off," Twist snarls.

Rasheed shrugs. "Just want to keep him quiet."

LJ nods. "This the best it's gonna get for this motherfucker."

Twist just shakes his head and stays quiet.

Tough talk, especially when neither one of them has had the kind of experience it takes to do the things they want to see and experience. Until minutes earlier all they had ever done was jack cars on South Orange Avenue across from Seton Hall University and try bump and run robberies on Eisenhower Parkway near the mall. Maybe pistol whip one of the junkies deep into them for street cash, and pull a gun on some suburban kid coming out of the Walmart. Or maybe roll a late night commuter hurrying out of an office building near Penn Station. But neither one knows what it really feels like to hold a .45 or a nine, point it at somebody walking down the street, and squeeze the trigger. Feel the power that comes from the gun. Feel the way it lurches and kicks in recoil. Smell that hard, nasty odor coming from the gun or the way your own sweat smells and how dry your mouth tastes when your finger is wrapped around the trigger.

Shake about it later when you're lying in bed trying to sleep. Feel it for days every time you open your eyes, and never get it out of your head.

Neither one of them ever watched the bullets they fired tear through flesh and bone and leave a hole the size of your fist in somebody's chest. Never seen the kind of damage it causes or know the hurt they're responsible for. And never realized the way they can change a world.

None of the blood they've ever seen in the streets has been on their hands.

Blood created by the consequences of their own actions.

He glances over at Cuba but he is silent, lighting another Camel and tipping the sunglasses off the bridge of his nose as he stares out the window. Whatever he can say about those kinds of things stay buried inside.

Twist draws a deep breath and keeps driving.

CHAPTER TWO

The night is no cooler than the day.

August is like that. There is no difference between night and day except for the darkness that closes in. Everything else feels the same.

"Too fucking hot for me," Rocco says, shaking his head slowly. "Can't stand to be sweating, you know? Not like this."

"It's summer. Gets hot in the summer."

"Ain't never liked summer," he says. "Be happier when it's winter. All that snow and shit, you know? I like that."

"That's fucked up."

Rocco shakes his head. "Nah. Just how it is, dawg."

He is black, like everyone who is a Skull. Tall, twenty, and built like a linebacker with broad shoulders and thick arms; when he enters a room he fills the door. Two diamonds in one ear and a thick gold chain around his neck. He moves with some flash but he's still just a soldier—not a leader. Another guy who reacts better than he thinks. Guys like him are valuable because he does what he is told to do and does it without questions.

He flashes a smile that is all teeth but no humor. "Need to navigate, if that's okay. Just get out of here and chill out for a while."

Twist nods but stays at the window, watching the street.

"You want something from downstairs? A beer? Weed? Maybe some more smokes?"

Twist shakes his head.

He can see his reflection silhouetted in the window. He takes in the face and the nose and the knife scar slicing across the cheek, soaking up the lines and the details on the skin. He stares at the eyes, trying to look beyond the reflection but he can never get close enough to see anything.

He stays where he is without answering.

Rocco finally shrugs and slips quietly out of the room while Twist stares out the window.

Somewhere a baby cries and the high pitched wail carries up and down the street. The noise gets in Twist's head as he finishes his Camel. At first it tears at him and he badly wants back the silence, but after a while he finds there is something comforting and familiar about it.

It is something that makes him feel like part of the neighborhood, and that he belongs.

It's the kind of thing he can grow to like if given a chance.

He stands at the window on the second floor, looking down on Murray Street. There's not much left of the neighborhood. A few houses and buildings scattered around vacant lots filled with weeds, trash, and broken glass. The street is quiet now. Down the block a couple of twelve-year-olds bounce a basketball, playing keep-away from a younger kid. The younger kid is too slow and short to have a real shot at getting the ball, and all he can do is wave his arms helplessly while racing back and forth between the older kids, always a few seconds too late. Missing by no more than an inch or two. A girl not much older than the twelve-year-olds skips rope on the pavement, hopping and bouncing to a hip hop cadence Twist can't make out. He catches an occasional word and phrase but nothing sticks.

The old lady across the street pokes her head out the door, tentative at first, then shuffles across the porch to peer at the kids. A couple of years ago she might have yelled at the boys to get out of the street or for the girl to hurry home, but that was when her life was different. Twist remembers how it was when they first moved into the building at 38 Murray. She was hard and tough then, standing on her porch waving a broomstick at them.

"Ain't gonna have you no good punks ruin my street," she warned. "Ain't no hoodlums taking over while I'm living here!"

The guys laughed at her.

"Crazy old bitch," they called her. "You don't know us to talk like that!"

"You stay away," she warned. "Keep your hands off what don't belong to you."

The guys just laughed more.

"I know what you hoodlums think you gonna do," she said. "And if the police won't stop you, I will!"

Although they laughed none of them doubted her seriousness; there wasn't a guy in the Skulls who didn't think she wouldn't smack that broomstick across somebody's head if given a chance. None of them ever challenged her.

But that was before her sixteen-year-old grandson took an unloaded .38 inside an all-night convenience store in Nutley. Before he ran out of the store with forty-two dollars from the register stuffed in a pocket and got gunned down in the parking lot by two white cops who claimed the kid pointed the gun at them. Cops who said they couldn't tell the gun had no bullets and shot him eleven times. Before the all-white grand jury refused to indict the cops by saying their actions were justifiable.

Now the old lady watches the street for a moment before hurrying back inside to lock her doors and windows against the night.

"Sure you don't want nothing?" Rocco calls again from the hallway.

Twist doesn't answer and the question dies in silence.

He can't see them in the darkness but there are others on the street too. Guys hide in dark corners, passing Marlboros and killing time. Corner boys watch the street, eyeing every car that slows in the intersection, fingers pressed against the speed dial on cell phones. Ready to run if they need to. There are two guys in the burgundy Sentra at the end of the block, wearing Skull colors and carrying guns, along with another guy downstairs in what was once the auto repair shop's waiting area, positioned behind the door with an AR-15. The gun is powerful enough to shoot a hole in the front of the old lady's house and take out somebody standing in the back yard.

All of them waiting—just in case something bad goes down.

Bone isn't saying anything but everybody in the building and on the street knows it's in case the Italians show up to take back their prisoner.

"They ain't gonna try nothing," Bone sneered earlier. "Not on our turf."

"Ain't got the balls to do that," Cuba agreed.

Twist isn't so sure.

"Be stupid, but you can't figure out the Guineas," he said. "All them rules about right and wrong. Same way we got respect for colors, they got their own code they live."

"Shit's fucked up."

"It's who they are and what they about."

Bone stared at him, looking for something in Twist's expression but Twist couldn't figure out what it was. "You think they that stupid? Try something like that with all the cops we got circling the block all the time?"

"Think we be stupid not to be ready," Twist answered. "Don't hurt none to ramp up security. Better to take no chances then get surprised."

"Word," Bone finally agreed, but the way he stared at him stuck with Twist for a long time.

There are no second thoughts and no second guessing about what has happened. Nothing has changed from the afternoon, except now they are in deeper than when it started and there is no turning back. If there was a chance to walk away, it's gone.

"No way this goes away by itself," Cuba said on the ride back, still smiling to himself.

"It was never gonna go away," Twist said.

Cuba nodded. "Not by itself."

"Ain't no more in-betweens," Twist said. "One way or another something happens but it don't go away."

Cuba bummed a cigarette from one of the kids in the back seat. "The Guineas gonna be looking at us different now. Ain't gonna be the same no more."

None of them can really know if that is good or bad.

There is a war council downstairs with Cuba and Bone and some of the older guys huddled around a kitchen table, talking about next steps. Tough talk and bullshit. They can't see it but it's still too early; there are too many loose ends and anything can happen.

All they can do is wait to see what develops, and see what the Italians want to do about Valentine.

Valentine.

Twist repeats the name softly to himself. That's the guy's name—Michael Valentine. He is upstairs on the third floor, tied up and locked in an eight-by-ten room at the top of the stairs. The room isn't much bigger than a jail cell, and the way the dormered ceiling cuts away chunks of space, there's barely enough room to stand up straight in most spots. The windows were bricked shut a year earlier, and the walls reinforced with extra studs and wire mesh, along with a heavier layer of thick sheet rock. There is no way Valentine is getting out of that room without somebody in the building hearing him.

There is also another guy standing outside the locked door, holding an AR-15.

Just in case.

A couple of months ago the guys hung a backboard and rim on the side of the building to shoot baskets, and Twist listens now for the occasional thump of the ball banging off the rim but hears nothing.

Just the sound of that baby crying somewhere down the street.

There is a bed in the room along with a broken black-and-white TV that had been there when they took over the garage, but Twist isn't sure about anything else. Some of the younger guys use the room to bang twelve- and thirteen-year-old neighborhood girls when there's no better place, but no one else has any use for the room.

Twist can't even remember if the bed has sheets.

Valentine is in the room, his hands tied behind his back, with duct tape across his mouth and the hood probably still covering his face. He has been that way for hours and nobody cares about him. What only matters is that he is alive; they have to do something with him to send the right kind of message to the Italians, and it has to be soon.

"Room up there gets hot," Twist said earlier. "I was one of the ones who bricked them windows last summer. I remember that."

Cuba shot him a look. "So?"

"So maybe we need to find him a fan," Twist said. "Or at least walk him into one of the other rooms every hour. Get him some air. Can't hurt."

"Fuck that," Cuba said.

"No danger doing that."

"What if he sees something?" somebody else put in.

"Like what?" Twist said. "The house down the street? Asphalt? A vacant lot? Ain't nothing to see that's gonna matter."

"Fuck him," Cuba said. "He don't matter. Who gives a fuck if the man is comfortable?"

"It ain't right," Twist said but nobody listened. "Leaving him like that."

"What's right don't matter no more," Bone put in. "Wasn't right what happened to Ice. And Spider. Wasn't right they got Malik."

"You forgetting that this is personal," Cuba said to Twist.

Twist shook his head.

"I didn't forget nothing."

"Then why the fuck you care about what's right?" Cuba said.

"Ain't for you to worry about," Bone told him. "Don't matter none if he's comfortable."

"You worry about organization and execution," Cuba added tersely. "Let me worry about taking care of the prisoner. That's my job, not yours."

It was right about then that Twist decided he had heard enough bullshit from them to last the rest of his night. He took his pack of Camels and climbed the stairs to the second floor, leaving them to argue about what might happen next. Sometimes he hears Cuba and Bone throw "organization and execution" at him like it's something old and dirty that doesn't matter as much as what they've got. And sometimes Twist asks himself how much more of Cuba and Bone he can put up with. But it isn't worth getting into it with them.

Besides, he knows Valentine is probably dead.

It is only a matter of time before they kill him. They didn't grab him off the street in the heart of his own neighborhood just to rough him up then let him go as some kind of warning. They are too far past things like warnings.

There are no answers that way.

Valentine is a soldier, just like Ice and Spider and most of the guys in the Skulls, soldiers turn into casualties in the blink of an eye. You expect to lose people every time you make a stand, the same way the Italians expect it.

Even though the losses hurt.

Now Twist walks around the building, lost in the silence of the rooms, thinking about what it will mean to each of them when that happens.

The old garage is cold and lonely, even when filled with voices, laughter, and music. It's a three-story brick building that had once been an auto repair shop owned by somebody's older brother but Twist has a hard time remembering who or whatever happened to the guy. The phone is still connected but nobody talks business on it; it's just a front, like the stack of tires in front of the garage bay doors and the sign over the door advertising $19.99 OIL CHANGE. It's the kind of place where there is always activity; guys coming and going at all hours, stopping by to shoot pool on the downstairs table or playing Xbox, pouring drinks, or crashing in one of the bedrooms on the second floor. It is in the heart of their turf, in downtown Newark, right off the intersection of Broad and Murray Streets, not more than fifty yards from the train tracks. Close enough to Penn Station that the Amtrak Acela and New Jersey Transit diesels shake the building whenever the trains rumble into the station.

There are guns on tables and hidden inside false walls, with bullets and ammo clips stacked in crates, boxes, and barrels in the basement. Guys sit in circles at tables with .22s and nines stuffed in their pants, using rolled up dollar bills to snort lines of coke or crystal meth stretched across table tops. Other guys sit slumped in chairs, absorbed in the games on their iPhones or the Xbox. There is a Jeep in one of the bays, with a tank of gas, keys in the ignition, and a loaded nine under the seat in case they need a fast escape. There are guards and sentries posted inside as well as somebody on the street watching for anything out of the ordinary.

Until this afternoon they watched for other gangs or worried about cops from the Major Crimes Unit busting down their doors.

Now they are waiting for the Italians and worried about what happens next.

There are a few neighbors but nobody gives them grief anymore or stops them from doing business. Sometimes the fathers of those twelve-year-old birds who wound up in that third-floor bedroom bang at the door, but staring down the barrel of a .45 and facing a line of guys can take away a man's courage. Those fathers were dangerous until they realized their little girls didn't belong to daddy no more. Then everything changed about the way they looked at the building.

38 Murray is everything to the Skulls. It is a place to meet and plan and organize their business. A place to plan for their future.

A place to decide how a man gets to live his life.

Or how his life is to end.

It's funny, Twist thinks, how things can fall apart in the blink of an eye.

It happened that way with the Italians.

The Italians used the gang to move coke, crack, speed, grass, meth, and heroin into schools and neighborhoods of Newark and

East Orange and Jersey City, and the Skulls shared in the profits. Anybody in those towns who wanted to score was a customer; from junkies looking for five dollar vials of crack to Rutgers law students buying nickel bags of weed and speed to suits at the Gateway Center discreetly buying dime tins of coke. The old Italian who put it together, Tony Giaccolone, got shipments of coke, heroin, and weed from the Colombians and Asians, cut it downtown and in safe houses in nearby Irvington, and used the Skulls to distribute it. The Italians were layers removed from the action on the street, and if anything went bad the cops would never spend the kind of time and effort it would take to trace it to Giaccolone. Corner boys who got busted knew how to deal with the cops; nobody snitched and nobody ever gave up anything that led back to the Italians. At least nothing the cops could ever prove. The drugs dwarfed what loan sharking, numbers, and pimping made them on other parts of the street. It gave Giaccolone's organization market share and control in Newark.

The Skulls got power out of it, and that was more important than the money they brought in.

"Ain't just about the Benjamins," Bone once said. "Be about the intangibles."

"Got to be all that."

All part of the game.

In their neighborhoods turf and space matter more than anything else. Every gang wants a bigger slice of territory than what they own, and battles rage over turf that at times could be as small and insignificant as a bus stop on Market Street, or as large as the acreage in Branch Brook Park. Fierce, bloody wars sometimes go on forever until nobody remembers how the fighting began. The drug money the Skulls earned created definite advantages. It financed guns and ammo, and superior firepower led to more control and more power.

That kind of control and power feeds on itself and makes everybody hungrier for more.

Twist saw opportunity—an opportunity to turn cash into legitimate businesses. An opportunity to get out of the game, or at least change it.

But others got greedy with power, even though it was disguised as ambition. They hungered for more—more of everything, including things others had. They started talking about cutting out the Italians, working directly with the Colombians and Asians while taking bigger chunks of the profits for themselves. And if that wasn't possible, then at least taking a bigger piece of the business than what they got.

The game would stay the same, only the playing field would get larger while taking on a whole new look.

They had been passing around joints and a bottle of Hennesseys downstairs in the kitchen while sharing two whores picked up off South Orange Avenue near Seton Hall in one of the upstairs bedrooms.

Bone took a deep drag off a joint before passing it to Cuba.

"Been thinking," he said. "Been thinking we working cheap for these Guinea motherfuckers too long."

Everyone just looked at him as he sat there in silence, holding the smoke in his lungs.

Nobody answered.

But it wasn't a new idea.

Bone is a year older than Twist, not much taller, with hard, sharp features and a large, flat nose. Hair that is short and cut in a wedge, wearing a denim jacket over a white Rum-D.M.C. T-shirt, with heavy chains around his neck. There was a murder conviction in his past that had been plea-bargained down to manslaughter with three years in East Jersey State Prison, along with some possession and felony assault charges that never stuck. There were other incidents and episodes in his past as well, but those were common things shared with the others at the table. Things guys wore as proudly as they wore their colors.

That kind of time in East Jersey State gives him an edge none of the others can match. It is an edge that is more than even Twist owns.

"Maybe we got to change things," Bone said. "Time to stop being their niggers and take a bigger piece of this action."

Ice looked up from his Bud. "You serious?"

"Serious like a heart attack."

There was silence. Guys thought about what that meant. Then slowly, all eyes turned to Twist at the other end of the table, waiting to hear what he had to say.

Twist remembers how simple it sounded when Bone spoke. How easily it seemed to fall into place as he listened. How it made sense to expand outside the drugs.

"You got an opinion?" Bone asked him.

Twist took a long time to respond, choosing his words carefully.

"No such thing as a fair and long-term partnership with the Guineas. Anything we got with them can never go far," he said.

"We doing all the work and taking all the risk," he added. "Never been the Guineas getting shot or chased by 5-0— when it turns bad. Never none of them watching cops cruising their houses. Don't make sense we're not taking a bigger piece than what they giving us.

"They giving us pennies on the dollar."

"Ain't giving us nothing," Bone said. "We earning it."

"Fo' real," Ice nodded. "Fucking right."

"If something goes wrong, we wind up in jail or dead," Twist said. "The economics don't make sense. Any of the downtown suits will tell you that."

"They be coming round, flossin' in their suits and Caddys and we the ones gave them the keys," Ice said.

"Time to stop being their niggers," Bone said more adamantly. "Time to stand up for us. Take what we can."

Twist shook his head. "Think it goes deeper than that."

"Don't matter much more than black-and-white," Cuba put in. "Not the way I see it."

Figures, Twist thinks, that he and Cuba can't even see something they agree on the same way.

The others waited quietly for details, thinking about possibilities as they sipped the Hennesseys and Buds and passed the joints. Waiting to know what was in it for each of them.

"Diversity and economics," Twist said. "That's what this about."

"What the fuck do you know about diversity and economics, nigger?" Cuba sneered.

"I read. Watch the news on TV," Twist shot back. "See shit on MSNBC."

"Nigger," Cuba said, "as long as I know you, you been wanting to be one of those business-suit-wearing motherfuckers standing on the PATH platform every morning. Taking a train to your office in some high-rise."

"Ain't nothing wrong with putting out some legit fronts," Twist said.

Cuba kept shaking his head.

"The Italians got no problem with us slingin' in Newark and East Orange and Jersey City, but they don't want to hear nothing about selling dope in Nutley or Belleville or Clifton neighborhoods," Twist said. "You know how many potential customers they got in those towns? But they don't want no part of it. Not for their kids."

"Fucking right about that," Ice said low.

"Just supposed to do it in the nigger neighborhoods where they keep the black people down."

Twist looked at the faces around the table, waiting for understanding. Then he looked to Bone and the smirk that was slowly stretching from ear to ear. Bone understood. "The white man's neighborhoods are where the real cheddar is."

"The same places the Guineas live and work and send their kids to school. They the places we should be," Bone said.

"But you and me both know it ain't gonna happen as long as the Guineas are the ones calling the shots," Twist said. "Ain't selling nothing to their kids.

"Got to expand the distribution," Twist said. "Grow the business. Take a bigger slice of the pie, then start putting the money to work for us. Take it outside the drugs and get it off the street. Buy real estate. Put that cash into real things."

"There he goes again," Cuba muttered. "Talking about being legit. Nigger, you dealing drugs. Not working some nine-to-five.

"Nigger never even finished high school," he added.

"We talking about a bigger piece of the profits," Bone asked, "or taking over everything?"

"Thinking we take over," Twist said. "Run it like it's ours and pay them a percentage. Be us taking the risk. Should be us calling the shots."

"Guineas ain't gonna give up nothing."

"Increase distribution. Build revenue. Then kick back a chunk of the cash to them," Twist said. "They don't got to do nothing but sit back and collect. Like a royalty. Be like a 7-Eleven franchise.

"Grow this right and they be getting a huge return," he added. "Maybe make more than they making now with less risk."

Cuba shook his head again. "Don't see them being so quick to give up something they already got."

"Got to sell them on the idea," Twist said.

"Renegotiate?"

"Only two ways to break it off with them," Twist said. "Words or action."

Cuba raised a fist. "Only way to break with the Guineas is to use this," he said, shaking it. "Take what we want instead of asking for it."

Twist looked at him. "That way causes problems."

"Something like that they know and respect."

"Better to chop it up first," Twist said. "Start with words and see where it goes. Don't want to get into a war with them."

Guys like Cuba and Ice were in favor of doing it the same way they took control of streets and neighborhoods. It was what they knew. Guns and drive-bys and violence worked best for them, and they figured there was no difference between the Italians and the Branch Park Bloods or the Blades on the other side of town. Words weren't necessary. All they understood was that it took power to get more power.

"Maybe there's another way to get what we want," Twist said. "Maybe talk and negotiations?"

But now he realizes how stupid it was trying to negotiate. There was too much at stake for the Italians to walk away from what they owned or allow the Skulls to stake out a bigger piece for themselves. The Guineas weren't giving up anything they owned.

Twist was wrong not to see that, even if he hasn't said that to anyone else.

For over a month they talked. There was grumbling from Cuba and Ice, but in the end they were willing to try it Twist's way: bargaining like business partners, talking about expanding the market and increasing distribution. Staking out the turf to build and manage as their own with the consent of the Italians; Twist thought they would be talking about things the Italians could understand. It was an approach that would create a profitable solution for both sides.

Instead the discussions went nowhere.

It was his biggest miscalculation.

A bigger miscalculation than thinking he could ever get out of the game on his own terms.

The Italians wanted bigger market share but only as long as the drugs stayed in local neighborhoods. Neighborhoods like the ones they already owned.

"Ain't gonna happen," they said. "Find more customers in the areas you already got. That's how you grow the business."

And the idea of giving up a piece of their business by turning it over to the Skulls made them laugh.

"Why you want those kinds of headaches?" they said, smiling the same way a parent smiles at a six-year-old who can't be taken seriously. "Things are good the way they are."

"Trying to make them better," Bone said. "Opportunity, you know?"

"No reason to change," they were told.

The Skulls pushed. The Italians pushed back.

The Italians sent two guys to talk. One was a big guy named Leonard, squeezed into a dark suit, short on words but with the kind of stare Twist saw often on Cuba's face. A guy who understood violence better than words.

The other guy was a Capo named Sally. He was Tony Giaccolone's right-hand man. He was black Cadillacs and two-thousand-dollar suits with matching ties and handkerchiefs, manicures, sunglasses, and dark hair greased back. Maybe forty but not much older. The kind of relaxed cool that hid the viciousness guys like Leonard and Cuba could not control. What always struck Twist was Sally's smile; no matter what he said or what he was told, his smile never broke.

Twist wondered what it took to make it fade, and what was hidden beneath it.

They met in the parking lot at the airport Marriott one rainy Friday night in late June. Bone and Ice stood in the rain, leaning against the side of the BMW, ready to try one more time. Twist was behind the wheel with Cuba next to him, cradling a .45 beneath his legs. Sally was all smiles as he came out of the Cadillac and crossed the space between the cars. Leonard stood close, holding an umbrella over his head as they faced Bone and Ice.

They got past the hellos with idle talk about weather, NBA lockouts, and the Mets and Yankees. Then Bone tried once more about taking a bigger chunk than what they had.

Sally's smile curled. "This again?"

"It's something we got to talk about."

"It's old news. Nobody wants to hear it."

Bone tipped his sunglasses to the bottom of his nose. "Time we took on more responsibility. Need to talk about that."

"You got responsibility."

"Time for more."

"Why you want more?"

"Figure with responsibility comes more money. Opportunity, you know. Be looking to build something for us. A bigger piece of the business."

Sally kept smiling. "Maybe you guys got eyes too big for your own good, know what I mean? Maybe you starting to get greedy."

"Maybe you don't see the opportunity."

"Maybe you aren't understanding that things are good the way they are."

"Maybe you're not listening?"

Sally spit out a toothpick and laughed. "This is getting old," he said in a tired voice, but with a tone that still had bite. "I'm tired of hearing this shit."

There was a moment where only the words hung between them.

Then Ice stepped across the distance and slapped Sally hard across the face.

His hand cracked the skin. Leonard was slow going inside his coat, and in the seconds that followed Cuba and Twist were out of the car, freezing him with their .45s and .22s. He held the umbrella tightly and let the other hand fall slowly to his side, keeping his eyes locked on Ice.

They stood in a silence that was crushing and heavy in its weight.

Slowly, Sally touched a hand to his face and the blood trickling from his nose. He drew it back, staring at the red smeared across two fingers. The smile stayed intact but there was no life to it any longer.

He pulled a handkerchief from inside a jacket pocket.

"What the fuck you doing?" he hissed.

Ice stared at him. "Maybe I'm tired of hearing you say no."

Sally shook his head. "You don't know what you're getting into. Don't know the kind of trouble you've created for yourself."

"Know enough," Ice said. "Know that the way things been ain't the way they gonna be no more."

"We ain't the stupid niggers you think we are," Bone put in. "Want more than what you giving us."

"You ain't listening. You think you know something—"

"That's the problem," Bone cut in. "We know a lot. It's you who ain't listening. You the ones who created the trouble."

"You cross the line with us, you more stupid than we thought," Sally said.

"Line's already been crossed," Bone said.

Sally's stare hardened. He and Leonard turned away.

"You ain't the only gang around wants to do business with us," Sally warned before getting in the Cadillac, still touching fingers to his face. He rolled down the window. "Plenty of guys hungry for what you got. Plenty of guys who want what you're walking away from."

"Ain't nobody walking away from nothing," Bone said. "It's you who's got nothing. We own this."

"What you think you own, you ain't gonna' own for long."

"Gonna be for as long as we want it."

Sally shook his head. Twist couldn't see more than the outline of his head inside the Cadillac but he knew the smile was gone. "You don't know what you're getting yourselves into," Sally said again. "Don't know how bad you fucked up."

It isn't until now that Twist realizes what Sally meant.

The threats started right away but nobody was worried; they were ready for war, if it came down to it.

The Skulls moved fast to make everything the Italians owned their own. There was talk about throwing in with one of Giaccolone's rivals, a guy named Joey Dogs who ran a crew out of Bergen County, but they figured it wouldn't be any better than what they had with Giaccolone—giving up anything they were trying to gain by trading one boss for another. Instead, Twist opened connections with the Jamaican crews in Queens that the Italians had set up for weed, negotiated with Columbian and Asian suppliers to get coke and heroin, and bought lab technicians inside Hoffman-La Rouche in Nutley to steal pharmaceuticals they needed. Worked out a deal with a biker gang in South Jersey to get meth and speed. Put it together the way he imagined businessmen did it in downtown office buildings. Allegiances didn't matter when you had money. Business went on like always.

It went that way for a few weeks until the Italians brought in the Bloods to take back corners and customers.

In the turf battles that go on there are always shaky cease fires negotiated between gangs. DMZs, treaties, and peace zones that allow colors to co-exist when they aren't at war; each giving the other enough to respect the lines drawn between them. The Skulls and Bloods had lived with a truce for almost a year. But the truce evaporated once the Italians brought in the Bloods.

"You can't win," the voices on the phone had warned. "You're in over your heads. You got to know when to walk away."

"You're gonna be dead."

Twist thought they knew what was coming. No surprises. Nothing unexpected. Nothing they weren't prepared to handle.

Nobody went out at night out unless they were armed and went in a group, and everybody always carried a burner. Nobody was ever out of touch. Basketball was out except on turf courts where players were surrounded by friends and where there were guys watching each other's back. Guys stayed with their colors and didn't take risks, even in familiar neighborhoods.

They figured it would start the way it always did, with the Bloods picking weak, random targets. First the youngest kids, pushing them around and intimidating them on the street. Then taking shots at guys stupid enough to walk alone or play ball at basketball courts in neutral turf. Someone was always foolish enough to take a risk, no matter how often you warned them. Then muscling in to bust up drug sales and random drive-bys at night. Maybe shaking down the Indian or Korean merchants on Skull turf who paid for protection, and if that didn't get the results they wanted, fire-bombing their stores. Just to make a point.

Nothing that hadn't been done before with the Blades or the Bloods.

Nothing the Skulls couldn't handle. Like always.

Looking back, Twist realizes now how big of a mistake it was.

"Ain't nothing we can't handle," Cuba said.

"Maybe you should think about walking away," the voice on the phone said. "Give it up now before you lose everything you got. Everything important."

"Think this is something we ain't never done?" Bone asked. "Think you're gonna show us something we never saw before and never handled?

"We can handle anything," he sneered.

Everything changed the night they popped Bone's younger brother, Spider. The kid was twelve years old; the kind of kid you sent on errands and had move extra nickel bags of weed to his friends for a couple of bucks. Nothing more than a corner boy. The gang taught him how to pop locks on cars and let him do donuts in the streets, but he was nobody important. Any importance was only because of Bone.

He was walking along McCarter about nine-thirty one night with friends, silver and black Raider's cap and colors in his back pocket, coming home from a ball game. He had the same toughness most twelve-year-olds have, and wore his colors proudly and defiantly. It didn't matter to him what kind of war they were fighting. And he didn't know that sometimes there were casualties, no matter how tough or good or young you were, or who your brother was.

A black sedan screeched to a stop alongside them and three guys jumped out, waving shotguns and .45s that chased away the other kids who had been with him.

One guy held Spider's arms behind his back while the other took out a long, thick hunting knife with a serrated edge. He sliced Spider's throat from ear to ear, ripping open the skin with one quick swing that showered the sidewalk with blood. Spider didn't die right away—he hung on for a minute, maybe two, reaching for his throat and sucking helplessly for air. It didn't do him any good to scream. They stuffed the bandanna from his back pocket in his mouth then left him dying on the pavement.

They wanted to be sure nobody misunderstood their message.

They got Ice a few days later as he was walking down Market Street with two other guys. It was probably the same black sedan with the same three guys who snuffed Spider. Three guys, dark windbreakers and .45s, took out the two kids before the car came to a stop, then dragged Ice into the backseat. Nobody got a chance to pull out their own nines. The two kids were clinging to life, hooked up to IV bottles and respirators in Beth Israel with cops outside their doors. More cops nosed around the neighborhood for clues, trying to find out what was going on and who was involved. Asking questions and knocking on doors. Looking for answers.

But Ice was gone.

"Maybe the nigger shows up in an oil drum floating down the Passaic," the voice on the phone said. "Or maybe he comes home. Piece by piece."

Two days later a package showed up at 38 Murray Street. It was found early in the morning but nobody saw how it got there. Inside the box they found two cracked, bloody gold-capped teeth that had been ripped out of someone's mouth. Underneath, wrapped in a piece of gauze soaked with blood, they found a long, bony black finger still wearing Ice's silver-plated skull ring.

"You're running out of time," the voice said later when he called. "Just like your friend who don't take no for an answer."

A day later they got Malik Mack coming out of an Irvington liquor store with an armful of six-packs he bought with a fake ID. The guys who were there said it went down so quickly he never had a chance, just like Spider and Ice. Three older white guys who looked just like the ones who got Spider and Ice surprised him from behind as he crossed the street and shoved him inside a car parked at the curb. The only things left behind were the broken six-packs that had been dropped in the street.

Malik wasn't yet sixteen. A smart kid who didn't need to be in the Skulls; even though he wanted to belong, Twist wouldn't let him join. He wasn't like other guys his age; he wasn't just book smart—Malik picked up on things others missed or didn't see. Twist liked the kind of vision the kid had. It was a skill that would be wasted in the Skulls, and Twist pushed him to be different. To finish school. To stay off the streets and out of gangs.

"You don't need this kind of life," he told him.

"Works for you," Malik said. "You been a Skull forever."

"Didn't have the choices and options you have," Twist said. "Been in the game too long. I'm running out of time and choices if I want to get out."

Malik looked at him. His expression curled. "Get out? What's that mean?"

"Means do something else," Twist said.

"Like what?"

Twist shrugged. "Maybe get my GED. Take some classes or something," he said. "Always been good with numbers. Wouldn't mind a different life where I had a nine-to-five in an office. Making deals."

Malik had grinned a wide, toothy smile. "Imagine you at some desk. Being a business executive."

"Be better than looking over your shoulder all day," Twist said.

"Besides," he added. "Stay in the game long enough and you wind up dead. Or doing time."

Malik had the potential to be more than some corner boy, or a guy working his way through the gang.

Now he was gone.

Twist wasn't certain he was dead, but he knew there wasn't a lot of time before Malik showed up in tiny pieces like Ice. If he even showed up at all. And with Malik's disappearance Twist came to the realization that he was stuck. He wasn't changing anything; nothing was ever going to be any different and they were never going legit.

"We got to do something," somebody said the night Malik disappeared, but nobody had any ideas. They were sitting around the table, voices soft and low, smoking Camels and trying to shape a plan. "Show them that we ain't gonna roll over and let them do this."

Bone had an intensity that burned in his eyes as he sat there, unloading and reloading the .38 in his lap. He examined each bullet in the light before slowly slipping it back in the gun chamber.

"We got to do to them the same thing they trying to do to us," he finally said. "Do it so they know we not just fucking around."

"How we gonna do that?"

"We got to hurt them."

"Make them fucking remember us. Make them give us fucking answers."

Somebody talked about taking out a group of them, and it was Cuba who suggested fire-bombing one of their social clubs or doing a drive-by through the streets of West Caldwell where Giaccolone was supposed to live.

"Nail the motherfuckers in their driveways when they bending over to pick up their Wall Streets in the morning," he said. "Take out the whole goddamned neighborhood before breakfast. Come back and finish their bitches by lunch."

"Do it like them Russians over in Coney Island do it," he added.

"Can't do it that way," Twist said, shaking his head slowly. "Wipe out ten of them and we'll attract too much attention. Do it one at a time and nobody notices it that much.

"Been able to avoid the cops so far. Something like that gets every cop in the county knocking on our doors with search warrants and questions. Kills what we got going on in the streets."

"You acting like this just business as usual for you," Cuba said.

"I'm not sitting on the sidelines," Twist snapped. "I'm in this one hundred percent."

"Besides," Bone muttered, nodding, "you kill ten in one shot, what you do the next time? Take out twenty?"

Cuba crushed out his cigarette. "Maybe you take out ten there won't be a next time."

Twist shook his head again. He wanted blood too, but he knew it never happened that way.

"So what we do?" Cuba asked Twist. "You been full of great ideas so far. What you think we should do?"

Twist felt Bone and Cuba eyeballing him across the table with the kind of stares that said he was to blame for what happened to Spider and Ice and Malik. Like it was his fault nothing worked out the way it was supposed to work. Like he didn't know what it cost and what was at stake.

"Eye for an eye," he finally said in a quiet voice.

"What that mean?"

"Speak so we can understand, nigger."

"Means we do it just like them. Same way they do. They take one of our guys, we take one of theirs," he said. "Revenge."

"What's that gonna do?"

"It makes it personal."

"Think that'll work?"

"Do it right and it will," Twist said. "We got to do what it takes to keep what's ours."

Cuba glared at him. "Glad you got that figured out. What we got to do is figure out how we gonna do it. And how we make it work."

"Grab one of their guys off the street and hold him until somebody comes forward with Malik and at least tells us where to find Ice's body," Twist said. "Even out the situation.

"Send them the same kind of message that says they ain't safe neither," he added. "Maybe it makes them think twice about what they got themselves into. Maybe it opens up dialogue about Ice and Malik."

Bone nodded his approval. "Get them to reconsider their position."

Cuba tossed off his cigarette butt. "Only one way to get them to reconsider their position, and it ain't with talk and bad intentions."

Now they have Valentine and his fate is in their hands.

Twist is responsible for him being here and he feels a link to Valentine, the same way there's a link with Malik and what happened to him. The crew is still downstairs talking about what to do next, but Twist knows Valentine is as good as dead.

Unless something else happens, it is just a matter of time before they execute Valentine. The only question is when it will happen.

And when that happens Twist knows he'll never get out of the game.

CHAPTER THREE

When Twist comes down the stairs the same guys are sitting around the table in the kitchen area. It's like he never left, except there are more Domino's boxes in the center of the table now. Other pizza boxes are scattered on the floor and tables throughout the building, along with empty plates, beer cans, and bottles, as well as piles of napkins crumpled into balls. Nines and deucey-deuces take up more table space. It's a weird scene; like he has suddenly walked into the tail end of a Sweet sixteen party turned nasty with pizza, party favors, and pistols. Guys continuously grab Buds out of the refrigerator, and a cluster of kids sit around the TV, watching the Mets game while passing lines back and forth on small mirrors. Others are slumped in chairs or on the floor, attacking slices of pizza the same way they attack the games on their phones. Guards stand watch at the door and windows, holding 16-gauges and ARs, but the feeling in the room has changed.

Twist can sense the difference.

The faces at the table are tired. Conversation comes in soft voices and halting, erratic bursts of words lacking emotion.

The Hennesseys is gone, replaced by warm Jack Daniel's they drink from paper cups without ice. Cuba grinds out a Camel in the ashtray and leans back in his chair, one foot propped against the table with his hands under his chin, barely able to keep his head from dropping. Bone grips his cup, expressionless as he stares across the room. He sits quietly between Dizzy and T. Capone as they carry on a conversation, but the words go right through Bone and he says nothing.

Everything at the table stops and all eyes turn toward Twist. He takes a Bud from the refrigerator and slides into the chair between Cuba and Eddie Dallas.

Cuba doesn't acknowledge him.

Bone nods. "Whasup?"

Twist shrugs as he pops the top on the can. Eddie opens the pizza box to offer a slice but Twist shakes it away. He hasn't eaten anything since an Egg McMuffin and coffee earlier in the morning and his stomach hurts, but he's not sure if that's hunger or because they need answers and time is running out.

He feels the weight of that on his shoulders.

"What you been doing the last hour?" Cuba asks without opening his eyes. "Taking a nap?"

"Did I miss something?"

"Talk, man," Eddie Dallas says. "Talk about the Guineas and about the guy upstairs and things we got to do. Talk about staying under the radar. Talk about how we gonna get Malik back."

"Want my two cents? Need my opinion?"

"Ain't nothing more than talk."

"We do anything besides talk? Accomplish something I should know about?" Twist asks.

"Nothing," Bone says. "Still just talk right now."

"Ordered pizza," Eddie adds, pushing the box toward Twist with a smile. "Did that without getting your fucking opinion."

Twist returns the smile, surprised it comes painlessly.

Eddie Dallas can do that. Cool and tough but the kind of guy who can find words that get a smile. He is the same age as Twist, with a long, hard body and biceps that bulge and flex as he bends forward in the chair. There's the touch of an accent, although he never gives a straight answer about where he's from so it's anybody's guess whether it's Jamaica, Haiti, the Virgin Islands, or some housing project in Queens. Long braids flow off his head, waterfalling to his shoulders and hang in front of Ray-Bans that never come off, no matter how dark it gets. Tan khaki pants tucked into his boots and a black Mőtley Crűe T-shirt.

A "rock n' roll nigger," Cuba once called him.

Eddie Dallas is the kind of person Twist can count on to be there when he needs him.

There is friendship and trust between them—Twist doesn't have to worry about getting a bullet between his shoulder blades when his back is turned. Eddie won't surprise him and he won't let him down when it matters. That counts for something.

He's a friend.

"What's going on with you?" Cuba tries with a little more edge to his voice. "You disappearing like that?"

Twist doesn't answer. He puts his mouth to the Bud can and throws back his head, letting the beer run down his throat in one long swallow. The Bud is drained quickly.

Cuba opens his eyes. Twist stares back but says nothing.

Cuba slowly turns toward him. "Where'd you go? Fading away like that?"

"You doing that all the time," Bone adds.

Twist turns with a stare but Cuba doesn't back down. He leans forward, closer to the table now, rocking back and forth with a motion that barely moves him. They lock stares. Twist wonders why it matters so much, and why he should even bother with an answer.

Some things are his and nobody else's. He shouldn't have to explain that to anybody.

"Wanted time to myself," he finally says, rolling the empty can to the center of the table. "Besides, ain't nothing going on here."

"There's things we got to do," Bone adds. "Things getting urgent."

"We can't do nothing until the Guineas come back with something," Twist replies. "Until then we just sit and wait. Try to conduct business as usual."

"That ain't getting Malik back," Dizzy says. "Ain't getting us no answers."

"Nothing we do now matters until we find out how the Guineas react and how they play it," Twist says. "Just got to wait."

Cuba isn't listening. "We got something going on here, and it don't feel like you want to be part of it."

"Been a part of this from the beginning," Twist says.

"You keep saying that but you ain't got no answers about where you been," Cuba says.

Twist doesn't answer.

"You hear me?"

"Valentine's here, right?" Twist finally shoots back. "If I didn't want to be part of this, he would still be walking down the street licking his ice cream cone and you'd be sitting here trying to figure out how to get back at the Guineas. I got something at stake here too.

"Don't be in my face, giving me shit, and telling me I don't want no part of this."

The table is silent and the words hang between them.

There is a look that goes from Cuba to Bone and then to Twist.

"Without me you don't have nothing," Twist adds.

Twist looks around the table for something from the others, but no one meets his stare or gets between him and Cuba and Bone. Eddie Dallas finally gets up, scraping his chair across the floor as he walks slowly to the refrigerator, taking out a six pack of Bud. He yanks two cans out of the plastic ring and hands one to Twist.

"Guess that's what it was, huh?" he tries. "You upstairs all this time patting yourself on the back."

This time Twist doesn't give him the same smile.

"Anybody check on that guy?" Eddie Dallas asks. "See how he's doing?"

Nobody answers. Curtis Granderson has just hit his second home run of the game for the Mets and the guys watching in the living room act like a meaningless late season baseball game on TV is the only thing worth caring about. The kids playing their games don't even see that. Michael Valentine doesn't mean anything to them yet; he is just a name. Dizzy and T. Capone look down at their plates in silence while Bone just shakes his head slowly, like he can't see the point of anything else.

Cuba seems surprised by the question.

"Maybe we should check on him," Twist agrees, with a nod to Eddie. "See how he's doing. Get him something to eat?"

Cuba glares at him, his expression hardening.

"You think they gave Ice something to eat before they pulled out his teeth?" he asks. "Before they cut off his motherfucking finger and mailed it to us?

"Think they're feeding Malik right now?" he adds and Twist turns quiet.

"Couldn't hurt to give him something," Eddie Dallas puts in. "Man's been up there a long time. Got to be hungry by now."

"So what?" Bone says. "Ain't our problem."

"We shouldn't have to feed him," Cuba adds. "Ain't responsible for that."

Twist shakes his head and kicks out a small laugh.

"Bullshit," he says. "We took him off the street and brought him here. He didn't come on his own. We took on that responsibility the minute we dragged him here. Owe him that much."

"We don't owe him nothing," Cuba spits back.

Bone is still motionless in the chair, his hand wrapped around the empty paper cup. "War's war, man. You know that. That's the way things go."

"War has nothing to do with it," Twist says. "War don't mean you get to torture somebody.

"At least not until you have to."

Eddie Dallas nods. "What's it gonna hurt to give him something?"

"He's our responsibility," Twist says.

"If it was me sitting up there in his place, I wouldn't want to eat," Bone says. "Too many other things going through my head to worry about food."

"That's you," Twist tells him.

"I ain't no different than nobody else."

Twist just shakes his head. Bone's the same guy who didn't cry when they did his brother, saying, "Tears are for bitches and faggots."

"If it was me," Twist says, "I'd want to eat."

He waits a moment but nobody moves or says anything else. They sit like statues, waiting, with the sounds of the ball game and the beeping of six different games filling the room. Twist pushes himself slowly out of the chair and stands, stepping away from the table. Eyes and heads turn to watch. He stops at the refrigerator and takes out another Bud, then moves toward the stairs, popping open the top as he goes.

Bone sits up straighter in his chair.

Cuba shouts out, "Where the fuck you going?"

Twist looks back at him over his shoulder. "Third floor. Gonna see how the guy's doing."

"Don't think you should be going nowhere," Bone tells him but Twist is already on his way up the stairs.

He hears them talking but ignores the voices following him up the stairs. There's nothing they can do to stop him, if that's what they are talking about. He's been in the Skulls as long as Bone—the only difference between them is that year Bone spent doing time. Nobody else has Twist's experience—at least nobody alive or not in lockup—and that gives Twist something none of the others can match.

It lets him come and go by his own clock, without worrying about the things Bone thinks and says.

It means most of the time Twist doesn't need to listen to Bone if he doesn't want to.

He and Bone are not so different. A long time ago they were both looking for something only the Skulls offered: a home and a chance. Twist just went at his life differently, without turning into the kind of mercenary like Bone who walked through enemy turf to take out a target to prove his toughness.

Either way, they are both at the same point in their lives, he thinks, only approaching it from different sides.

He is the same as everybody in the neighborhood—just luckier to get where he is now.

If where he is means something.

There was nothing about Twist's life that was so different from other kids in his neighborhood. He had a mama who was never around and a junkie father he never knew, and the cops started hassling him the day he turned ten and stole some kid's ten-speed near Woodland Cemetery. Twist was always in trouble. Stealing cars to race through the streets late at night and turning donuts in the intersections to impress the girls watching from apartment-building windows before their mothers pulled them back inside. Jumping late night commuters coming out of the Gateway buildings with friends, stealing and robbing whatever they could get their hands on. Doing whatever it took to find enough money to buy two-hundred-dollar pairs of Nikes and Reeboks at the sneaker shops along Market and Raymond, and then playing basketball for hours once he put on the shoes. He smoked and drank and fought and cut class whenever something better came along, until the tenth grade when he decided being out of school was better than being there, and never went back.

No one missed him.

"The usual story of another nigger's life in the city," he said when somebody from Social Services got around to asking. "Ain't nobody down there at school even knows who I am."

"Everybody matters," he heard again and again.

Twist knew better.

The Skulls changed that. They gave him a home, along with a chance to belong and make a difference and be somebody.

Somebody who was important.

He had never had that, and it was the most important thing anybody ever offered him.

Bone found the same thing with the Skulls. There is time and history between Twist and Bone, and that counts for something.

It gives him what they have in common.

Bone will never take him out. He knows Twist, and knows Twist is not somebody who would challenge his authority. There's no chance it will ever be Twist's body the cops find stuffed in a dumpster or face down in an alley in the Ironbound section with bullet holes in the back of his head. At least not by Bone's hand.

Bone doesn't work that way.

It is Cuba who Twist is not too sure about.

Cuba would take out anybody who stands in his way and do it without hesitation if it got him where he wanted to go.

Twist climbs the stairs, slowing on the second floor to finish the Bud before tossing the can to the floor before continuing. There's a light bulb hanging from a cord in the ceiling but the stairs are dark, and Twist keeps one hand on the railing to guide himself to the third floor. The plaster falls from the ceiling in huge chunks and the walls are a mess; the paint is cracked and peeling in spots, the wallpaper falls away in ripped strips, and there is graffiti scrawled in pen and ink. Only the walls around the bedroom door look solid and clean.

LJ stands in front of the door, a cigarette dangling from his mouth. No shirt now, a black bandanna tied around his head, with the black sweat pants tucked into his high tops. He has the AR under one arm and raises it slightly as Twist comes up the stairs.

"Whasup?" Twist asks as they bump fists.

LJ shakes his head. "Ain't a lot he's gonna be doing, you know? Not a lot of places he can go."

"Hear anything in there?"

LJ shrugs. "Not for a long time," he says. "First hour or two he was kicking at the walls but it stopped. Probably got tired."

"What's he been doing since then?"

"Sitting on the bed, I guess."

Twist looks at him. "You look in on him?"

"Some," LJ mutters, like it's something that takes a lot of time and energy to do. "Been a while."

Twist nods like he understands. "Let me in there."

The kid turns and does it without question. He unlocks the top two dead bolts and steps back a foot, aiming the gun at the door as Twist turns the last lock.

He pulls open the door and steps inside.

Behind him the door slams shut and the three bolts lock in place.

The room is as dark as the stairs and hallways, and stifling hot. There is a small lamp on a dresser but the bulb flickers without giving much light, and without windows the days probably run into the nights in here. There is no way to tell the difference between the two. The black-and-white TV is perched on a plastic milk crate but the knobs are gone and the cord is cut and frayed. The thin layer of dust that covers it is smeared with fingerprints. The dirty floor is bare wood and creaks as Twist takes two steps further into the room.

The bed is against the far side of the room, tucked beneath the overhang of the ceiling. A jacket and tie lie crumpled on the floor, tossed aside in the dust and dirt. Michael Valentine sits on the bed, watching silently with that same hard stare he had burned into Twist in the car. It is the stare he wore before Cuba rapped him with the butt end of the gun. The hood is gone now, as if it doesn't matter whether he can recognize anyone or not. His white shirt is open, unbuttoned, torn, and stained with blood. There is a bruise under his right eye and his cheek is such a dark shade of purple that it's almost black around the edges. The steel duct tape that covers his mouth is tight, and when Twist moves closer he can see broken strands of hair stuck behind the tape—like the hair got caught beneath the adhesive when they taped his mouth, and every time Valentine turns his head now more strands are ripped from his scalp.

They face each other.

Valentine is a good looking guy. At least for a middle-aged white guy. Broad shoulders, thick arms, and long legs stretched out in front of him on the bed. Most of his hair is still tied in the ponytail, and he looks strong and powerful, as if Twist can tell that from looking at the shape of his body and the way the shirt hangs on him.

But it is those eyes that haunt Twist as they exchange stares.

They hook into Twist, plunging into his chest like six inches of steel blade, slicing everything inside.

Twist watches him, trying to understand everything about Michael Valentine. He wonders who he is and what his life is all about. If he is happy with what he has or just living from moment to moment, taking whatever he can find to fill the empty spaces. He thinks about Valentine's world and the people who fill it, but can't imagine anything about them or what they mean. To Twist they are like the people he passed on the street in Belleville, but to Valentine they must mean everything.

Valentine's stare is filled with none of those thoughts.

All Twist can see in his eyes is rage and hate.

He leans forward. Valentine tries jerking his head away but Twist puts a hand to his face that stops him. Something passes in the touch of his fingers to Valentine's skin, but it goes by too quickly to last.

Twist tears the tape off Valentine's mouth with one hard pull.

There is nothing at first, then the silence is ripped open. The scream starts low and hard, like a rasping cough deep in Valentine's chest, and when it comes out it is sharp and piercing, and moves Twist back a step.

Valentine finally sucks in a deep breath and shakes his head as the sound echoes, then dies.

"Okay in there?" LJ calls from the other side of the door. "Everything cool?"

"No problem," Twist says.

"You need me, you call me," he hears him say. The suggestion is almost worth a smile. Twist can't imagine a situation where he is will ever need the kid's help.

His mouth is puffy and swollen, and there is dried blood on Valentine's lips and chin. He moves his mouth back and forth, like it's something new he's learning to use for the first time. Valentine works his lips and jaw, turning his head from side to side, readying everything for a test drive.

Twist is still staring at him.

"Couldn't figure out why you kept that fucking thing on me anyway," Valentine finally mutters. "Didn't think you'd be stupid enough to keep me locked up someplace where people who could give a fuck would hear me screaming."

Twist stands with arms folded across his chest and says nothing. He keeps the distance between them short. The space and the quiet of the room work better for him than words.

"You want something to eat?" he asks finally.

Valentine eyes him again.

"You're one of them," he states. "One of the guys who grabbed me off the street."

His voice is flat and emotionless, without any trace of anger, and what he says comes out more as a statement than a question. Twist nods his head just the same.

"I was driving," Twist tells him.

Valentine nods his head, remembering that detail.

Then something clicks and the stare cools, and he trains his eyes on Twist like he is taking in every feature of his face for the first time and hating what he sees. Twist sees something change. Valentine's face reddens, and his nostrils flair and the stare gets a different edge.

"You're the one who pointed a gun at Angelina," he says slowly. "Threatened to put a bullet in her."

Twist returns his stare in silence.

"That was you, wasn't it?"

Twist says nothing.

"You motherfucker!" he cries. "I'll kill you!"

Valentine starts forward but his legs don't have the same kind of jump they had on the street. He strains against the ropes that tie his hands behind his back but he can't get free, no matter how hard he struggles, and Valentine can't move fast enough to stand. He can barely get to his feet as he lurches off the bed. Twist shoves him with two hands to his chest and sends Valentine back across the bed, hard into the wall.

Valentine lands backward on his shoulders and neck.

He kicks his feet slowly and rights himself. His face is still red and his breath comes in hard, labored bursts, and his stare doesn't change.

Twist doesn't move.

"You want something to eat?" he asks again when Valentine finally stops struggling.

Valentine doesn't answer.

"Man, it don't matter to me one way or another," Twist says. "You want to be a fucking hard-on, that's up to you. But I ain't gonna stand here begging. You want something to eat or not?"

Valentine nods his head slowly but nothing in his expression is any different.

Twist turns and goes to the door, thinking about what he sees in Valentine's face. The floor creaks and sags under his weight as he moves. He raps once on the door and tells LJ to open it.

He can hear the dead bolts unlocking and he steps back, looking one last time at Valentine upright on the bed.

"I wasn't going to shoot her," he says before leaving. "Figure you should know that."

◆ ◆ ◆

Valentine sits on the bed, surrounded by empty Big Mac wrappers and cardboard French fry containers, sipping hard on a straw. He sucks the last drops of the vanilla shake from the bottom of the cup and wipes a hand across his mouth. Twist watches from across the room, the nine tucked in the waist of his pants, still poking against his back. He keeps his back to the wall and his hands closer to his sides, a little more cautious and careful now.

Valentine's hands are untied. Cuba and Bone would have bitched about it, but Twist knows Valentine isn't going anywhere. Even if he gets past him, Valentine still has to get past LJ and the AR-15 at the door, then a whole building filled with gangsters and soldiers who would love to ice him.

Besides, Valentine has to eat and there's no way he can do that with his hands tied behind his back. And no way Twist is feeding him. Not like some candy striper working the geriatric ward at Beth Israel.

He watches Valentine eat, tentative at first as he pokes through the burger, lifting the bun to pick off the chopped onions and pickles before biting into it. Wincing as the salt stings the cuts in his mouth. Nothing more is said and Valentine eats in silence, only now and then shooting looks at Twist.

Twist stares while Valentine eats and wonders what's going through his head. If he knows why he's here, and if he knows anything about Ice or Spider or Malik and who they are. Twist wonders if Valentine really knows why he's stuck on the third floor of the garage at 38 Murray Street, although Valentine has probably figured out most of it by now.

Some things can be figured out by instinct and gut feeling.

Twist thinks again how lives had gone in separate directions until this afternoon, and how everything has changed since then. Nothing is the same. There are scars they will each carry until they die.

Valentine breaks the silence. "It's boring sitting here like this with nothing to do."

"No fucking picnic for me either," Twist says. "Got better things to do than watch you eat."

"You guys think about what I'm supposed to do if I got to take a leak or something?" he asks. "I'm not some kind of camel who can hold it for days, you know?"

Twist shrugs. "I'll see if maybe I can get you a tin can or something to use."

Valentine crinkles his face. "Be nice if you can let me use a toilet," he says. Twist shakes his head no and Valentine frowns.

"Come on. A toilet ain't much to ask."

"Too risky."

"No way I'm taking a leak in a can," he says.

"No other choices for you. It's either that or in the corner."

"Can't see what the big deal is," Valentine says. "It's not like you guys won't be following and watching every step I take."

"I'll see what I can do about it," Twist says after thinking about it.

They fall back into the quiet again and Twist doesn't say anything. Valentine is upright against the wall, pressing his back into the sheet rock as he eats, locking eyes with Twist. Twist returns with his own stare and they stay that way, holding stares and flexing their toughness.

Twist is calm. Being the one in control gives him that advantage.

"A TV that works would be nice, too," Valentine tries after a while.

Twist shakes his head. "Ain't gonna happen."

"In case you didn't notice, there's not a lot to do in here," Valentine says. "What am I supposed to do—read the fucking McDonald's bag?"

Twist shrugs.

"If I've got to sit here staring at the walls with nothing to do I'm gonna go fucking nuts," he adds. "I thought maybe I could catch some of the Mets game. Like to see how they're doing. Need a TV to do that."

Twist still doesn't answer and Valentine's words fall away.

"You play baseball?" he asks Twist after a while.

"Basketball," Twist says. "Why?"

Valentine shrugs. "Just wondering. Probably think you're good, huh?"

"I do okay. What's it matter to you?"

"That's what everybody says. Guess talk's cheap with you guys." Twist glares at him.

"Suppose you think you're Kobe or LeBron on the courts, huh?"

"Maybe I am," he says. "Guess we'll never know that."

Valentine says nothing else and Twist accepts the silence that follows. He eats quietly, without a sound, as if table manners are still important. There are a few fries stuck to the bottom of one container and they disappear quickly as Valentine curls them between his lips and takes one last breath before swallowing. He rolls up the empty wrappers and napkins, stuffing them down inside the shake cup, then puts the cup in the McDonald's bag on the floor by the bed. There's still one burger left in its wrapper, unopened, and he sets that on the far corner of the bed, leaving it for later.

"What time is it?" he asks, looking up.

In a quiet voice Twist answers that it's after nine, wondering why it really matters.

Valentine looks at Twist then rubs his hands and wrists together.

"I suppose you want to tie me up again, huh?"

Twist thinks about it. He knows he should, and he knows that's what Cuba and Bone would want, but he doesn't see the point.

"Think you'll be okay. Ain't going nowhere, right?" he says.

Valentine doesn't answer. He looks away to the darkness in the corners of the room, rests his head against the wall, and closes his eyes.

◆ ◆ ◆

"Thanks."

Twist nods, thinking Valentine is talking about the food.

Valentine picks up on that and shakes his head. "Talking about Angelina," he says.

"It has nothing to do with her, right?" Twist answers. "She ain't a part of this."

Valentine nods as if he understands. "I appreciate it."

◆ ◆ ◆

49

Nothing has changed downstairs in the garage.

The TV is on but nobody pays attention to it. When Twist asks, somebody says the Mets blew the game in the ninth, even with the two home runs by Granderson, and now the guys are listening to WBLS. The game kids are still into their own action, barely aware of Twist. There are different guards at the door but they stand with the same expressions, peeking through windows with their fingers curled around triggers, ready for action. The kitchen area is hot and filled with cigarette smoke that hangs in the air. Eddie Dallas is gone but the other guys at the table haven't changed positions. The mountain of empty Bud cans and bottles in the center of the table is higher and the Jack Daniel's is almost gone, but if anybody notices, nobody cares.

Twist wonders if the Italians are sitting around a house like this place, with Sally the Capo and Tony Giaccolone doing what the Skulls are doing. Wondering if Malik is locked in some kind of upstairs bedroom prison cell like the one Valentine is in.

If they fed him the same way the he just took care of Valentine.

"I'm Audi 5-0—," he says and everyone looks up. "Time to split."

Bone sits up straight in his chair. "Where you going?"

"Home," Twist says. "Nothing else to do. Any more minutes at this table are just a waste of time."

Twist doesn't need the Skulls to help him do that; he can waste time by himself.

"Ain't nothing going on here that won't be happening tomorrow," he adds. "Just the same shit a day later."

"Word," Dizzy mutters with a sip of his Bud.

Bone lights up a Camel and lets the smoke curl to the ceiling. There's that look again in his eyes that Twist can't figure out, and it stays with him. "Think maybe tomorrow we'll have something? Get some kind of response?"

"Takes time," Twist tells him. "Let's wait to see what happens."

"Be nice to have some answers," Dizzy says. "Find out how we're gonna go forward with this."

"Try Malik's cell phone again?"

Dizzy shrugs. "Same as before. Sometimes it just rings and rings. Other times it just cuts right to voice mail."

"Fucking waste of time," Cuba says. "Ain't like he gonna answer."

"Just reaching out," Twist says. "Trying to take all the right steps."

Cuba returns the same hard stare that hasn't changed.

"Business as usual tomorrow," Twist says. "That don't change."

"Same as always," Bone says, still watching the smoke spiraling and drifting through the air. "Keep going hard. Watch each other's back and don't be doing nothing that gonna create problems. Don't be taking no more risks."

Twist nods. "Makes sense."

Cuba stirs in his seat and sits up, fumbling for a cigarette and matches. "Just got to make sure nobody does anything stupid."

That would be a first, but Twist keeps those thoughts to himself.

◆ ◆ ◆

It's after eleven when Twist gets off the bus at Springfield Avenue but the night still hasn't cooled off. It is hot and doesn't feel like the heat will ever end.

The bus pulls away with a shudder and Twist starts cautiously down the street.

Walking alone on the street is stupid, and knowing that makes it worse. There is too much happening with the Italians and too much at stake, and even with the nine tucked inside his shirt Twist needs more than the gun can offer. The ride home that was offered would have been smarter, he thinks; Twist would have insisted on it for anybody else. He had only grudgingly agreed to an armed escort to Penn Station, figuring that the usual rules didn't apply to him, and nobody pressed him about it.

Most of those rules didn't matter much any more.

If the Italians want him they will find him, and it doesn't matter how late it is, who he is walking with, or how many guns he carries. The way they got Ice, Spider, and Malik proves that.

Besides, Twist wants to be alone without four or five kids talking trash and trailing step for step. It is quieter on a bus than in a car filled with sixteen-year-old soldiers and corner boys.

He hears the sound of dogs barking and babies crying, and somewhere in the night voices are raised in anger, raging loudly, shouting to be heard over one another. Other voices come in spurts above music from the radios and CD players stuck in windows and propped up on the stairs he passes. Far away the siren from a cop car or ambulance rips open the night but gets no closer; it just whines on and on until finally fading away.

Twist knows this street; it's a part of him and the memories left on the pavement feel comfortable. They mean something, even if he doesn't always remember why.

The buildings in this part of town are older than the houses and buildings on Murray Street. Some are turn of the century brownstones, slowly falling apart and even though others are newer, they are in no better shape. Most windows are open, with the curtains knotted and fans balanced on the ledges and sills, stirring hot air as they teeter and shake. The front steps that wind down to the sidewalk are filled with old people and young mothers and kids who sit waiting for the next breeze to come along. Guys hang in cars at the curbs, radios loud, talking trash while trying to pick up girls walking past.

He sees faces that glance quickly at him then turn away and Twist feels that surge of power, same way he did that first day he proudly wore his Skull colors. The way all eyes turned to him when he got on the cross-town bus, checking him out before looking away or down to the floor to avoid his stare. Even then it was about power and respect.

Being somebody; somebody who matters.

There are faces in the shadows watching him as he walks. Familiar faces, like distant memories lost in the back of Twist's head that he can't pull out any more, but ones that are still there. Eyes follow him in the darkness but there's nothing to the stares.

At least nobody looks at him like a target.

He wonders if that's how Michael Valentine looks at him, or if there's something more to his stare.

He doesn't slow or even hesitate at the spot on the corner of Springfield and Waverly where the Bloods killed his brother twelve years earlier. There are no reminders left there. The blood washed away a long time ago, the building on the corner burned down two summers later, and none of the neighborhood faces who still live on the street would remember anything about it. It was nothing that would stand out—no reason to remember. There is nobody to blame any more, and nobody who can do anything for Twist or what is left with him.

That makes it easier to walk past the corner.

Tayshaun is dead because he talked to a girl who was fucking two guys in the Bloods. It wasn't political or territorial, and had nothing to do with revenge. It was all about sex. Tayshaun didn't even know anything about her when he stopped to talk, except she looked like somebody he could party with and have a good time. Probably figured it was worth his time to try. The four guys who jumped him and crushed his forehead with bricks and a Louisville Slugger made sure he never got that chance.

Sometimes things like that happen.

Twist remembers one of the cops saying that, like it explained away everything, and he can't shake the cop's words as he crosses the street.

There are times when the memory feels like such a long time ago, in such a distant part of Twist's world, that Tayshaun was never even real. Never flesh and blood and bone; just somebody he made up. It's those times when Tayshaun seems like another character on a TV show; somebody who's pain doesn't bother you. The only thing that keeps it real for Twist is the pain he feels from his past.

Even though he can get past it now, the hurt hasn't gone away.

Home is just two blocks away on Rose Street, but instead Twist crosses Springfield and goes toward Woodland Cemetery. The street changes a little with each step and there's a different kind of activity. The faces aren't as familiar and the rap and hip hop turn to a salsa beat; Spanish voices build in intensity and the atmosphere spins differently. The guys who look at him and follow his walk with stares don't give him the same respect the faces on his street did. There's a heavier sense of danger. He turns down Fairmount. To an outsider the neighborhood and its street could be identical to the ones Twist passed on Springfield. The noise and atmosphere can feel the same.

But he knows the difference.

The street is a DMZ; one of those edges between Blade and Skull turf where the wrong look or a hard stare can start something. Guys walk a delicate balance to hold their own power and cool without getting into something more with strangers. Three guys on the corner eye Twist as he passes. He feels a surge of anticipation and adrenaline that puts him on edge. Their conversation quiets and their words drift into silence as they watch him.

Twist slips his fingers around the nine in his pocket.

Just in case.

He goes up the stairs at 1117 Fairmount. The building is like others on the street; brown and dirty with bars across the windows on the first two stories. Twist nods to the old Cuban sitting on the steps in his white T-shirt, black hair slicked back, sipping a can of Pabst while smoking a cigarette. The guy turns his head to watch him pass in silence.

The lights inside the first glass door at the top of the stairs are dim, and the air is heavy with the sweet smell of weed when he steps into the hall. Twist climbs up four flights, past closed doors that muffle the sounds of TVs and radios and conversations and lovers having sex. At the top of the stairs he goes to 4-K and quietly lets himself in with a key.

The apartment is dark as he steps inside and eases the door shut. Twist slides down the hall quietly, moving slowly and softly. The bedroom door to his right is closed and the only light comes from the glare of the TV in the living room. The windows are open, the curtains pulled back, and a fan on a pole stand blows hot air that doesn't cool the apartment. Twist is aware of the sweat on his body, inching down his back and clinging to his T-shirt.

He's also aware of the nine tucked close against his skin—his fingers still wrapped around the gun.

The girl is sitting on the couch, drifting in and out of sleep. Her eyes are barely open and she doesn't pay attention to the *Friends* rerun on Channel 11. Her head nods backward slowly, just enough to wake her so she catches herself with a jerk. In the light that comes and goes Twist can see her tanned skin, soft and smooth. Her face is thin, with a small round chin and light brown hair that barely touches her shoulders.

He feels something stir inside as he takes another step forward. She doesn't know he's there.

Twist feels her turn as he slips around the couch and eases down next to her. Her Yankees T-shirt is bunched around her thighs and her bare feet are tucked beneath her. He runs his hand softly along her skin, tracing a pattern with his fingers from her thigh slowly up her leg to the soft cotton of her panties.

His fingers caress slightly and he pushes her T-shirt further up, working both hands along her skin as he slips a few fingers inside the elastic waistband.

Twist feels her arms coming forward and she turns her head toward him. In the light from the TV he sees the slight smile that crosses her mouth as she opens her arms and pulls him closer.

In that moment nothing else from his day matters.

CHAPTER FOUR

Twist wakes up hard and stiff on the couch.

At first he's lost and confused, unable to find anything familiar or recognizable about the morning. A moment of panic grabs his throat and chokes him with fear. A hundred thoughts scream at him but move too fast for comprehension, making it impossible to hold onto anything that makes sense.

Mornings go like this sometimes but there's no comfort in that knowledge.

At least nothing to calm the fear that comes with it.

He squeezes his eyes shut again and tries pulling back whatever memories he can, grasping for help. It takes time drawing everything into focus; time for clarity to return.

His muscles and joints hurt, and Twist is aware of the sharp pain shooting through his shoulder. It's the only thing that is constant and familiar; it's been that way since the day he got shot. The emergency room doctors told him that he would have to live with pain, and mornings since have been filled with accurate reminders of those predictions. He hears the sounds and chatter of cartoons and turns his head far enough to see a Rugrats cartoon on TV across the living room.

The couch is rough corduroy, scratchy against his bare skin. The room is hot and when Twist rolls off a damp spot in the fabric he can feel the sweat sticking to his back as he struggles to sit up. On the floor a few feet away, a little girl sits with her back to him while a small Puggle named Hobo nestles its head into her lap, watching cartoons like Twist doesn't even exist. She has long, straight hair that falls down her shoulders and pale skin. A long white Winnie-the-Pooh T-shirt, like the kind of shirt every other six-year-old wears is pulled down to her ankles.

"Morning, Angel," he croaks.

She and Hobo look up. She has the same deep blue eyes as her mother, with a small round chin and a gap in the smile she flashes before turning back to the TV.

Twist swings upright, letting his shoulders sink backward into the cushions as he finds the floor with his feet. One of his high tops is across the room but he can't see where the other one has been kicked, and his T-shirt is knotted in a ball on the side table, rolled up and tossed aside.

Twist shakes a cigarette from his pack of Camels and hunts for the lighter.

"About time you got up," a sharp voice comes from behind him.

Twist turns, wincing at the shooting pains movement creates.

Maria is standing barefoot in the kitchen wearing the same Yankees T-shirt she had worn last night. In the morning light Twist can see the outline of her body in the shirt. She wears a pissed off expression as she pours a glass of orange juice, then kicks at a roach scurrying across the linoleum.

Twist is thinking that the orange juice and a handful of aspirin will help him ease into the morning.

Maria finishes the orange juice herself and puts the carton back in the refrigerator without offering him a glass.

There's a message there that he misses.

She stares at him with her hands on her hips. Her skin is light and fair, but with that weekend tan she gets on the beach at Seaside she can pass for one of the WASPs walking the streets in Nutley or Belleville. She doesn't look like a Puerto Rican from Jersey City—somebody who's got no place in towns like Nutley or Clifton or Belleville. His eyes move over her. Short and slender with a tight ass and curvy, hard breasts that push out beneath the shirt. Somewhere in his memory of last night Twist can remember the feel of his hands against her skin as they pulled closer on the couch, but most of that is still a blur. Something else lost to the morning and not yet recovered.

"Morning," Twist says, but she doesn't smile.

This time he catches the warning and his own smile sags.

"What's up, baby?"

Maria's stare is cold enough to freeze him in his tracks. "Don't give me that baby shit," she snaps.

"I'm getting real tired of your act, Twist."

"What the fuck you talking about?" he says, rubbing his eyes.

Angel sits a few feet away, too caught up in the cartoon to care about the words passing between them. Hobo rests his chin in her lap and shuts his eyes.

"You know what I'm talking about," Maria says. "Ain't like this is something new."

Twist shakes his head. It is too early to figure out bad moods and guess what he might have done wrong this time. He has no time for games. If it's not black-and-white there's no way he's got what it takes to figure it out—no way he even feels like bothering.

"Too early for this shit."

"You always say that."

"Maybe you can spell this out for me."

She burns that stare into him and for a minute he gets that same edgy feeling he got the first time Valentine nailed him with his own look. "This coming around all hours of the night, letting yourself in here like you own the place," she says, with her voice rising and falling as the words come out faster. "Thinking that the key you got gives you some kind of privilege."

"Ain't just the key. I pay the rent. Don't that count?"

"So you think your eight hundred dollars a month gives you the right to come in here whenever you want," she says. "Just to grab a piece of ass when you feel like it."

Twist shuts his eyes.

"I'm not your slut," she tells him. "I don't sit around here waiting for your dick.

"That ain't the only thing I want in my life, Twist."

Twist keeps his eyes closed tight but the words still cut and slice. While she's going on he's thinking about mistakes he made; not the selfish ones when he ignored her or treated her badly, but the times when he showed Maria he cared. Those times when he let her know that she and Angel meant something; when she got to see his feelings and know his heart. Giving up that part of himself was a mistake, and now that he's lost it, Twist knows there's no way he'll ever find even ground with her.

Once you lose that kind of thing it's gone forever.

Twist shakes his head. All this shit and aggravation because a year ago they were at the same party in Jersey City. She was a hot twenty-two-year-old hard body in a tank top and shorts who was leaning against the wall with a bottle of Corona in one hand, fending off the three guys hitting on her. The first time he saw her, Twist knew he had to have her, and he did what he had to do to get her.

Sometimes he forgets that sex causes more problems than what it gives back in return.

Got to remember that next time.

"You even listening?" she asks.

"Wrong time for this," he tries, searching the floor for his pants. "Got too much going on. Too much for me to get into all this with you."

"All you got is excuses."

Twist shakes his head. "Ain't a good time right now."

"It's never a good time."

"Not now."

"So when is a good time for you?" she shoots back. "One o'clock in the morning when you show up here looking to get laid?"

For a moment he thinks that maybe he can tell her about Ice and Spider and Malik and the Italians. Tell her about Michael Valentine sitting on the third floor at 38 Murray, dried blood caked on his shirt, counting the hours he's got left until somebody comes in the room and puts a bullet in his head. He thinks about explaining how they're trying to get back Malik but knows none of it would make sense to her.

He asks himself again if some things are worth the price you've got to pay to get them.

"You got any ideas about what it is you want?" Twist asks, tired and weary. "I spend time with you."

"If you wanna call it that."

"Do the best I can."

Maria crosses her arms. "Maybe your best isn't enough."

"What's that mean?"

"Means I told you when we met that I wasn't just some neighborhood girl. Not the kind you're used to," she says. "I put myself through Hudson Community. Got my Associates Degree at night then got a nine-to-five downtown with no help from anybody. Did all that before I met you."

"What am I supposed to give you?" he asks.

"I want a life."

"And what's that mean?"

She stares at him.

"It means I'm tired of what I got here," Maria snaps. She goes on without waiting for an answer. "I want something real."

"What's real? What do you mean by that?"

She looks at him, like he can't see what is so clearly obvious. A tired, impatient look like the kind he would expect from Angel crosses her face. "'Real' means a house in a nice place and a man who spends time with me. Treats me like I want to be treated."

"And how you supposed to be treated?"

The pause is too long. The silence too hard.

"Fuck you, Twist. Fuck you if you don't know!" she finally says, turning away.

Twist slams a fist on the table. "I'm asking questions and I ain't getting no answers. How the fuck am I supposed to talk about this if I have to guess what you want?"

Maria turns.

"I want someplace where I don't have to lock the doors and windows all the time. Someplace where Angel isn't afraid to go outside when she want to play," she says. "Someplace nice with somebody who's gonna keep me safe."

And where, Twist asks, is that? What does safe even mean? Ice figured his protection would keep him safe but he's coming back to the Skulls in chunks. Malik thought it was okay to grab a six pack but he's gone. Even Valentine and his old lady probably thought they were safe. He imagines Valentine walking down the street in Belleville talking about how good he's got it, with no idea somebody like Twist can take it all away.

Funny how things like that go.

And funny how it changes so quickly.

◆ ◆ ◆

He knows nobody will answer, but Twist dials the number anyway—the same way he's done it ten times a day since Malik disappeared.

It doesn't even ring once before going to voice mail, with Malik's voice telling him to leave a message.

"Holla back or hit me on the hip," he says.

In his voice there is no trace of fear or worry. No drama. He has no idea of the things that lie ahead or just how badly it will all turn.

Twist feels the knot in his stomach tighten and the hopelessness of everything kicks in.

◆ ◆ ◆

Twist is on the basketball courts, moving back and forth on the asphalt, taking fifteen-foot jump shots. He feels good driving to the net, cutting between guys trying to slap the ball out of his hands, and then pulling up quickly to take his shot. The ball hits nothing but net every time, even if that hot streak doesn't last.

The courts aren't much. A small strip of asphalt behind the Martin Luther King Elementary School, surrounded by a rusted eight-foot-high fence with gaps large enough to drive a Honda through. The paint lines on the court are faded, the white washed off the backboards a long time ago, and there are holes in the blacktop where guys have kicked up chunks of asphalt with the toes of their sneakers. These are Skull courts and Twist has spent his life here. He was Kobe on these courts when he was a kid, practicing and shooting and hustling games against guys in the neighborhood every day he could. Playing for five and ten dollars a game, scraping together enough money for a new pair of Nikes every couple of weeks and a dime bag of weed whenever possible.

The courts are familiar and he likes that comfort.

There are guys shooting baskets, bouncing balls and hustling games wherever and with whoever they can, trying to be Durant or Curry or LeBron. Each pretending like basketball is the only thing that matters.

There are two sixteen-year-olds with guns, their backs to the courts, eyeing the neighborhood. They watch for cars cruising the street too slowly or for stares from strangers that linger; always aware of everything and everybody around them.

It's only a matter of time before the Italians take another shot at somebody. When Twist got shot it was random and quick, and he never saw it coming. He was lucky the drive-by shooters didn't have better aim. All that's left is the scar where the doctors pieced him together and pain that wakes him most mornings.

He knows guys who point to their bullet holes and knife scars like they are meaningful. For Twist, all his scar means is that he was stupid and unaware; nothing more than that. It makes him cautious now. Reminds him that he's not immune to anything around him.

"Your own fucking fault," his older brother told him. "You in a place where you should have seen it coming."

"Can't see everything," Twist said.

"Something like that you got to know what's going on," he told him. "Got to have eyes on both sides of your head.

"You know better next time."

For a while Twist has one of those "can't miss" mornings where every shot he takes falls. He's in the middle of a three-on-three, playing against a couple of older guys nobody knows too well. Somebody on the sidelines said they were cops but Twist knows cops in this neighborhood have better things to do then play pick up ball games against gang bangers. These guys play a slow, physical game with bumping and banging and picks that take you off your feet when they roll into you. They set hard screens that knock you on your ass every time you go up for a rebound, and use their elbows to jockey for space. But it's the kind of game where Twist can use his speed to move, pass to a teammate, or hit an open shot that takes away any advantage they have.

The game is close but then it turns—Twist's hot hand turns ice cold quickly. The bumping and pushing wear him down and it gets tougher finding the seam between players to work his way toward the basket. Nothing comes easily. Twist tries a simple shot with nobody in his face but the ball bounces off the backboard. One of the other guys chases down the rebound, grabs it, and does a spin-around jumper over Twist that hits nothing but net from twenty-five feet.

It quickly deteriorates into that kind of game.

A few minutes later Twist is on the sidelines watching another game, lighting a Camel and waiting his turn for the next game. There are no shortage of guys ready to take his place—barely off the court, three or four others quickly angled to take his spot.

"Game got brick," the kid next to him offers.

Twist shrugs. "It happens, you know."

"You was good. They just better, man."

"Can't get too hung up on it," Twist says. "Shit like that happens."

"Hear about your action on the street yesterday. That true?" the kid asks. "You snatched a Guinea?"

Twist looks at him. He's no more than twelve or thirteen. Small and thin, with the same kind of tough cool guys like LJ and Rasheed have but with the kind of inexperience Spider showed. Twist knows him without knowing his name. He's one of the kids the Skulls use to sling nickel bags and push dime tins in schools. Not ready to be a corner boy but somebody they can use. He's hungry to do things so he can belong. Maybe someday the kid gets his chance but if something happens before then you don't mind losing him.

He's the kind of kid who can be replaced easily.

"Who you hear that from?"

The kid smiles a mouthful of white teeth. "Man, that's all anybody talking about."

"What they saying?"

"Saying it's gonna be a war. Take no prisoners kind of thing, you know?"

Twist watches the games on the court. He can't see the kid's expression change but he can hear the eagerness in his voice. Like he wants badly to be in on something, even if he's not sure what it is or where it'll lead.

"That what you think?"

"Everybody knows what happened to Ice. Know about Spider and Malik. Everybody knows the score," the kid says. "Won't blame you none for what you gonna do to him because of Malik."

Twist turns to face him.

He doesn't think it has anything to do with blame. It's about protecting turf, taking pride in what they got, and sticking up for each other. What they're doing has to do with not letting the Italians walk in and take away everything the Skulls worked hard to build. It's about a future.

At least a chance at one.

He wonders again if Valentine has got to the part of his morning where he sees things like that a little clearer; where the questions fall away and what's left is black, white, and definite.

If he can see what everybody else already knows.

"What you think we're gonna do to him if we don't get Malik back?"

"You frontin'?"

Twist shrugs. "Tell me."

The kid laughs. "Ain't a guy on Broad Street who don't know the Guinea's a dead man. Don't need Geraldo Rivera to tell me that."

◆ ◆ ◆

Twist calls Murray Street from his burner while keeping his back to the brick wall and his eyes on the street while he dials. The two guys are on the edge of the blacktop, just inside the chain link fence, with their .22s tucked against their shirts covering the parts of the street he can't see. One of the game boys answers the phone. He tells Twist that Bone and Cuba are out and nobody's seen Eddie Dallas since early that morning.

"Everything's cool," he says. "Just waiting to make it happen."

"Is that what you think?" Twist asks. "Or is this what you hear the others saying?"

The kid doesn't reply and Twist lets the moment pass.

"You check on the guy upstairs?" he asks instead.

The silence is enough of an answer. Twist pictures the kid standing in the living room, holding the phone in one hand, searching for the words he's supposed to repeat but drawing a blank. Afraid to say the wrong thing, he says nothing instead.

"Either you got a yes or a no," Twist says. "Ain't no multiple choice question."

"Cuba says he's okay," the kid finally replies, drawing out the words.

Twist frowns. "How's he know that?"

"He was up there this morning," he says. "Said everything's okay."

Twist is still frowning when he hangs up, not sure if the situation has changed at all, or if it's got better or worse. He doesn't like the feeling washing over him. He knows that he and Cuba share a different definition of what "okay" is.

When Twist returns to the courts Eddie Dallas is leaning against the side of a dark green Cadillac Escalade. It has the kind of dealer plates on the front and back that traffic cops rarely check, and a Metallica song blasts through the open windows. There's a six pack of Bud cans on the hood. Eddie has a proud, smug expression and Twist knows the cars hot, only an hour or two at the most. He's still in the same khakis and boots Twist last saw him wearing, but now he's got on a red Limp Bizkit T-shirt with a black bandanna tied around his dreadlocks. The same sunglasses are angled down low on his nose. He takes one last puff on a Marlboro then crushes the butt beneath his heel.

He flashes Twist a grin.

The two kids with the .22s give him a nod and move farther down the street, taking up new positions on the sidewalk.

"Knew I'd find you here," Eddie Dallas says, holding out a hand for Twist.

Twist returns the grin. "Better than being on Murray Street."

"Word," Eddie says, looking around as he shakes another Marlboro out of the pack. "At least here you take on the assholes one-on-one. A good beating on the court and you don't have to listen to motherfuckers who can't back up their words talking trash for days afterwards.

"Like they know something you don't and can do something you can't."

"Too bad I can't get Cuba and Bone out here," Twist says.

Eddie Dallas shrugs.

"Ain't the kind of place where they can be in control," he says. "If they don't have control, they don't have nothing."

Twist doesn't say anything but he knows it's true.

He leans against the car, next to Eddie, and wipes the sweat from his face. The morning is already hot and when he looks across the courts he can see the heat curling off the asphalt in waves but it's not hot enough to slow the games that continue on every court.

"Where's the action?"

"You tell me," Twist says.

"Ain't nothing changed since last night."

"I hear Bone and Cuba don't have nothing yet," Twist says. "No word from the Guineas."

Eddie Dallas nods. "A lot of nothing going on right now."

Twist takes one of Eddie's Marlboros. "Just waiting for something to happen."

"Cuba and Bone don't see that as a good thing. They're itchy to do something."

"They still thinking we should be out making something happen?"

Eddie shrugs. "Guess they figure snatching the guy off the street ain't enough. Need to be pulling a trigger."

It suddenly comes to Twist that nobody in the Skulls refers to Valentine by name. In every conversation Valentine is "the guy" or the "Guinea"; like he doesn't have any other name. Or that he doesn't need the one he has. Whatever identity he used to have is nothing now.

That sticks with Twist and bothers him.

"What's going on with Valentine?"

"Nothing much," Eddie answers. "He's okay."

"You saying that because that's what Cuba says," Twist asks, "or you telling me that because you know it's true?"

Eddie's expression curls into a grimace that fills with anger in an instant. A weird look crosses his face. His eyes narrow as he pushes the sunglasses back up his nose with his thumb.

"Fuck Cuba," he spits out. "You know the only time he gives a fuck about Valentine is when he gets to put the bullet in his head. Until then he don't matter.

"I know he's okay because I looked in on him this morning."

That makes Twist feel better. "How's he doing?"

"Same as yesterday. Pissed off and bored," Eddie Dallas says, taking one of the Buds from the pack. "I brought him coffee and he bitched that it was too weak. Took him to the can and he bitched that I should've been there sooner. Said he wanted a TV and a radio and a newspaper so he could see how the Mets did last night."

"Tell him about the game?"

"Didn't want to fuck up his day," he said. "Figure things are bad enough for him already."

"Get him anything else to eat?"

Eddie shakes his head. "Nah. Figured maybe you and me could get something before we go back. Bring him back a sandwich. Be like two Mother Theresas doing our good deed."

The thought of food reawakens rumblings in Twist's stomach. It's close to eleven and he still hasn't had anything to eat since yesterday's Egg McMuffin and cup of coffee. The last time he thought about food was when he was squared off against Maria, watching her finish that orange juice he wanted. On a different day he might have taken her and Angel out for breakfast but this morning he was too pissed off and left quickly, and by the time he got to the courts he had forgotten about food.

Now he can't think of anything else.

"Sounds good to me," he says, rapping Eddie in the shoulder with a fist.

"Could use a couple of subs and a slice of pizza," he adds. "Maybe pick up a newspaper for Valentine if we got time."

Eddie smiles. "We got as much time as we want, right?"

Twist just nods his head.

◆ ◆ ◆

The deli is a few blocks past Seton Hall, on the part of South Orange Avenue that dips beneath the railroad tracks along the edge of the business district, in a neighborhood where even modest houses are expensive. It's a small store, with a few chairs and tables and a long glass and chrome counter displaying salads, meats and cheeses. Two racks of chips and pretzels when you walk in the door and three large soda cases against the far wall, filled with Cokes and Snapple and bottled water. The kind of soft rock—Adele, Taylor Swift, and Jessica Simpson—playing on the radio that makes them both cringe. Twist and Eddie Dallas wait at the counter, wearing shades and chain smoking Marlboros. They're as out of place in the deli as they are driving through Belleville and Nutley but nobody says anything to them, and they wait in silence.

There's a college kid behind the counter, white, geeky with glasses and acne scars, making their subs as fast as he can. Twist thinks that if he were to pull out the 9mm the kid wouldn't be too surprised. It would just feed into his expectations. The kid peeks up at them like he knows it can happen. Like he's ready for it.

Eddie and Twist exchange glances, both of them thinking the same thing.

Twist keeps going back to Valentine's execution, knowing it will quickly turn into a reality, even if nobody else has admitted that yet. It's that obvious. The only questions are when it will happen and who will pull the trigger.

The way Twist has it figured, it will be Cuba; he's the only one who gets off on things like that. And he's the only one with a burning desire to do it.

But somehow it doesn't seem right to Twist that Cuba is the one who pulls the trigger if they don't get Malik back.

He wonders what it feels like to shoot a man up close and see the life drain out of his body; if it's any different than doing it from far away or if it's the same kind of feeling. Watching everything fall from a man's expression as he's dying leaves something that lasts. Twist has killed before, but he was never close enough to see what it's like when the victim's face twitches and his body shudders while the bullets take away his last breath.

He would remember something like that.

The same way he still remembers his first time.

He was eighteen, willing to do anything to prove himself. He did everything without question. Actions had a definite purpose and there were none of the shades of gray like the ones he lives in now.

It was a spring night when he and some other Skulls went after the Bloods. There weren't many Bloods left by then; the gang had been ripped apart by internal wars, rumbles with other crews, and big time trouble with cops. The Asian gangs had been kicking their asses on one side of town, the Jamaicans were cutting off their dope supply, and the Russians in the Ironbound were chipping away at their turf. Jail, death, and attrition left them desperate to hold on to the fragments of the neighborhood they still controlled. What they had wasn't much, but it was enough that the Skulls wanted it for themselves.

None of that mattered to Twist.

It was about revenge. Getting back something for Tayshaun.

.45s, shotguns, and good timing made it easy. Nobody saw the car with Twist and Stinger Brown leaning from the passenger's side, aiming their guns. They took out five soldiers standing on a corner as they sipped Buds and listened to BLS on their boxes.

Twist can remember the feel of the gun spitting backward in his hand every time he squeezed the trigger. The way the bullets tore into flesh. The screams that stayed with him as their car raced away into the night. There were stories in the *Ledger* over the next few days; kill five gang bangers and the cops don't look the other way. There were names and ages and backgrounds about the dead crew, but none of them meant anything to Twist.

He never saw their faces. Not close up. He never saw how death looked in their eyes.

That makes it different.

He wonders now if doing Valentine will feel the same way. If revenge will be different this time.

Twist and Eddie walk out of the deli, going down the block toward the Escalade. Twist sips a Snapple while Eddie carries the bag with the sandwiches, mouthing the words to a Michael Jackson song that had been playing on the radio station. He looks both pissed off and amused that he can't shake the melody.

"Fucking antiseptic rock shit."

Twist just smiles. "Who you kidding? You probably got that CD at home. Or on your iTunes. Be listening to it late at night."

"Fuck you, nigger."

Twist stops. "Forgot to get a paper," he says.

"What for?"

"For Valentine. Remember?"

Eddie Dallas smiles and shakes his head as he keeps going to the car. "Probably just want an excuse to hang in there and listen to that bullshit song on the radio."

"Yeah, you on to me," Twist says with a smile.

Twist sees the black BMW racing around the corner as he turns and knows in a heartbeat that it's trouble. It's moving too fast and too recklessly to belong on this street, and Twist is moving before the two black guys come through the windows with guns in their hands. Everything goes from zero to sixty in that one moment of time, although it feels like it takes hours to chip away each second that passes. Every detail is graphic and intense.

Their movements stay frozen in Twist's head forever.

When the first bullets explode on the concrete at his feet he yells at Eddie to get down while diving for cover. Dust and chips of concrete spray him. He hears the ping of bullets ricocheting off cars and storefronts.

It is chaos around him. Some people freeze while others drop to their bellies on the sidewalk, covering their heads with hands and burying faces in the concrete. The glass in the store windows shatters and rains on the sidewalk, and there are screams as more bystanders tumble to the ground. Traffic on South Orange Avenue screeches to a stop as the BMW weaves around cars. Twist rolls across the sidewalk, grabbing for his 9mm while turning his head to follow the BMW.

He sees Eddie crouched behind the Cadillac, flat against the metal, reaching a hand inside an open window.

A bullet takes off the side mirror by his chin.

"Motherfuckers!" Eddie yells.

Another bullet ricochets off the concrete by Twist's cheek.

The BMW never slows. It's through the intersection before the two gunmen slide back inside, cutting across the left lane and accelerating down South Orange Avenue.

Twist comes up with his gun, braces his arms, and fires.

Eddie gets inside the open window and yanks out a sawed-off, shoving two shells into the breech and lurching into the middle of the street. He straddles the yellow line in the center of South Orange Avenue, raises the shotgun, and pulls both triggers.

The blast shatters the back window of the BMW. The sedan fishtails hard to the right then back to the left—although it slows for a second, the car never stops.

Twist sees one of the guys in the back slump forward and the guy from the front seat starts back to get him, but nothing more after that. The car is too far away and moving too fast to see anything clearly. In another second it runs a red light and disappears in traffic.

"Think I got him?" Eddie yells as he runs back to the Cadillac.

"Got at least one," Twist says. "Saw that."

"Good."

The whole episode has taken no more than thirty seconds but it feels like it's been hours. Like any minute now five or six cop cars will race around the corner, uniforms hanging from the doors like the cops on TV, guns out and pointed at the two of them. Looking for an easy reason to kill two niggers.

He and Eddie are inside the Escalade in seconds, cutting across the street and heading in the opposite direction toward Newark.

"You see faces?" Eddie yells. The engine kicks hard from gear to gear as he accelerates. "Colors? Something?"

"Happened too fast. Didn't see shit," Twist yells back, although later when he sits down he'll pick out the smallest details as if the whole thing had passed in slow motion. He'll remember the car and the two guys with the guns pointing from the window, as well as the crack of the bullets against the concrete and the sounds of the glass shattering around him. He'll hear voices screaming and remember their cries. Those memories will stay with him.

"I think we got an answer from the Guineas," he says.

Eddie nods.

"Tough to know what this means," Twist says, "or where we go from here."

They drive in silence.

Eddie cuts down Irvington Avenue and takes that to Clinton, slowing enough to blend in with the rest of the traffic. Twist sits back in his seat and closes his eyes. Eddie eases his foot off the accelerator and looks at the bullet holes that strafed the car and cracked the windshield, shaking his head slowly from side to side.

"Fucking shame," he says dejectedly. "Kind of liked this car."

CHAPTER FIVE

It's after one when Eddie Dallas steers off McCarter onto Murray Street. Twist has his eyes closed again and his head back against the seat, although he's too wired to sleep. For the past hour it has been impossible to relax. They've killed time taking the Turnpike south to Woodbridge then driving slowly back along Route 1, zigzagging up and down side streets to shake any tails. Every car was a threat. Every traffic light another ambush to fear. Making sure there were no cars following them back to the garage, no sign of the BMW, and no gunmen hanging out open windows or lurking in the shadows.

The bag with the sandwiches rolls back and forth on the floor between Twist's feet, on top of copies of the *Star Ledger* and *New York Post* they picked up at a deli near Irvington. This time Twist ran inside while Eddie sat in the car, watching the street with the shotgun in his lap and a finger on the trigger.

Taking absolutely no chances.

At the deli Twist used a pay phone to call the garage. He stayed off his cell and didn't give any details—nobody was ever sure if the cops had a wire on their numbers or what could be heard if they were listening. Conversations were always risky, and it was better taking no chances.

He told the Game Boy who answered, "911. Guineas tried to clock us."

A guy in long shorts and a Yankees' shirt leans against the Sentra on the corner and watches the Cadillac approach with a wary stare, turning to follow the car as it slows near 38 Murray Street. Eddie waves a hand through the open window and the guy returns the wave, but his stare never fades until he's sure about everything. Twist's eyes are still closed as Eddie pulls the Escalade to a stop. Twist's jeans are ripped at the knees, streaked with blood, and the skin is warm and sticky when he touches a finger to it. There are sharp, new pains in his shoulder and his elbow throbs, but nothing he's concerned about.

Worries for another day and time.

Neither one of them has spoken in a long time, not since Eddie steered off Clinton toward the Irvington deli, and Twist was grateful for the silence. Sometimes he welcomes that more than words and conversation. He used the silence to think about the guys in the BMW, the bullets that chipped up the concrete at his feet, and the windows that shattered on the street behind him. He thinks about where this drive-by is going to lead.

And where it will take them.

It wasn't random—not just about two guys in the wrong place at the wrong time. There is no way that this is an isolated incident, and no way it doesn't purposely involve them.

And it is only the beginning.

Eddie leaves the car double parked and they get out slowly. One of Cuba's boys, a nineteen-year-old named Boo comes off the porch to meet them. Short and wide, with a gold-capped smile and a shaved head like Cuba, he stuffs a .45 in his belt the same way Cuba does. Twist can already see that little bit of Cuba in the way Boo carries himself, although he hasn't seen him pistol whip a corner boy and his stare doesn't yet have that same nasty edge that Cuba's does. Not yet, anyway.

"Nice whip," he says, grinning. "Fine looking ride."

Twist walks past him without a word and quickly crosses the sidewalk.

Eddie comes around the Escalade and tosses Boo the keys.

"Make sure it ain't ever found." he says.

Boo shakes his head. "A car that fine, a fucking shame to get rid of it."

"You hear what I said?"

"Heard you. Just saying that the cars serious."

"When I look out the window in ten minutes, I don't want to see the fucking thing on the street," Eddie Dallas says over his shoulder as he catches up to Twist.

Twist turns and stares down the kid. "Don't want to drive past your mom's apartment one day and see you out there putting a coat of wax on it, neither. You make it disappear permanently. Ain't never gonna be found by nobody."

"You understand that?" Eddie asks.

"It's cool," Boo says, beaming that smile as they walk away. "No problem."

Twist and Eddie Dallas both stare at him climbing into the Escalade, each of them thinking that Boo is the kind of kid stupid enough to keep the car for himself. Stupid enough to never realize the consequences of something like that.

"You ever think that no brains are better than bad brains?" Twist asks.

Eddie Dallas just shrugs.

The garage feels different. There's music playing upstairs but the rest of the building is quiet. There aren't many guys inside and those who are there look edgy and tense, like they've lost whatever cockiness and confidence they wore last night. Two guys are hunched over a mirror on the table, using a rolled up twenty to snort fat white lines laid out in front of them, and another guy takes apart his automatic, methodically cleaning each piece. Two kids stand guard at the window and door with rifles. The rest are on the street, moving drugs in teams, collecting protection money and loan payments, and taking stolen cars to neighborhood chop shops where nothing interferes with the mechanics of business.

The realization that they're in deeper than they expected to be has sunk in.

The kids at the window don't have the same toughness as the guys on the basketball courts. Twist wonders how many more times the phone will ring this afternoon with stories like the one he and Eddie have to tell. If these kids are the kind of mercenaries they need at the door; the kind who can react without waiting for orders when something bad happens.

For a moment Twist thinks about bringing that up to Bone, but he tables the idea almost as quickly as it comes. It's a security issue. If Bone says something about Twist's concerns, Cuba will get in Twist's face. Cuba doesn't take well to suggestions; not from anybody, but especially not from Twist.

Sometimes suggestions sound too much like threats to Cuba.

Bone comes slowly down the stairs wearing black shorts and no shirt, with a can of Bud in one hand and a 9mm in the other. He sits down at the kitchen table and shakes a Camel out of the pack, lighting it slowly before leaning back in his chair.

He eyes Eddie and Twist but says nothing.

Twist sees the girl behind him. She's no more than sixteen or seventeen, in shorts and a halter top, creeping down the stairs in her bare feet like she doesn't want to be seen. She's a face from the neighborhood—someone Twist has seen on the corner making time with the crew. She stares at the three of them for a moment, then turns and walks slowly toward the bathroom in the back of the shop.

"Yo," Bone mutters, ignoring her. "Whassup? What's this 911?"

"Kid give you the message?" Twist asks.

Bone stares at him. "Didn't say nothing except you and Eddie got a 911 and you coming back to the place."

"Shit," Eddie mutters.

"Fucking kids can't get nothing straight," Twist says, glaring back at the faces in the living room. "Can't do nothing right, even something simple like pass on a message."

"So?" Bone asks. "Whassup?"

Neither says anything.

Twist leans a shoulder into the wall and returns Bone's stare, waiting. Eddie Dallas crosses the room, drops the bag with the sandwiches on the table, then takes a Bud out of the refrigerator. He pops open the top and tips it to his lips, draining most of it in one long swallow.

When he finishes he wipes a hand across his mouth and stares at Bone.

"Fuckers took a hit at us. Tried to take us out."

Heads turn with a jerk. In the living room the faces crowded around the mirror snap up, the guy cleaning his automatic starts to his feet, and the two kids standing guard at the window peer across the room with an intensity missing from their stares only seconds earlier.

Nobody says anything but Twist sees what it does to them.

Bone's expression changes too. It's nothing too noticeable— nothing the others see. But in that moment Twist catches a trace of something that comes and goes, even though it doesn't last. He recognizes the uneasiness Eddie's words have unleashed.

Bone quickly recovers his cool, but Twist knows what was there.

Bone's fingers tighten around the beer can. The words come haltingly. "What the fuck happened?"

"It was a drive-by," Eddie says. "Happened fast. Like they was waiting for us. Knew we were there."

"Middle of the day at that deli on South Orange Avenue we go to sometimes. Right past Seton Hall. The one that's open all night." Twist looks at Bone and says, "The place you and me went last Thursday."

Eddie sucks the last drops out of his beer can. "Couple of shooters in a BMW. Looked like Blood colors but we couldn't tell for sure. Came after us when we were walking out the door."

"Why the fuck you up there?"

Twist keeps his stare locked on Bone's eyes. "Getting something to eat."

"You can't go someplace around here?"

"I like that place. I like their subs," Twist says. "You do too. You kept talking about it for hours last time we were there. Acted like you never had a sandwich that good."

"Tried to pop us while we're walking across the sidewalk to the car. Think we got one, but they were driving away too fast and it was tough to tell for sure," Eddie says, looking first to Bone and then back to Twist for confirmation. "You think we got one of them?"

Twist nods.

"How they know you up there?"

Twist shrugs. "Figured they must've tailed us. Maybe saw me on the courts. Caught up to us when we weren't looking."

"Could've been me," Eddie says.

"Means you weren't careful," Bone says.

"My bad," Eddie says with a shrug. "Been careful. Just didn't catch the tail."

Bone smiles something that's not really a smile at all. "That's fucking stupid being up there."

The edge comes through in Twist's voice before he can contain it. "Ain't like it's some place new. We go there all the time," he says. "Know the street and know the territory."

"Stupid being up there."

"We knew what we were doing. Knew our steps."

"Still stupid."

"Give me a fucking break!"

Bone glares at him. "Give me a fucking break, Twist," he spits back. "Going up there don't show brains. Not with Ice and Spider dead, Malik nowhere to be found, and us holding one of the Guineas upstairs. Not with all this shit going on."

"Going up there had nothing to do with this."

"Everything you do from now on got something to do with this. You got to be smart enough to realize that," he says.

The words hang and Twist feels the sharpness that comes with them. Eddie Dallas looks first to Bone and then at Twist, and then back to Bone again, waiting for what's between them to pass. The rest of the Skulls watch from the other room but nobody says anything. Bone holds the gun in his hand with a stare that grows harder and colder. Whatever crossed his face moments earlier is gone now.

He's back in control.

He runs a hand across his face and leans back in the chair.

"I guess this means the Guineas getting worried," he says. "Maybe this their way of getting back some of what they lost."

Twist doesn't see it that way, but he keeps that to himself and doesn't share it with Bone.

"You hear anything?" Twist asks later. "Got any kind of response?"

Bone shakes his head as he takes a long drag on his Camel. "Nothing. Guys hear rumors and talk," he says, "but if you asking whether we got something from the Guineas, the answer is no."

"Anything in those papers you picked up?"

Twist shakes his head. There is nothing about Valentine, but nobody expected headlines or page four stories detailing what happened in Belleville. Newspapers are like that; the same way nothing was ever written about Malik getting snatched off the street or the Bloods snuffing out his brother years earlier. Even when they took out Ice and put two other Skulls in Intensive Care, there was nothing. It was what cops called "non-news"—incidents that rarely made it into print, at least not right away. Maybe if Twist had taken out that old couple coming out of the bank or if Cuba had killed that geek with the briefcase who was trying to help Valentine it might have made the front page, but stories about guys like Valentine, Twist, and Malik never get told unless there are corpses and clues cops can figure out.

"Cuba been hearing things on the street."

"Like what?"

"Guys telling him the Guineas saying we won't kill this guy because we don't want to start something we can't win."

Bone takes a deep drag on his Camel. "Say we're afraid of them."

"You believe that?" Twist asks.

Bone shrugs. "That's what he telling me he hears."

It sounded too much like Cuba talking. The kind of words Cuba wanted to hear. The kind of tough talk that starts him up the same way a slap to the face or a kick in the ass does it for others. Those are words that create excuses and reasons to take action; if that's what Cuba is looking to find.

Most times Cuba doesn't even need reasons or justification.

"They got to be thinking we just a bunch of stupid niggers too dumb or too afraid to pull the trigger on this guy," Bone says.

"That don't sound like them," Twist says. "Not from what we know."

"If that's true, them saying that," Eddie says, more to himself than either Bone or Twist, "they're throwing lit matches at gasoline. Just waiting for some kind of explosion."

Twist shakes his head. "It ain't them. They've been doing business with us too long to say something like that."

"That don't mean nothing. That's long ago," Bone says.

"They know us. We know them," Twist says.

Bone shrugs and the way he does it tells Twist that he's past the point of caring what Twist has to say.

"Anybody make any decisions about him?" Eddie Dallas asks, nodding upstairs. "Think about what we're gonna do with that guy?"

"I figure we wait until later, when everybody gets back," Bone says but Twist knows that really means 'when Cuba gets back.' "Give us some time to hear if the same shit happen to anybody else. Maybe we hear something from the Guineas by then."

"Maybe decide something to do."

He looks at Twist and asks again, "You hear anything?" This time he's not asking about the rumors and gossip on the street.

Twist knows what he means.

Twist shakes his head. In the past day he's only been home long enough to shower and change clothes. There haven't been any messages; nothing on his cell and no call backs on his pager, but Twist doesn't expect anything. The way he figures, he won't get a phone call from his older brother Raphael yet. There are too many ears inside the joint; guys who listen to conversations that don't involve them, trying to find information they can use to drop on somebody else. Information and what you know inside is important. You can use information in East Jersey State the same way you use a shank, so most times you wait until you know nobody else can hear what you're saying. There's too much risk in talking unless it's face-to-face, and that can't happen until visiting day on Saturday.

Whatever Twist hears from his older brother won't matter much by then. Saturday is too late. Valentine is probably a dead man if Saturday is the soonest Raphael can tell him what he thinks they should do.

Twist stands up and pushes away from the table, taking the sandwich bag along with three cans of Bud that he yanks out of the refrigerator. He feels the eyes following him to the stairs. Eddie Dallas says something but Twist doesn't catch the words, although he hears Bone's voice loud enough.

"What I still can't figure out," he's saying, "is why the fuck the two of you got to go to South Orange to buy sandwiches. Still don't make no sense to me."

Twist lets it slide as he starts up the stairs, tucking the paper under an arm.

◆ ◆ ◆

There's a different kid at the third floor door. Twist has seen him around but can't remember his name; sometimes there are so many wannabes drifting in and out of the garage that he can't keep all the names and faces straight. Some days it seems that everybody wants in.

Each of them is willing to do anything it takes to prove they deserve to be there.

This kid is short and thin, flat top hair cut shaved close and tight on the sides, with a broad face and a flat nose. The nose has the kind of lumps that come from being slammed into the pavement or the sides of police cruisers too many times. Heavy chains hang around his neck, like the ones used to lock bicycles on the street, his shirt is open and unbuttoned to his belly, and a black Raiders cap is turned around backward on his head.

The halls are littered with more cigarette butts, empty Coke cans, and candy bar wrappers. The trail of graffiti stretching across one wall continues to grow.

He needs to tell somebody to clean up the mess. And to start respecting the building.

The kid looks at Twist and tries pushing out his shoulders. He turns up both his cool and toughness a notch, bringing up the gun and waving it back and forth.

Twist looks at him. "Anything going on in there?"

"Not a fucking thing."

"Open the door," Twist says. "I'm going in there."

The kid moves to the door, fishing the keys out of his pocket. "When we gonna waste this fucking guy?" he asks. "We gonna do it soon?"

Twist takes a step back and eyes the kid in silence. The kid feels the stare as he fumbles with the locks.

"What the fuck's your hurry?" Twist asks. "You got some place you want to go? Something you got to do, that this is keeping you from doing it?"

"What?"

"Asking why it's so important to you to ice this guy?"

The kid doesn't have an answer but that doesn't surprise Twist.

Most times nobody ever does.

♦ ♦ ♦

Michael Valentine is sitting on the edge of the bed, stiff and tense as the door opens, and when he sees Twist he lets out a breath and eases back on his elbows. There is a look on his face that says he's glad it's Twist coming through the door and not somebody else. Nothing is said or spoken but Twist can see it in his expression. Valentine looks up at Twist with a nod.

The door closes but Twist waits until he hears the kid bolt the locks before moving further into the room.

He hands Valentine the bag with the sandwiches and two cans of Bud, then tosses copies of the newspapers on the corner of the bed. "Thought you might want something to read," he says. "Help pass the time."

Valentine's face cracks slightly. "Appreciate that."

"Figure it's got to be pretty boring in here, huh?"

"Got that fucking right," Valentine says.

Twist goes across the room and drags a chair out of the corner, putting the can of Bud at his feet. He turns the chair so the back is facing the bed, then straddles it with both legs, leaning on his elbows as he watches Valentine tear into one of the wax paper sandwich wrappers. The way he goes after the sandwich, taking big bites that fill his mouth and cheeks makes Twist wonder what kind of breakfast he got. Cuba probably didn't offer him more than coffee and candy bars.

The night and the morning have not been good to Valentine. His face is pale and drawn, and beads of sweat dot his forehead and ring his neck around the shirt collar. His hands shake slightly as he holds the sandwich, but when he catches Twist staring he turns a shoulder to block the view. The bruise on his face is still dark and nasty, and in the dim light it looks worse now than it did yesterday. The lines in his face are more pronounced and his whole body looks ragged; there is a weariness about him. His eyes are bloodshot; lifeless the way a junkie's eyes get after a bad string of crack-filled days, and it takes a long time before his stare returns.

Valentine looks over at him. "You got a name?"

"They call me Twist."

"Why?"

Twist shrugs. "Just do."

"No reason? No meaning to it?"

"Nothing that matters to nobody else."

Valentine accepts it without pressing; satisfied with the answer. He tries out the name between bites from the sandwich, connecting the name with the person across the room to see how it fits.

"Guess you already know my name," he says.

"We needed your wallet," Twist tells him. "Wanted something to prove we had you. To show your people, in case it ever came to that."

Valentine takes another big bite from the sandwich and washes it down with a gulp of Bud, letting his thoughts kick around in silence. " Did you know who I was when you took me off the street?" he asks. "Or did you take a shot at the first white guy you saw and figure the odds were on your side?"

"Wasn't a guess." Twist shakes his head. "One of the guys seen you around with Sally. Made the connection. Knew you were one of them."

"Got lucky finding me on the street?"

Twist shrugs.

"How did you know I wasn't just some guy? A delivery guy or a driver or something?"

"Told you. Knew you were a part of this."

Valentine looks at him. "That made me important?"

"Enough to matter."

"Wrong place at the wrong time?" Valentine frowns. "Or wrong place at the right time?"

"Something like that. Know most of you guys live in Belleville. Figured we'd keep looking until we found one of y'all."

Valentine just shakes his head and goes back to his food.

It's hot and stuffy and Twist feels the suffocating strength of the heat the longer he sits in the chair. Somebody had brought up a fan from one of the downstairs bedrooms and plugged it in by the bed but it doesn't do much—it blows the warm, stale air from one corner of the room to the other. Twist turns in the seat, feeling his shirt sticking to his body as he moves with the weight of the 9mm still heavy against the small of his back. He draws the gun from his waistband and positions it in his lap.

"Is that for show?" Valentine asks, gesturing toward the gun. "Or maybe you're thinking about using it?"

"You thinking about giving me a reason?"

He shrugs. "Maybe if you didn't bring me these papers I might've considered it," he mutters. "But now we're talking a different situation."

Twist doesn't answer.

"You can't believe how fucking boring this is," he says, finishing the Bud. "There is nothing to do. Not a fucking thing. I watch the blades turning on the fucking fan and if I'm lucky I get to step on all the bugs and roaches running across the floor. That about covers my excitement for the rest of the day."

"Figured the papers might make it better," Twist says. "At least give you something to do."

"Maybe you can do something about getting me a TV?" Valentine asks, but Twist just smiles and slowly shakes his head.

"Not like this is the Holiday Inn and we got to entertain you," he says. "You know what the situation is."

He wonders if Valentine really believes he'll stay in the room long enough to watch a few days' worth of summer reruns. If he's still holding out hope that something's going to happen that will get him released—that he's not a dead man after all. Maybe that kind of hope keeps him going.

Twist wants to ask him about that but says instead, "You don't give up, huh?"

"I never do," Valentine states.

"There's been other guys coming up here," Valentine says a little while later with the *Ledger* spread out in sections in front of him on the bed. He's reading slowly through the different pages, soaking up the words while Twist gives him the space and the quiet to do it. "Guys checking in on me. Walking me down to the bathroom. Making sure I'm not doing something stupid, like trying to make a weapon out of the fan or slashing my wrists with the blades.

"One of them was that guy from the car," he adds, and Twist knows it's Cuba he's talking about.

He looks up. "He say anything? Do anything?"

"Eerie motherfucker, that guy," Valentine says, rocking his head back and forth, stretching the neck muscles. "He comes in here and stares at me, and you can tell right away he wants something more. Like he's willing to take everything I got until he finds what he wants, or until he finds something better that he can take from somebody else. Doesn't matter who it belongs to or what he has to do to get it.

"He looks like the kind of guy who doesn't care about things that aren't his. Not if he wants them."

He just described Cuba as well as anybody ever did.

"That's why I was glad it was you who opened the door," Valentine says. "Out of everybody who's poked his head in here, you're the only one who's bothered trying to have a conversation with me."

"He say much?"

"Nothing I didn't expect to hear," Valentine says, "from a guy like him."

Twist reaches down and takes a Bud, popping open the top as he brings it to his mouth. The beer hits his throat and the rush feels good. Valentine sits with his back against the wall and opens his second can of beer, pushing the papers aside with a foot and looking over at Twist. "That guy somebody important?" he asks.

"He's somebody," Twist says with a toss of his shoulders, "but he ain't much for making decisions. At least not the kind of decisions where you got to look at all the choices and figure out which one is better."

Valentine nods as if he knows guys like that too.

"Always easier to use a fist, huh? Eliminates the debate and makes it simple."

"That way you don't look stupid if you make the wrong choice," Twist agrees.

"Guys like him don't like to make the wrong choice."

"Guys like him don't like to look stupid."

Valentine cracks a brief smile. "Funny how somebody like that worries more about looking stupid then he does about anything else, huh?"

Twist takes a sip from his Bud and leans forward, resting his chin on his forearms as he nods.

Valentine looks at him. "You one of them?"

"What do you mean?"

"You one of those guys who worries about looking stupid?" he asks. "Or are you the kind of guy who does things and gets respect from the guys you know?"

"Maybe I'm neither one."

"You're either one or the other. And you ain't one of the others who just follows orders and does what he's told."

Twist stares back at him. "What makes you think that?"

"I saw that already."

Twist keeps space between them.

"What kind of guy does that make me?"

"Somebody who's got more going on than what's happening with this gang. Anybody who's got a brain can see that."

Twist shrugs and Valentine comes back with that stare, harder now and more focused. "You telling me you were born to do this?" he asks. "That getting in this gang was all you ever dreamed about as a kid? This is your life's ambition?"

"What I wanted don't matter much now. Besides, I'm not one of those guys who lives for respect," Twist tells him. "Giving somebody that much respect just makes him think he's something he's not. All I am is a guy who'd rather be playing basketball most days."

"None of this is important to you?"

"Didn't say that," Twist corrects. "Just said I'd rather be playing basketball."

"You play a lot?"

Twist shakes his head. "Been dealing with too many other things to get out on the courts the way I want."

"You any good?"

"Good enough for the courts around here."

"What's that mean? You're either good or you're not."

"What it means is what I said. You think I'd be sitting in this building, staring at you if I was any good," Twist says. "I'd be banking my multimillion dollar contract from the NBA, owning a sneaker contract with Nike, wearing my Gucci, and driving a Benz in a neighborhood a hell of a lot nicer than this one. Maybe even live down the street from all you motherfuckers."

Michael Valentine smiles as the words come out.

"What about you?" Twist asks with the hint of his own smile. "You do something with your life before this?"

"Before what?"

Twist shakes his head and forces his own laugh. "Man, you gonna sit there and tell me you don't know what the fuck I'm talking about?"

It takes a while for Valentine to respond, like he's thinking about what is true and what's not. Finally he shrugs. "It's different. What I got ain't like this."

"How? It can't be that different," Twist says. "Same game. Just different sides. Know where the line's drawn and when it's been crossed. What else is there?"

"Things like family and honor and respect," Michael Valentine says.

"Shit," Twist says. "Here comes that fucking bullshit."

Even Valentine cracks a smile.

"So what did you do?" Twist asks again. "Before this."

"I used to fight," Valentine says. "Spent time as a middleweight. It was a long time ago. Like thirty years ago, but it was something to do."

"You any good?"

"You think I'd be walking down the street in Belleville if I was that good? Think I would've let you fucking clowns wrestle me inside the car?" Valentine says, still smiling. "I had some fights. A couple at Ice World up in Totowa before they turned it into a hardware store and some undercards in Philly and Atlantic City. But I never did more than bounce around from fight to fight. Finally came a day where I figured out I wasn't going to get the big time shots other guys were getting and that it was time to get out. One of the promoters who did fights was this guy who owned a bar in Madison, and when boxing was going nowhere I got jobs driving him around and doing stuff for him."

"One thing leads to another, you know?" he says and Twist nods.

"This guy connected with Giaccolone, huh? That your way in?"

Valentine nods. "That and family and the neighborhood. Guess it was one of those things that was bound to happen, no matter how much I dreamed about doing other stuff."

Valentine stares at Twist. "Too bad you can never do things the way you set out to do them, huh?"

Twist nods.

Sometimes it happens that nothing you wish for comes true; at least not the way you want. But he always figured that the secret to getting by was making the best out of what you got and dealing with the fallout later.

At least until everything went down with the Italians.

Even through the smile Twist can feel Valentine's eyes coming at him. And when the smile fades Valentine's stare narrows, although it is still strong and intense. "Maybe what we got here are two guys who can't do what they really want to do," he says.

At least not good enough to do it for real.

"You hear anything?" Michael Valentine asks, waving around the room. "Anything about this?"

"Only been a day," Twist says. "Still early."

Valentine runs a hand through his hair, untying the band that knots his ponytail and shaking free his hair. "That eerie motherfucker told me this is about getting back one of your guys," he says, closing his eyes for a moment. "Told me you guys figure taking me is gonna force some kind of trade."

"Something like that."

Michael Valentine shakes his head and lets the hair fall over his face. "I guess it doesn't matter if I tell you I don't know anything about the guy who's missing."

"You saying you didn't have anything to do with it?"

"Would you believe me, if I said that?"

Twist shook his head. "Know you were one of them. That ain't a discussion."

"Okay. I'm just saying I don't know where he is," Valentine says. "If you're thinking I know something like that. Or if you think it's some kind of bargaining chip I got."

"You guys never thought about that, huh?"

Twist rocks back in the chair. He kicks the empty Bud can with his foot and watches as it rattles and rolls across the floor until it hits the wall.

"Figure maybe it doesn't matter what you know. Or what you did," Twist says finally. "Maybe somebody who wants you back knows enough to make it happen. They want you back the same way we want our guy back."

Valentine doesn't answer right away.

Valentine eases back on the bed and lays down, locking his hands behind his head and stares at the ceiling. He clears space on the bed by kicking away the papers, the beer cans, and what's left of the empty sandwich wrappers. Twist watches, uncomfortable and tense, like he's seeing something in Valentine that he's not supposed to see.

He has an idea about the emotions Valentine feels but there's nothing he can say to him about any of it. There is nothing he can offer to make it better or change what he's feeling—whatever is there is Valentine's. Twist knows it's something that doesn't belong to him.

Michael Valentine lays motionless on the bed.

After a while Twist gets up, scraping the chair across the floor as he stands, but still nothing comes from Valentine. It's only when he takes the first steps to start across the floor that Valentine turns his head.

"Hey Twist," he says in a low voice.

"Yeah?"

"You got anybody important in your life? Kids? A woman? Somebody like that?"

Twist thinks about it and nods. "Yeah, I guess so."

Valentine doesn't move.

In the quiet of that moment Twist can feel Valentine's pain, and something comes over him that makes him want to reach out and make it the same for both of them. He doesn't know anything about what Valentine has or needs, and he doesn't know the words Valentine needs to hear, but Twist thinks he should try.

"When's your wife due?" he tries quietly and immediately hates himself for saying those words.

Valentine looks at him so long that Twist is sorry he asked the question. The rage and hurt in his stare make Twist realize he can never know anything about Valentine or what it takes to make everything better, the same way Valentine will never know what Twist has. Twist can see that he's made the hurt worse.

"She ain't my wife," Valentine says.

Twist stares at him.

"She's not my wife," Valentine says again.

"That was my daughter."

Twist doesn't say anything else.

"Couple of months," Valentine finally adds. "She's due in October."

He turns his head again to stare at the ceiling and doesn't look up to watch Twist leave.

◆ ◆ ◆

A half hour later Twist is alone in back of the garage at the basketball court. He bounces the ball back and forth between his legs and turns, driving toward the net in two long steps. The ball rolls off his fingertips and drops softly through the net like it usually does but the shot doesn't matter to Twist. He's stuck on that image of Valentine on the bed, staring at the ceiling as he wrestles with the grief and rage inside.

Twist can't get that picture out of his head.

He keeps coming back to how not having the people who are important to him probably hurts Michael Valentine more than any bullet ever will.

He grabs the rebound before it bounces away too far and dribbles back toward the foul line where he takes a fifteen-foot jumper. Everything feels right about the shot and the ball banks easily against the backboard and drops into the basket.

Sometimes life should be as uncomplicated as basketball, but it never works out that way.

CHAPTER SIX

The same kids are still inside the garage. Nameless, faceless, and tough, they pass from room to room sharing cigarettes or playing their games. Trash is everywhere. Garbage cans overflow, cans and bottles litter the floor, and newspapers lie open, crumpled and torn apart. Twist has to make his way carefully down the stairs, picking his spots to walk.

Bone is at the bottom of the stairs, scowling and angry, directing two kids upstairs. One of them is Boo, carrying an AR-15 in one hand as he curls a slice of pizza into his mouth with the other.

"Take them gats upstairs and find yourselves positions at the windows," Bone says. "Got better sight lines up there."

Bone turns. "Ain't taking no chances," he says and Twist nods his agreement. With night coming anything can happen.

"Keep your eyes open," Bone says. "Stay frosty."

Boo's face opens into a slow smile. "Ain't nothing to worry about."

"Don't be so sure about nothing," Twist says.

"Man's right," Bone snaps in a voice that wipes away Boo's smile. "Too much going on for you to be strutting around here like you cool. "You feel me?"

The guy nods. "True dat."

Twist follows as Bone goes toward the bedroom in the back of the garage, swinging his shoulders and moving quickly as he walks. There's music from a radio downstairs but it's soft and low, hard to hear through the walls. Long, tense faces pass with serious expressions and screwed up looks that peer at Twist. Eyes touch his, looking for something in his expression he can't give.

"He tell you anything?" Bone asks over a shoulder.

"Who?"

"The Guinea," Bone mumbles and Twist shakes his head, even though Bone is too far in front to see that now.

The first floor bedroom is as sparse as the rest of the building. At one time it had been the auto repair shop's office. Now there's a mattress on the floor, some plastic milk crates stolen from Pathmark dairy trucks, a wooden nightstand, and a battered old chair that's pushed into the corner against a window. The fifty-inch plasma positioned on one of the crates is the only new thing in the room. The window has iron bars from top to bottom and two-by-four slats crisscrossing from corner to corner, and up close Twist sees the words and initials that guys on guard duty have carved into the wood. Like the rest of the house, there are empty pizza boxes, McDonald's cups, burger wrappers, beer cans, and bottles on the floor.

Bone is bent over the nightstand, tearing quickly through the drawers. He straightens, holding a small glass bowl, a four-inch pipe, and a small plastic baggie filled with powder.

"That Guinea got anything to say for himself?" he asks. "He singing a different song yet?"

Twist eyes the pipe and the powder, and takes a few seconds before answering. "Nothing's changed," he says. "He's uncomfortable. Maybe the space upstairs is starting to get to him, you know? Staring at the walls all day is probably doing things to his head."

"Fuck him. Don't give a shit he's uncomfortable," Bone says.

Twist shrugs. "Other than that, he's getting along okay."

"That supposed to be good or bad?"

"Considering everything, I guess he's okay."

"Thought maybe he'd be up there crying by now," Bone says, a smile curling up a corner of his mouth. "Begging to cut a deal or asking for help. Maybe crying for his bitch."

"That ain't him," Twist says. "He's not that kind of guy."

"They all the same. Start crying cause they ain't so tough."

"Valentine's different."

"Cuba figures he be losing it inside another twenty-four hours."

Twist wonders if Valentine has that much time. "Where's Cuba?" he asks.

"Still out on the street," Bone says. "When he gets back we can sit down and talk about what we gonna do."

"Didn't think we were making any decisions until we know more about Malik," Twist says.

Bone stares at him. "Talking about the 'what if's.' What we do," he says. "You know. Nothing more than that."

"I know."

"Looking at our options," Bone says.

"Fucking Guinea should be dead, no matter what happens next," he adds. "That's the bottom line. You don't make things right, you got no balls to go on."

Twist doesn't answer. He just stands there.

"It ain't just about dollars and turf no more," Bone mutters. "You know about that, same as me, Twist."

Twist stares at the bowl and baggie in Bone's hands, and when Bone sees that he stuffs it in a pocket as his expression turns into one that says what he has is none of Twist's business. For the moment it's nothing Twist wants to challenge—just something else to walk away from.

"Maybe you and Eddie got all this time on your hands you should be out there like Cuba," Bone says, locking his stare into Twist's eyes. "You should be out on the street seeing what's going down. Checking on what is ours and what we still got."

"We can do that," Twist says, still holding Bone's stare, "if that's what you're asking."

Bone steps slowly around Twist, their shoulders brushing as he passes and starts toward the living room alone.

Twist stares after him.

In those few seconds that pass Twist thinks again how he has the ability to change lives as well as people and the worlds they live in. He knows he can change things the same way that everything changed when Ice slapped Sally in the airport parking lot. He wonders about the possibilities he holds in his hands.

And for the first time in his life Twist thinks about what would happen if he did Bone.

He feels the 9mm snug between his pants and skin and knows how easy it would be to empty the clip in Bone's back. He can picture it so clearly in his mind that he sees the bullets ripping out chunks of Bone's flesh and spraying blood on the walls. Twist thinks about the changes it could create. It would alter the world of every Skull, the dynamic of their gang, and even change what goes on with the Italians and Michael Valentine. That might not be such a bad thing.

None of it would come without problems and complications; Twist carries a hard, vivid image of Cuba that he can't shake, but every important decision comes with consequences.

It could be the kind of move worth trying, no matter how bad those consequences. You weigh the good with the bad then decide which works best.

But in the end Twist does nothing.

Bone walks down the hall and Twist follows, telling himself that at least for now he'll let everything stay as it is. But he likes having that option—if he ever needs it.

◆ ◆ ◆

Twist and Eddie Dallas are in a dark blue Toyota. There's a car seat in the back with a diaper bag and baby toys, a pair of woman's high heels in the front, and a JESUS LOVES ME bumper sticker on the dashboard. It's the bumper sticker that bothers Twist the most, but it's been hardened and baked too long by the sun, and it's impossible to peel off the dash now.

One of the Skulls had driven it away from the Garden State Plaza in Paramus that morning, no more than ten minutes after the mother went inside with her two-year-old. Once they popped the door with a screwdriver they needed less than thirty seconds to hot-wire and crank the ignition until it started. The car was on Murray Street before the mother and the mall cops even realized it was stolen.

Twist hears Bone's voice behind them as they leave, saying, "Be nice you do this without nobody taking shots at you."

He turns with a "fuck you" stare but the moment is lost. Bone has something he can use like a switchblade, sticking it between Twist's shoulder blades and digging and turning until it gets the reaction he wants. They both know it, and they know Bone will keep using it until he finds something else that works even better to get under Twist's skin.

He wears the kind of satisfied smile that makes Twist reconsider the idea of doing him.

He wonders if he'll regret that decision not to pull the trigger.

The afternoon is still hot, although there are dark clouds in the sky to the west and the air holds the kind of heavy stillness that comes before a storm. The car windows are down and the air conditioning is cranked up as Eddie slows at Market and Raymond. Conversation is brief; one or two words, phrases, and subtle nods each recognizes and understands.

Twist doesn't ease off his edge, staying guarded and cautious as he looks for signs of trouble and danger.

Eddie Dallas drives with the sawed-off in his lap, taking no chances. A black-and-white eases alongside them in the next lane but the cop ignores the Toyota. At the next intersection the cop makes a turn while Eddie continues forward.

Twist lights a Camel and sits back, stretching his legs and propping one Nike on the dash to cover most of the JESUS LOVES ME sticker.

The late afternoon traffic is heavy, stop-and-go on every street, and intersections are gridlocked. Cars are bumper to bumper, angled between taxis, buses, and trucks, horns blaring as drivers try maneuvering ahead whenever they can find a foot to move. Eddie flicks his cigarette butt through the window and shakes the braids from his face.

Sitting in traffic carries too much risk and danger. There's not much that can be done to protect themselves; it only takes one guy sneaking between cars with an automatic stuck inside his pants to carry out a hit and Twist knows they're both fucked.

"I don't like this," he says. "Last place I want to be is stuck like this in traffic."

Eddie Dallas nods. "Makes it too fucking easy for any dick with a heater to take a shot."

There's a long pause and Eddie turns in the seat to stare at Twist. He's looking for something in his expression or hidden behind the words. "Ain't like it was a couple of years ago, huh?" he says. "Not like it was when Raphael was on the street."

Twist shakes his head. "Ain't changed that much. Game's still the same."

"Feels different now," Eddie says.

"You didn't hear from him yet?" Eddie asks.

Twist takes a deep drag on the cigarette and shakes his head again.

"A guy like your brother, what he says means a lot to guys. He's an original. Guys respect Raphael. Respect his opinion," Eddie Dallas says. "What he has to say about what's going on with the Guineas has meaning. Guys want to hear it."

Maybe, but it's not the same any more. What his brother says would carry more weight if he wasn't doing a seven-year stretch for manslaughter at East Jersey State. Being one of the original Skulls gives him something in the gang he'll never lose, and something nobody else has over him. Guys like Cuba and Bone will never have it, no matter how much they strut or how hard they try to impress people with their cool. The kind of respect they get isn't the same as what his brother earned.

But once Raphael slit that faggot's throat in the Broad Street theater everything changed, Twist thinks. Any real power he had disappeared.

Being behind bars means he is as good as dead, at least when it comes to things that matter. He can talk about next steps and voice his opinion, but he's not a part of what they got going on and everybody knows it.

"It means something when guys like Cuba and Bone still want to know what he says," Eddie Dallas puts in. "Says something about respect."

That's not the way Twist sees it. It says less about Raphael and respect, and more about what Cuba and Bone don't have and don't see.

"How about that guy?" Eddie Dallas asks. "What's he like?"

"What guy?"

"The guy in the building. You got more than one guy that you don't know who I'm talking about?"

"Valentine?"

"Yea, the Guinea. Valentine," he says above the guitar chords from a Red Hot Chili Peppers song. "What's he like?"

Twist shrugs. "What makes you think I know anything about him?"

Eddie laughs. "You the only one who's spent more than thirty seconds in his room. Figure you got to be talking to him all that time you're up there," he says. "Maybe you got some kind of idea who he is and what he's all about."

"He's a soldier," Twist says. "Not much different than you and me."

Eddie Dallas shrugs. "We're different worlds, us and them," he says, watching a bus closing the distance behind them in his rear view mirror and measuring threats. "Guys like him do things none of us know anything about. Live in a world that ain't the same as ours."

"The way I see him, he's just like you and me," Twist says, staring out the window at the street. "Just a guy doing a job. Nobody important."

Eddie doesn't say anything. He drives the car.

"I guess you know that Cuba and Bone got something to say about you and Valentine," he says after a while.

Twist closes his eyes. "Those two got something to say about everything that goes on. Never paid much attention to it before. Not gonna start now."

"Bone don't like you spending so much time with him," Eddie says. "It don't look good to him. Thinks you should be focused on Malik instead."

"Nothing I can do about Malik. I got to do that on my own terms anyway," Twist says. "I do it my way. Bone does it his."

"The way Bone sees it, it don't look good."

Twist lifts a foot and props it back on the dashboard. The car feels cramped and tight. He searches his cigarette pack for another Camel but comes up empty, and has to bum a Marlboro from Eddie.

It doesn't surprise him much about Bone and Cuba. Things Bone can't control turn into threats very easily.

"That's the dope talking," Twist says. "It's making him paranoid. Everywhere Bone looks he sees something or somebody else out to get him."

"Been that way forever."

"Just getting worse now."

"This don't make it no better."

"Nothing's gonna get better between him and me, no matter how this turns out. We see the same things different ways," Twist says. "I figure he's already blaming me for what happened. It was his idea just as much as mine, but all he's gonna remember is how I agreed to do this and how that makes it my fault."

Eddie looks over at him. "I heard Cuba go along with this plan. He's a partner in this like you and me and everybody else who wanted in on the decision."

"He ain't gonna remember it that way either."

Eddie shakes his head. "Memories get real short when the shit turns bad, huh?"

"Bone sees everybody as either a friend or an enemy. No in-betweens with him," Twist says. "I think he's got me in the enemy category."

"Cuba don't even have that many categories."

A long white limo cuts in front of the car and Eddie hits the horn and eyes the car the same way he took in the bus. "What they saying is that you hanging with Valentine don't look good."

Twist frowns. "Not like we're whoring with the same women or shooting hoops together. We're talking. Nothing more than that."

"You getting close to him or something?"

"I only talked to him a couple of times," Twist says. "Not much to know.

"Although I'm pretty sure I like him better than Cuba and Bone," he adds, "if that's what you're looking for."

Eddie smiles as he keeps beeping the horn to get the limo driver's attention, then pops him the finger when the guy glances his way. "Man, liking him better ain't saying nothing. I like that fucking Guinea Sally better than I like the two of them guys," he says. "That don't mean nothing."

Twist doesn't answer. He doesn't talk about what he knows or what he thinks he knows. It doesn't seem right telling things like that to Eddie, no matter how close they are. This is between him and Michael Valentine, and it should stay between them. It's the kind of thing that doesn't belong to anyone else.

It probably doesn't even belong to him, so he says nothing.

The closest Eddie comes to bringing it up again is when he says, "Got to be tough on him."

Twist nods, saying, "You got to do what you have to do. Don't matter what side you're on."

◆ ◆ ◆

"Ain't nobody been hassling us," Jamal says. "Nothing going on. Nothing happening out here. Nothing we can't handle."

"Just because nothing's happened yet don't mean you got an excuse to be stupid," Twist says.

Jamal nods but Twist and Eddie Dallas see he's not caught up in their dialogue.

Eddie leans over. "What's your count?"

"A little slow right now," Jamal says. "Off, but nothing that matters too much."

The Toyota is parked on the street at the Pennington Courts apartments—a brick housing project between Independence Park and Penn Station. There are two hundred forty-eight apartments with over thirteen hundred people living in them, ranging from single parents with infants to extended families of eight or nine people. The largest apartments have two bedrooms, and close to sixty percent of the residents survive on food stamps, welfare, and Social Security. The courts are comprised of three eight-story buildings built in the late sixties, obsolete and dirty and crumbling to pieces now. Even the cops have given up on the apartments; single cop patrol cars pass only once or twice a day and foot patrols are even rarer.

Pennington is the type of community that makes up the guts of the Skulls drug operation. There are always guys in colors, ready and available to sell whatever someone wants to buy, whenever they want it. The Pennington operation is run with four teams working the hallways, sidewalks, and courtyard, and two other teams taking up positions in separate apartments in different buildings. It's a twenty-four hour convenience store.

Armed Skulls watch the street as carefully as they guard the garage on Murray Street. Ready for cops that might show up along with soldiers from another gang.

Jamal stands by the Toyota on Eddie Dallas' side while three guys from his crew fan out carefully around the brick and asphalt courtyard, making themselves seen without being too obvious. Twist recognizes one of the faces from the stairs outside Valentine's door and the other kids he knows from the garage. He watches a guy approaching, late thirties, dressed in greasy mechanics overalls and a dirty white T-shirt. He passes dollar bills to one guy then follows the kid from the stairs across the sidewalk while the third guy watches for eyes that shouldn't be staring at him. A different guy passes him his purchase. The transaction is fast and smooth, and doesn't take more than thirty seconds for the mechanic to score what he needs.

He stuffs a dime tin of powder in a pocket and hurries quickly away.

"You heard somebody took shots at us?" Eddie says but there is nothing in Jamal's expression.

"It's summer, man," Jamal says. "That kind of shit happens sometimes. Got to figure on it, right?"

Twist and Eddie exchange glances, and Eddie rolls his eyes and shakes his head.

Jamal rolls the toothpick from side to side in his mouth. He has a cocky smile and a "what, me worry?" expression. He drops the sunglasses down to the tip of his nose and leans down further into the car.

"Ain't nothing we can't handle," he says in a tough voice, flashing his twenty-two out in the open like a proud father showing off his kid. "Take care of business if it comes to that."

Twist wonders how Jamal will ever see nineteen.

He turns and looks away. The sky darkens and Twist can see the storm clouds moving closer, like a hard, heavy rain is about to fall. The rain won't be such a bad thing when it happens.

Eddie Dallas and Jamal are still talking about the Italians but Twist has stopped listening.

An old lady shuffles by the car with her head down, clutching a shopping bag tightly with both hands. A ten-year-old runs past in shorts and a pair of sneakers, yelling for his friends. There's a group of Hispanic women about twenty feet from the car. Their conversation is loud and animated and Twist doesn't understand much of it, but he watches anyway, checking out the hard bodies in shorts and Lycra. They are late teens and early twenties, talking and gyrating to the music from somebody's radio. None of them pay attention to the Toyota, Jamal's twenty-two, or the network of Skulls circulating throughout the yard; it's nothing they don't witness every day.

One of them starts toward the car and Twist sits up straighter.

She's tall with long dark hair and a thin face. No more than twenty-one or maybe twenty-two, with fine, delicate features. A hard body squeezed into black Lycra, cutoffs that barely cover her ass, and long, tanned legs on spiked heels. It's the kind of body Twist can easily imagine beneath his, locked together in a long, steady rhythm. He takes off his Ray-Bans for a better look.

She brushes long strands of hair from her face, cracking gum as she walks. Each one of them follows every step with their stares, imagining themselves with her in the back seat of the Toyota or on a mattress back at the garage, listening to her moan their name into a shoulder. Conversation between Eddie and Jamal slows as she passes. Jamal leans against the roof of the car, leering at her.

"You don't put your eyes back in your head they're gonna fall out on the sidewalk," she tells him.

"Be worth it just to have you pick them up, baby," he says with a toothy smile.

She shakes her head and keeps walking.

Twist turns his attention back to the courtyard.

"Stay on your game," he tells Jamal. "Want you and everyone else her to be sharp."

"On it. Got nothing to worry about with 5-0—," Jamal says.

Twist slams a fist into the JESUS LOVES ME sticker on the dashboard.

"Damnit nigger!" he yells. "Ain't just worried about heat from the cops!"

Kids in the courtyard turn their heads.

"Been talking about what we got going on and you're too busy pressing your cool to understand the seriousness of this situation."

"Pay attention," Eddie says.

"You supposed to be ready for this. Told you and your young'un's about this for days," Twist says.

"You can't fucking handle this, I'll get somebody down here who can," Twist says.

Twist unfolds his Ray-Bans and slips the sunglasses back on his face.

"Fucking amateurs going to get killed," he says as Eddie pulls away.

◆ ◆ ◆

August thunderstorms are quick and violent.

Hot days turn dark, skies blacken, and a stillness hangs on everything. It's an eeriness that can get inside and stay there, just long enough to make everything uncomfortable. The rain comes down hard, dropping in torrents that flood the streets and back up sewers, sending garbage and trash floating along curbs in dirty brown streams. Umbrellas, rain coats, and hats are useless, and everything that moves grinds to a stop.

The sky lights up with streaks of lightning then a long, slow clap of thunder rocks the street as the Toyota moves ahead an inch at a time. The rain drops pounding off the car roof sound like .45 caliber slugs popping metal. The noise is too vivid and real, at least for Twist; there's more comfort in silence.

But that silence is gone.

The rain falls harder and the pounding noise gets louder.

Twist sighs and drops his head backward to the seat, closing his eyes. Eddie Dallas lights up a Camel and takes a deep drag on the cigarette. Neither of them has anything to say. The day has gone on endlessly—it's been an afternoon filled with conversations, retelling the story about the BMW and the shooting so many times that the words lose their feeling and emotion.

It turns matter-of-fact too quickly.

Except that Twist knows a part of it will stick long after the story's over and other guys have forgotten the details.

Time won't make it go away.

With the radio off the only sound in the car is the noise the wipers make as they slap back and forth across the windshield. The windows fog up quickly and when Twist opens his eyes he can barely make out the tail lights of the car ahead. Eddie cracks a window and cranks up the defrosters but the windows don't clear fast enough, making it impossible to see without wiping a hand against the glass. Sometimes the rain can be relaxing; Twist has always liked the sound it makes splattering against windows or splashing in puddles on the street. It washes away anger and trouble, and makes everything better. Something about it makes everything clean and new.

This time it is just noise.

◆ ◆ ◆

"If they want a fucking war, we give them a motherfucking war," Cuba says. He pours the vodka into a plastic cup and drinks it in one swallow. He shakes away the burn with a grimace, then finishes the rest before the burning stops.

"Do it to them before they do it to us," he rasps.

Dizzy nods. "Ain't nothing more important than that."

They are sitting around the table. It's close to eight o'clock and for the first time everyone who matters is there. Outside the rain has turned into a slight drizzle, nothing steady and not as hard as it had been earlier. Inside everyone has an opinion but there's little action and nothing gets done. There are bottles of Stoli, Jack Daniel's, and Johnnie Walker Red on the table, as well as empty, grease-stained buckets from KFC with the remains of bones and biscuits. Guys chain smoke Marlboros and Camels and whatever else is handy. There's an empty chair next to Twist where Ice usually sits, and although nobody really expects him to reclaim it, it stays empty.

Bone sits at the head of the table, his eyes watery and bloodshot, barely able to hold the edge he's riding. The lines in his face look deeper and hardened. His hands are curled into tight fists that stay on the table, close to the silver-plated .45 and the ammo clips stacked alongside the gun.

Twist takes a deep breath and leans forward into his Jack Daniel's.

The conversation has gone on forever but they are nowhere. It was supposed to be about Valentine but instead they're deep into discussions about how to take out Giaccolone and his group. Cuba sees doing Valentine as only the first step; not enough to make the kind of statement he wants. He wants to take out as many Italians as possible, no matter how many Skulls it costs. To him, doing it that way shows strength and power. Doing it like that is the only way he understands.

Twist is tired of the talk and the endless debating that has them stuck in neutral—tired of the voices and tired of the questions. He knows guys like Cuba never hear anything but their own voices. He is tired of everything.

He crushes out his Camel in one of the fried chicken buckets. "You're talking about starting something we can't win," he says in a hard voice that carries. "Ain't our kind of war. We don't have what we need to win.

"We got no shot."

His voice is sharp and the words have bite. Heads turn when he says it.

Cuba stares at him.

"What's that supposed to mean?" Bone asks, looking up from his bottle.

"You telling me you don't think we good enough?" Cuba asks, his stare narrowing across the table. "That the Guineas got something more than us?"

"Bullshit," Dizzy puts in defiantly.

Eddie Dallas tips down his shades and stares over the top at them. "That ain't what I just heard him say."

"Don't matter what he said. What matters is what he means," Bone says to Eddie although his eyes are still hooked into Twist. "What you trying to say?"

Twist reaches slowly for the Jack Daniel's and feels every eye at the table burning a hole through him, waiting for his answer. He wonders if anybody ever hears him or if most times he just wastes time and words. He takes his time uncapping the bottle, measuring the whiskey as he pours out a glass.

"Been through this before," he says, first to Cuba then Bone. "You know what I got to say. Said it already at this table."

"Say it again," Bone says again, hard and tense. "So it's clear. So we know what you mean."

"And where you stand," Cuba says.

"It means the same thing it meant the first time I said it," Twist says. "You try taking on the Italians the same way we took on the Bloods and we lose. You playing by their rules in their game. They got all the advantages, like guys and dollars and things we can't ever have.

"Ain't gonna come out of that on top. Not that way."

Cuba is still staring at him, his smile stretching thin and tight across his face. "Then what else we gonna do? Just give up?"

"Did I say that?"

"Ain't sure what you're saying."

"Got to give them the kind of fight that wears them down slowly, a little bit at a time until they don't want no part of it any more. Until they're looking for reasons and excuses to quit," he says, looking across the table to meet Cuba's stare head-on. "Give them their own Iraq."

"Man," Cuba says, shaking his head slowly but still holding his smile, "sometimes all you good at is talking bullshit. Sometimes I think you got nothing else."

The room gets quiet and the sounds of the TV and radio disappear. The silence is sudden, and around the table each guy looks down at plastic cups or studies details on their fingers and hands. Only Bone watches with eagerness and anticipation.

Twist locks eyes with Cuba, feeling the flash of something building inside and moving quickly to the surface.

"What's that mean?"

"It means you good at talking," Cuba says without backing off as he pours himself more vodka. "You sitting here talking about Iraq the same way you always talking about business and economics, but there ain't a goddamn nigger here who knows what the fuck that means.

"Maybe what it really means is that you ain't got the balls to get into this," Cuba says, "the way we supposed to get into it. The way you supposed to get into it."

Something passes between Cuba and Twist with those words. Twist feels the edge inside sharpen, ready to slash if he lets it go. That voice in his head wonders if he can take out Cuba first before Bone can load that .45 and put a bullet in his chest, then get off another clean shot and do Bone the way he should have done it earlier that afternoon. There's a challenge at the table that can't be ignored; Cuba's words are the kind that don't go unanswered. At least not without a heavy cost.

Twist never takes his eyes off Cuba.

"You got a problem with the way I do things, I can respect that. Don't like my ideas or how I want to do this, that's okay," he says, drawing out the words evenly and slowly. "Got a problem with me, that's different.

"If there's something between us here, be a man and say it. Don't act like a bitch and do some kind of dance I'm supposed to figure out," Twist says.

Cuba smiles. His expression and his stare remain icy and cold. The challenge will still be there, even after he's done talking.

His voice is apologetic but he's made his point. "I'm saying the Guineas won't understand your way. What we got going on now needs more than that," Cuba says.

"What makes you think you know a better way?"

"Yours ain't the only way," Cuba says. "There's nothing that says something else won't work, just because it ain't something you thought up."

Bone crushes out the stub of a Marlboro. "You think we got time to do it your way?" he asks Twist. "We got to make the Guineas realize that they into something here they can't win. Got to make our point in a big way. Got to do it now."

"You got to project strength. Show them you got the balls it takes," Cuba says.

T. Capone nods his head and opens his mouth for the first time. "Let them know we mean business, right?"

"Balls," Cuba repeats. "It's called balls."

"You saying again I don't have balls?" Twist asks. "That what I hear?"

Bone takes a sip from his glass. "What we saying is we got to do something big if we want to hold on to everything we got."

Twist shakes his head. He can see that he's losing whatever grip he had, and he doesn't like the turn the conversation has taken. "You're gonna turn this into their kind of war. Something we can't carry."

"Man, it's already hunting season out there," Bone shoots back. "Any Skull walking the street is an open target."

"We expected that," Twist says.

"Ain't nothing gonna get better until we make a stand," Bone says.

Cuba smiles. "The first step is doing this Guinea upstairs."

Twist looks at Eddie Dallas but there's nothing there that will make it any different. The expressions around the table tell Twist where he stands. And it's then that he knows that Valentine is a dead man, no matter what happens to Malik; Malik no longer matters to anyone at the table except him. If there was ever any doubt, or even the slightest chance of trading Valentine for Malik, it is gone.

"We make that decision?" Eddie Dallas asks. "It's already decided that we're gonna ice the Guinea without waiting to find out what's up with Ice or Malik?"

Bone and Cuba exchange looks, then Bone nods.

"What about his brother?" Eddie asks, nodding toward a sullen Twist. "We want to wait so we can talk with him?"

"He ain't a part of this," Cuba says. "It's decided now. We want to take care of the Guineas and turn this around, we ain't got time for no more opinions."

Bone finishes the vodka in his glass. "We do the Guinea," he says. His voice is flat and emotionless, but something in it is decisive and firm.

Everyone stares at him. Nobody says anything.

"Tomorrow," he says. "Before midnight tomorrow."

Twist shakes his head. "Just like that?"

"Just like that," Bone states. He looks slowly to each guy, waiting them out—looking for something in their expressions the same way

Cuba stared across the table at Twist earlier, flexing his power and searching out challenges.

His eyes hold on Twist.

"We get the word out. Guineas want to talk and negotiate," he says, "they got all day tomorrow to do it. They want to bring us Malik, we got something to talk about. Tell us if Ice is a corpse and where they dropped his body, fine. But Valentine's only got those couple of hours. After that, he's dead."

Twist knows there won't be anything the Italians can offer that will measure up to what Cuba and Bone want. Even if Malik turns up, it won't matter.

"Problem with that?" Bone asks, still staring at Twist.

Twist simply returns the stare.

"Who's gonna pull the trigger?" Eddie Dallas wants to know.

Something passes again between Bone and Cuba. They exchange looks and turn until they are both staring at Twist.

"Twist," Bone says. "Twist gonna do it."

Twist stares back at Bone.

"You got a problem with that?" Cuba asks with that smile still on his face. "A reason you don't want to do it?"

Twist takes a long time to answer. His mind is numb even with all the thoughts and words, and nothing comes out. "No," he finally says. "Ain't no problem."

"Ain't nobody better to do it," Bone says with his own smile matching Cuba's.

"Twist got a personal interest in this because of Malik," Cuba says. "Makes it good that way."

There is more than just a personal interest because of Malik but Twist lets it go. Instead he says, "Everything's been personal for all of us."

"Better for you to do it," Bone says.

"Everything balances out if you pull the trigger," Cuba says. "Know what the boy means to you."

Twist just shakes his head slowly. "You want some kind of ceremony that everybody can watch? Do it so it gets seen?"

"What's that mean?"

"Means you're acting like this is some kind of public execution," Twist says. "Thought maybe you want me to call CNN or Fox."

"Don't matter about nothing except he dies," Bone says. "Just pull the trigger and do it. It don't matter what happens or where we dump the body. Just matters that we do it."

"Am I supposed to say anything to him?"

Bone shrugs. "Like what?"

"You tell me," Twist says. "Read him a list of his crimes or something? Make some kind of statement? Say something you want him to hear?"

Bone pours himself another cup of vodka, stirring the ice cubes and vodka with a thin long finger. "You got your own thing you want to say to him, that's your call," he says. "Don't matter one way or another what words you got for him."

"He got to have it figured out he's gonna be dead," Cuba puts in. "If it was me, I'd tell him exactly what I was gonna do and why I was doing it, then watch how the fear fucks with him.

"But that's me," he adds. "You and me are different. Got our own ways and our own reasons. You got to do it the way that works best for you."

Twist doesn't know which way will work best for him.

He sits there are the table wishing it could end.

CHAPTER SEVEN

It's ten o'clock and Murray Street is quiet. Sounds and noises fill the night but there's nothing out of the ordinary; trains rumble slowly along the Northeast Corridor tracks, cop cruisers and ambulance sirens wail on Raymond and McCarter, and a dog barks somewhere down the street.

Twist stands on the second floor, smoking a Camel and staring out the window. The rain has stopped but the brief comfort created earlier is gone, and the oppressive heaviness is back. He feels the sweat on his back and neck, inching down the skin. Nothing is cooler and nothing has changed. The rest of the Skulls are downstairs talking about where they're going to dump Valentine; where the body is found matters almost as much as killing him does. But Twist passed on that conversation.

All he can think about is killing Michael Valentine and how it will feel to pull the trigger.

A guy like Cuba would look forward to it. Getting a chance to see death up close and being the one to do it creates an adrenaline kick for him, and Twist knows some guys like that. They live for everything that comes with that feeling.

But there are none of those feelings for Twist.

He imagines Valentine's body stuffed in a dumpster behind one of those Portuguese restaurants in the Ironbound section. That image makes his guts tighten. The feeling starts deep in his balls, squeezes his insides, and gets stronger as he thinks about snuffing out Michael Valentine's life. Twist wonders about Valentine's daughter and the baby she's carrying. If the kid will grow up asking about his grandfather. If the kid will ever understand why he died. If the only knowledge of his grandfather will be that he was killed and his body stuffed in a maggot-infested dumpster filled with garbage.

Bone and Dizzy come through the door. Bone moves slowly, hugging the wall with his shoulder. There's a cigarette hanging from his mouth, a can of Bud in one hand, and a pair of dark Ray-Bans covering his eyes. Dizzy hangs a step behind as they stand in the doorway, watching Twist looking out the window.

Bone eyes him carefully. He looks him up and down like there's something wrong that he's trying to figure out but can't get a handle on what it is.

Dizzy moves around Bone to the window. "What's going on out there?"

He frowns, expecting something more than what he sees; like he's afraid he's missing something.

"Came up here to get you. We going out," Bone states, his voice low. The way he says it means it's not a request or an invitation with options about attending.

"Viper Club," Dizzy adds, cracking a wad of gum in his mouth and moving back behind Bone. "All of us."

"Think that's smart?" Twist asks. "Doing that tonight, with everything going on?"

"Fuck the Guineas," says Dizzy. "Cops too."

"Easy to say when you didn't have somebody popping slugs at you," Twist says.

"Ain't doing this just to get our G on," Bone says. "Got business there."

Twist stares back.

"Time to talk to that guy, Cooper, about getting some better firepower," Bone says, staring Dizzy back in place. "Things heating up, got to start thinking about buying us some heat."

Twist is thinking that bigger guns won't solve the problems they face.

Instead he frowns and says, "Been a while since we did business with Cooper."

"Don't have a lot of choices."

"Sure we can trust him?" Twist asks. "Things change."

Bone shrugs. "You asking me if I'm one hundred percent positive he's straight, you ain't gonna get me to bite. But we don't got any other place else to look," he says. "Not enough time to shop for bargains."

"Yeah, but doing it at the Viper Club?" Twist says. "It's a sweat box. No space to move in there."

"Need to be out in public. Ain't there to be getting buck," Bone says. "Gives us a chance to make a statement that we ain't afraid. Don't look good if we holed up inside where nobody sees us. People get to talking trash. Can't have that, you know?"

"Ain't a good thing," Dizzy adds.

Neither is being a target.

"Important we do this. All of us," Bone says before turning to go downstairs, with Dizzy two steps behind him. "Be leaving in ten minutes."

Twist nods, taking another drag on the Camel as he turns back to the street.

◆ ◆ ◆

The Viper Club doesn't look like much, just another old store front no different than any others on the street. The front is brick and cinder block, stained and dirty near the corners from years of drunks staggering out of the club and pissing on the bricks. There are no windows and none of the neon beer signs that dot other local bars and taverns; not even signs advertising the bar. Only a small red cobra coiled and ready to strike painted on a piece of wood bleached white and tacked above the door. To casual passerby it's nothing more than another James Street store struggling to survive—the kind of place that doesn't get a second look from most people. But tonight a crowd stretches from the open door halfway down the block, and the street is bumper to bumper with big bodies with twenty-inch anchors and metallic spinners. The curb is lined with BMWs, Infinitis, and Range Rovers. Dance music pumps through the door, and across the street teenagers who aren't allowed inside shake and groove on the sidewalk, sharing cigarettes and cans of Buds. They watch the crowd and talk about getting fake IDs to get inside.

Two black guys, late twenties with hard stares and nasty East Jersey State attitudes, eye the crowd from the doorway.

Nobody says anything about the .45s tucked in the back of their pants that keep problems from getting out of hand.

The Skulls show up after ten in a three-car caravan. Three guys with shotguns ride in the Toyota in front, while a GMC Suburban trails behind with four more guys carrying automatics, shotguns, and .22s. With all that firepower the police will have a field day if they get pulled over, so the drivers have been cautious since they left Murray Street and made their way downtown. Twist sits in a Ford Explorer sandwiched between the two cars, along with Eddie, Bone, and Cuba; one of the sixteen-year-old soldiers is hunched behind the wheel and another is slumped low in the back with a sawed-off double barrel and two boxes of shells. The procession pulls up outside the club, double parking in the street. They stay in the Explorer while guys from the Toyota take up positions across the street. One kid waits on the sidewalk while two others enter the club, nodding to the bouncers as they push past the crowd at the door.

"It's good we doing this," Bone says again, this time to Eddie and Cuba.

Twist stares out the windows at the crowd on the sidewalk, looking for something in the faces of the people who return his stare.

When one of the kids returns with an all clear they ease out of the Explorer and cross the sidewalk, slipping wordlessly past the crowd waiting in line. Their rides stay double parked in the street.

The bar is long and L-shaped. The dance floor is alive with bright colored lights that flicker and revolve on people bumping, sliding, and spinning. There are girls in spandex, leather, and lace, and guys in jackets wearing three hundred dollar Ballys, heavy rope chains, and weekend bling. There's a long bar against the far wall with two bartenders serving drinks to a crowd three and four deep in spots, while another guy guards the register, wearing the same look as the bouncers at the door. His expression is mean and nasty with rough edges that nobody misses. His .45 isn't obvious but it's there.

The dance floor swallows most of the space while off to the side in a small booth a DJ named Fly spins records and raps with the crowd as he controls the flashing lights and strobes. Twist knows him from the basketball courts. He's an okay guy who grew up in Blood turf and still lives there, but isn't somebody who lets colors get in the way of what's important to him, like spinning records and making a statement with his music. He's got his own set of priorities.

Twist hears him, funky and loud, over a P. Diddy song. His voice has power and commands the same kind of respect the Skulls get from people when they cross the street. Twist sees it in the way heads turn to watch him and how people hang on his rap.

The room bootlegs to the left past the bar. Back in that corner there are VIP tables and chairs, along with a standing room only crowd watching the action on the dance floor, too unattractive, afraid, or unavailable to be out there themselves.

The kids who had checked out the bar push through the crowd and move toward the reserved table in the back. Bone and Cuba stare straight ahead as they make their way to the seats. Heads turn and eyes follow as they pass, and Twist gets that familiar twinge of importance that accompanies those stares. There's admiration, respect, and envy; hands reach, touching shoulders and slapping palms as voices call out names, looking for recognition.

Twist is cautious. A hand reaching out to slap skin could just as easily be holding a twenty-two.

He doesn't relax until they're sitting at a table with their backs to the wall.

Cuba slides into a chair next to Bone, and they both keep their backs to the wall to face the door. Cuba takes out his .45 and lays it across his lap, keeping it close. Twist sits next to Eddie Dallas, leaning back in his chair and feeling the weight of his own nine against his skin, sharing the same sense of comfort that Cuba does from having the .45 in his lap.

A girl in high-heeled pumps, shorts, and a red Viper Club T-shirt comes to the table to take their orders. She's light-skinned, lighter than Maria, with long legs and soft skin. She spreads a smile around the table as they call out drinks. The smile says it all.

"Gonna be falling in love with you," Bone says to her as he reaches for her hand. "For a little while, anyway."

She just laughs and turns away.

Four sets of eyes follow when she moves, watching her ass shake and dip as she walks from the table.

"Shit," Cuba says with a low whistle, shaking his head.

"Been a long time since I've seen something that fine," Eddie Dallas says. "A long, long time."

Bone leans forward to watch her ass disappear into the crowd. "Want to hit that," he says. "Tonight."

Cuba's eyes jump from a tall girl in white spandex and red lipstick to another girl with blonde hair cut short and spiked, to a third who's shorter, dressed in a leather vest, cropped T-shirt, and denim skirt. "Check out them squirrels. They be potent."

"Shit," Eddie Dallas says in a long, drawn out voice. "Maybe even an ugly nigger like you got a shot at hooking up tonight."

Even Twist breaks a smile as they all laugh.

Twist lights up a Camel and waits for his drink. He catches a glimpse of Dizzy skirting the edge of the dance floor, cutting a wide path toward the table and trailed by the same Murray Street girl Bone had that afternoon. Women pass, searching the table for the guy with the power; trying to decide if any one of them is worth the effort and looking for a reason or an excuse to chance a hello.

Twist is still thinking about pulling the trigger. And consumed with thoughts about Valentine, and thinking about where they will dump Valentine's body.

It's funny how something like that matters. The Italians don't give a shit about chopping up guys and sending body parts through the mail or floating corpses down the Passaic in oil drums. There's a message doing it that way. But leaving a body in the wrong part of town is worse than icing the guy in front of his family.

Some things with them you can't figure out.

He has always known that somehow it would come down to him being the trigger man. Malik is on him. From the reaction it got at the table no one else thought differently; nobody challenged the decision. Cuba might have been disappointed, but only because he lost the chance to snuff someone.

Dizzy finds a seat at the table, leaving the girl on the fringe of the crowd. Twist remembers when she used to be one of the quiet kids jumping rope on the corner and playing hopscotch with friends. Now she's the kind of girl who will go through the gang quickly, looking for love and friendship. She won't ever find that with any of them.

He catches a glimpse of her head turning from Bone to Dizzy and then back to Bone, but Bone won't ever acknowledge her again. Once he's done with somebody they disappear.

The girl doesn't meet Twist's stare when she turns back to the table.

"Won't be able to take much of this hip hop dance shit," Eddie Dallas bitches. "Listen to it too long and it'll have me putting a bullet in my ear."

Twist leans back in his chair. "Could be worse."

"Ain't nothing could be worse than this."

"Could be country and western, right?"

Eddie's face scrunches into a frown. "You're right," he agrees, taking a swallow of his Jack Daniel's. "Five minutes of those hillbillies yodeling and I'll be loading clips in the automatic."

It gets hot and noisy in the club quickly. Twist's T-shirt is wet and heavy with sweat and his head hurts with the kind of dull, throbbing ache that comes from too much drink, not enough sleep, and worrying about too many things. He nurses a watered down Jack Daniel's and stares quietly into the crowd.

Cuba puts down his Stoli in one long gulp and flags the waitress. She throws him a casual smile but keeps moving toward other tables.

"Whassup with you?" he asks Twist.

"Who said something's wrong?"

Cuba smiles a grin that has no humor. "Man don't know how to have fun no more. Anybody can see that. That's the problem," he says. "Man thinks too much about everything."

"I'm tired," is all Twist says.

"Got to get past it and enjoy the night. Take advantage, you know?"

"Who the fuck can have fun with all this noise," Eddie Dallas puts in. "The music sucks. Need something with balls and kick to it."

"You another one," Cuba sneers, "to be talking about balls."

Eddie Dallas lets the remark pass, giving a little laugh along with the others and passing it off as the vodka talking. But the comment stays with him, long after Cuba moves on to the waitress. Twist knows the look in Eddie's eyes and the way that stare turns and darkens.

"How you think the Guineas gonna react?" Dizzy asks Bone as he settles into his chair. "What you think they gonna do?"

"Fuck that," Cuba cuts in. "Tonight we just chillin.' Gonna enjoy what's going on here. Guineas gonna get what's coming to them soon enough."

"Ain't talking about none of it no more tonight," Bone agrees. "Done planning and talking. Time for action."

Twist takes a deep drag on his cigarette and says nothing. The things he wants to talk about and the words he has stay inside. They're important only to him.

When the waitress brings more drinks he doesn't return her smile.

"You know this guy?" Dizzy asks Twist. "What's his name? Cooper?"

Twist nods slowly. "Me and Bone and Raphael met him a couple of years back. Did some business with him when we had that situation with the Bloods," he says. "But kind of lost touch since then."

"Haven't had the need," Bone says.

Dizzy looks to Cuba. "You weren't there?"

Cuba shakes his head and jerks a thumb toward Twist. "Mr. Businessman here wanted to handle it," he says. "Said it was all about negotiations. Be like Donald Trump and the art of the deal."

"Worked out fine," Twist says quietly.

Cuba downs the rest of his Stoli and sneers.

Dizzy takes a long sip of his drink. "He got a story?"

"Good guns. A little bit pricey," Twist says slowly, staring into the crowd on the dance floor. "He's got a decent selection but it can cost you."

"Price ain't what's important," Bone barks. "What matters is what he's got. And that he don't fuck us."

Cuba looks up from his Stoli. "What matters is that he got what we need to bring the Guineas to their knees. That's the only story I need to know."

"Heard he used to be a state cop," Eddie Dallas puts in, poking the ice in his glass with a finger. "Heard he was dirty. Did side jobs then took up with some prostitute he was banging and got booted off the force when the bosses found out."

"Big time fuck up," Bone says.

Twist shrugs.

"He straight?" Dizzy asks. "Don't fuck you over. Gives you an honest deal?"

"He the best thing we got right now," Bone says.

◆ ◆ ◆

Cooper comes through the crowd slowly, shoulder to shoulder with a black bodyguard, his eyes carefully searching the darkness for a recognizable face. His is the only white face in the club yet he looks comfortable—almost cool and nonchalant moving along the edge of the dance floor in jeans, black T-shirt, and Armani jacket. An inch shorter than Twist, Cooper is late thirties with broad shoulders and a thin waist exaggerated by the cut of his jacket. His hair is dark blond, short and spiked to frame a receding hair line, with three days' worth of stubble on his chin. Something about the way he carries himself still screams "cop," no matter how long he's been off the force.

Once a guy carries a shield, he never loses that attitude.

The bodyguard is shorter and stockier and his eyes jump uncomfortably from face-to-face as he pushes forward. He wears a plain jacket over a T-shirt. His hair is cut low and his face is hard and square, and when he turns three diamonds in his left ear sparkle in the lights. He is polished but tightly wound, tense like a coiled spring.

"This got to be the guy, huh?" one of the Game Boys against the wall says.

Eddie Dallas looks up. "You see any other white guy looks like he belongs in here?"

Bone gives Cooper a small nod.

Cooper catches the look and quickly changes direction toward the table.

"This my show," Bone says quietly as Cooper approaches. "Don't want to hear everybody's opinion about what's going down. Let me tell him what we need. Make it brief and simple."

It is said to everyone but Twist feels the words are meant only for him.

Bone's voice is firm but his face carries a trace of a smile. "Cooper. How's it going, bro?"

Cooper extends a hand and slaps it lightly against Bone's, then slides easily into the empty chair between Cuba and Eddie. "Hey Bone," he says. "Good to see you."

He looks around the table, nodding to Twist as well as other faces he recognizes. He offers a smile as he eases backward in the chair, keeping enough elbow room between the Skulls flanking him. The bodyguard stays stoic and expressionless, backing up three steps to the wall and standing with his arms crossed over his chest, watching the table as well as everything around them.

"Been a long time," Cooper says. "Lost track of you. Guess that means things have been good, huh?"

"Things change and things stay the same," Bone shrugs. "You know how it goes sometimes. Staying fluid."

Cooper smiles and nods.

"Business been okay?" Bone asks, tipping down his shades to stare at him.

"Tough economy," Cooper replies. "I'm doing whatever I have to do, just to get by. It's not like it was a couple of years ago."

"You want something?" Dizzy asks. "A drink? Beer? Smokes or something?"

Cooper shakes his head. "Not gonna be here long. Figured we're just talking, right?" he says. "Give me an idea of what you want and I'll see what I can put together for you. We'll have drinks another time."

"We just shopping right now," Bone says, slowly and carefully. "Ain't nobody ready to pull out cash and start placing orders, looking for delivery if the product ain't right. We have a problem we need to deal with. We trying to get an idea what kind of options we got available to us if we looking to spend some dollars."

"What kind of money?"

"Fifteen grand," Bone answers. "More for the right kind of package."

"You can do a lot with that kind of cash," Cooper says, leaning carefully back in the chair. "I can get creative. Put together a number of options to deal with your problem."

"We need something with an edge," Bone tells him, knocking back the last of his drink then looking for the waitress while he talks. "Looking for a package that has pop, power, and coverage. Want heat that's got more than we can get from AKs, ARs, and the .22s we carry.

"Got in the middle of a situation that requires more than negotiations," he adds.

"Results," Cuba adds. "We looking for results."

"What we looking for is something that can change the odds," Bone tells Cooper.

Cooper sits back with a serious expression, keeping his eyes focused on Bone. The attitude and cool he carries don't change; Twist thinks it must be something all cops take to the grave. Cooper doesn't say anything for at least a minute and all eyes at the table stare at him. The music is loud, but it's deathly still at the table. Twist takes another drink and rattles the ice cubes around the empty glass, first watching Cooper then turning to Bone and Cuba, and then back to Cooper again.

Finally Cooper leans forward again and plants his elbows on the table. "I've got some ideas," he says slowly, "but it could run you a little more than you want to spend."

"Maybe price don't matter as much as what you got. If it meets our needs."

"Flexibility gives us options," Cooper says with a smile. "Give me the night and let me work on this. I'll put together a package. Come by tomorrow and check out what we've got. See for yourself if it will change the odds."

"Ain't gonna make us wait?"

"Cash and carry," Cooper says. "Bring the cash and carry out the hardware."

"Give us something to dream about tonight," Bone asks. "What you thinking about putting in this package of yours?"

"Giving you that maximum firepower you're looking for," Cooper says with a smile.

"Like what?"

"Imports," Cooper says. "You ever hear about Galils?"

Twist looks up. "Israeli guns, right?"

Cooper nods. "They're .308 caliber semiautomatic rifles with detachable twenty shot magazines. Put together a couple hundred round mags and you can shoot over six hundred rounds per minute. Expensive but effective."

"How expensive?"

"Fifteen hundred per gun plus ammo," Cooper says and Bone whistles. "You want something with even more pop, maybe I can get my hands on some Steyr AUGs."

"Fuck is that?" Bone asks. "Ain't never heard of them. Better than ARs?"

"German guns. Run you four grand each but they're worth it," Cooper says. "Give you thirty to forty round magazines with easy loading. Do a little tinkering and you can even set them up to launch grenades."

Everyone at the table sits up. Cuba's expression turns into the kind a kid wears on Christmas morning when he sees presents under the tree.

A dozen questions get fired at Cooper. He smiles and nods, holding up a hand to quiet them. "Think that'll give you the kind of results you're looking for?"

"You got our interest," Cuba says.

"Sounds like we can deal," Bone says.

Cooper stands up and steps away from the table.

"Call me in the morning," he says. "You give me the night to work on this and I'll see what we can do, and how fast I can put it together for you."

"Need to make this happen," Bone says.

"I won't disappoint you," Cooper says.

They shake hands.

"One more thing," Bone says, leaning forward on his elbows and locking Cooper with his stare. "We involved in something that needs to be settled quickly but discreetly. Don't need nobody knowing our business."

"You and me have always been straight with each other," Cooper says. "I respect you and respect your operation. All that matters to me is moving product and getting my price."

"Just want to keep everything on the table," Bone says, and Cooper nods like he understands. "Got to be sure you got no kind of conflict dealing with that."

Cooper shakes his head. "I don't take sides," he says. "All I do is move product. How you use it and who uses it doesn't concern me."

Bone exchanges looks with Cuba and smiles.

"Think we ready to do a little more than talk," he says. "Think we ready to do business."

CHAPTER EIGHT

Twist lives on a quiet residential street near Rutgers. The block has the same haunting, eerie silence of Murray Street. Faces peek out from doorways and bodies dart quietly through the shadows but none feel the same tension and stress that Twist knows. The kid behind the wheel of the GMC Suburban slows at the end of the block and steers to the curb, parking behind a Chevy that has its back end propped up on blocks. He turns to Twist, waiting for something without knowing what it is he's looking for.

Twist takes one last drag on the Camel then flicks the butt through the open window. He checks the clip in his nine and sticks it inside his jeans before opening the door.

He never bothers looking back at the kid.

It went that way during the drive back from the Viper Club, with the kid anxious and edgy, desperate for a common link to create conversation and break the quiet, but he got nothing from Twist. The kid looks like he needs to say something but doesn't open his mouth.

Instead he watches Twist looking up and down his street before walking toward the building. It doesn't feel right but the kid doesn't know enough about how things work—he's not sure what's expected of him and what he's supposed to do, so it takes time to find words.

He finally sucks up his courage enough to poke his head out the window. "Want me to wait or something?"

Twist keeps going without answering.

The kid just watches and waits without a clue about what to do next.

Twist's black Pathfinder is parked on the street, same place it's been for two weeks. There are no new dents or scratches. No broken windows where some junkie tried getting at the radio, or nail holes ripped into the tires by kids looking for smiles and laughs. Things like that don't happen much to him. Guys on the street know Twist and know his colors; he's never had a problem with anybody messing with the car. It's wedged between an old Impala and a Dodge minivan with a stack of wet, soggy parking tickets curled underneath the wipers. Twist takes the tickets and crumples them into a tight wad. The ink on the paper is blurred and impossible to make out, and he drops them to the street and keeps going.

His apartment building is typical for the neighborhood. Prewar brick and mortar, four stories high with long, wide stairs to the sidewalk like most buildings lining the street. There are trash cans and fire hydrants, with trees dug into three-foot squares of dirt crisscrossing the sidewalk. The street is an urban renewal project that never came off as planned. Twist remembers bits and pieces of those ambitious plans to convert buildings into low-income housing and his family was one of the lucky few who got a rent subsidized apartment before it all fell apart. The renovation money got tight soon after the project started, and then new mayors with new administrations created their own agendas that needed additional funding. Old programs died and tax dollars dried up, and things like rec programs for kids and neighborhood renovations disappeared.

Nothing really changed.

Not that any of it ever made a difference.

Most of that happened while Twist's mother was still around. Before she figured out she was just thirty-five and that there was more to her life than what she had with Twist and his brothers in a city-owned apartment. Before she took off for Atlantic City with some trick she said she loved; someone who mattered more to her than Twist and his brothers. It wasn't like they had a lot of memories together. At first there were phone calls and an occasional letter but nothing more than that. It's been five-years since that last letter. But there's nothing in his life to remind him of her and no reason to think about her.

Whatever reasons he used to have for remembering her are gone.

He hears the GMC Suburban's engine kick to life behind him as the kid takes the big body down the street.

Twist feels the silence in the building as he enters. It's after midnight, and with the late hour there's a quiet to the building that's troubling. At other times he can hear voices and noises that make the building come alive; televisions, music, dogs barking, and babies crying, but there is nothing now. The situation with the Italians has him on edge and the silence gives him pause. There are no gangsters here, only families, and Twist likes that. The people who live here keep their distance, and he likes being alone. It's more than respect. It's normalcy.

His apartment is on the fourth floor, the first of three apartments at the top of the stairs. There's a middle-aged couple, no kids or family, at the end of the hall, and a young mother with five year-old twins who lives next door to him. She's an assistant manager at the Rite Aid drug store across the river in Harrison; cute, petite, and in her early twenties, and she can always find a smile for Twist when they pass in the hall or on the stairs. Her husband split a year ago and Twist hasn't seen a man at her door since. He's been wishing he could find the cool it takes to do more than smile, like chancing a hello or finding a reason to invite her inside his apartment for a beer, but the time is never right. She's not someone like Maria, and the words and actions that would work on Maria don't seem appropriate. Twist doesn't know anything about this woman but he's sure that saying the right words are important to her.

He stops at the top of the stairs. There's a light visible under her door but the sounds inside are low and muffled. He's tempted to take a chance but the moment passes and Twist keeps going.

His apartment is dark and quiet. Twist steps inside the door and punches in his four-digit code to turn off the security system, double-bolting the door behind him. He waits in the darkness for Adonis but his dog never comes. It's another bad habit that's still too fucking hard to shake, Twist thinks, flicking on the light. It's been six months since a drunk ran the stop sign and hit the Rott as he ran between two parked cars. It wasn't the drunk's fault; he wasn't the one who let the dog run around without a leash. It wasn't the drunk who was careless.

Six months of emptiness and solitude.

Maybe it's time to get another dog.

The living room is long and spacious, with fourteen-foot ceilings and hardwood floors that are dark with age. Twist never paid much attention to furniture and his home is sparse; only a couch and two chairs on a small braided rug. There's a plasma TV on one side of the room hooked up to two different Xbox and Wii consoles along with a DVD player. The walls are covered with framed horror movie posters and the glass-doored book case is filled with horror flicks, Sonny Chiba movies, and sex tapes Maria never likes watching with him.

Twist goes through the living room and down the hall to the bedroom, stopping in the kitchen for a Bud from the refrigerator.

The bedroom is furnished with the same kind of casualness as the living room. The walls haven't been painted in five or six years. A long walnut dresser that's chipped and scratched on the edges is angled against the wall with a small matching table by the bed. The finish on both is stained, many of the knobs on the dresser drawers are missing, and the ones remaining are loose. There's a stereo in the corner, with each component set up and arranged carefully on the floor, surrounded by CDs and empty plastic cases. The poster of Malcolm X that his aunt from North Carolina sent a long time ago is tacked up on one wall, although the top corner has dropped and the poster sags in half. On the other wall there are posters from movies like *Aliens* and *Friday the 13th*, as well as one of Bruce Lee in mid-kick that faces his waterbed.

Twist kicks past a pile of jeans and worn T-shirts on the floor to get to the closet.

Inside are empty Nike boxes, old karate magazines, and albums he used to play on his brother's turntable. Clothes he never wears anymore and things that don't matter fill up the space. There are boxes that belong to his brother; a few possessions that mattered enough that he saved them before he got sent away. Twist moves them to one side and goes deeper into the junk.

It takes time to find the boom box. It's been years since he last used it and Twist pokes at the knobs and dials, checking the batteries to make sure it still works. The small plastic door that holds cassettes is broken and one of the side speakers has a quarter-sized hole in the grill, but the radio works well enough. He keeps turning the knob until he finds something more than static and chatter.

It's good enough for what he needs.

He carries the radio to the window and holds it to his chest while looking into the night. Twist takes another sip of the Bud and stares into the darkness. He has no problem killing Valentine, but decides that he won't let the Skulls just casually dump the body. He draws the line at leaving the corpse in a trash can or in a plastic bag out in a drainage ditch near the airport.

Things like that matter.

At least it matters to Twist.

◆ ◆ ◆

Twist returns to the building on Murray Street.

It's silent. Nobody has returned from the Viper Club and he knows the outings can last all night. The vodka, cocaine, and tight-assed women can keep the crew there for hours. The kids downstairs are too wrapped up in a late night rerun and the last few lines of white dust on the mirrors to care about Twist or anything he does. He's just another face passing through the house. There are a couple of nods when he comes in but nothing more than that. Twist doesn't command respect without the others around unless he pushes it.

It goes that way.

When the phone rings none of them hurry to answer it. They leave that for Twist, like it's his privilege. Or his obligation.

"You somebody?" the voice on the phone asks.

When Twist hears the voice he knows that whoever is calling has been watching the garage and saw him enter.

"Or just one of them guys who all he knows how to do is dribble a basketball and fuck fourteen-year-old welfare babies?"

Twist recognizes the voice. "Got something you want to say," he says, "might as well say it."

The line is quiet and Twist waits, hearing the sound of his own breath coming in short bursts.

There's nothing but breathing on the other end.

"Things gonna get worse. You know that, right?" the man finally says.

"That's what you're saying. Don't mean it'll happen."

"You don't do something to change it, pretty soon it's gonna be like one of those plane crashes. A thing that can't be stopped," the voice says. "Maybe you starting to get in too deep? Maybe if you want to pull back, you got time now."

Twist doesn't say anything.

The man goes on in a voice that sounds like it has a smile attached to every word. "Figure something like that could happen, right?

You get into something over your head and all of a sudden you start thinking that maybe it's time to get out before it's too late. Like you made a mistake and need to reconsider your choices.

"What I'm saying is that it ain't too late right now," the guy says. "But pretty soon, before you know it, you gonna crash and there ain't nothing gonna stop what happens afterwards.

"You know what I'm saying?"

"I hear you," Twist says.

"Good," the man says. "Because pretty soon you gonna lose this thing you got. Unless maybe you do the right thing and this don't get any worse than it already is."

Then he hangs up.

◆ ◆ ◆

Twist goes up the stairs slowly. He's aware of every noise the floors and walls make as the building shifts and settles. Nothing feels safe anymore and there's suddenly too much danger in the silence. He reaches the second floor and turns quickly when he hears a door hinge creak.

One of the Game Boys is coming out of a bedroom. He stumbles through the door, with his T-shirt pulled out of his shorts and his Nikes open and unlaced. Another kid comes out of the bedroom behind him with his head down, pushing past quickly to move down the stairs. Twist steps to the side to let him pass.

The first kid nods to Twist, holding a dopey smile on his face while leaning into the wall.

"Hey," he says.

There are footsteps behind Twist and another kid rushes by, hurrying down the hall toward the bedroom. The first Game Boy holds open the door and lets him in.

"What's going on?" Twist asks, approaching cautiously. He feels the hairs on the back of his neck standing at attention and he looks around warily.

"Shit," the kid says in a long, lazy voice. "Just stickin' it with a neighborhood piece."

Twist stares at him.

The Game Boy motions Twist toward the bedroom, giggling like a ten-year-old with a secret he needs to share. His eyes are open

wide with a smile stretching across his face. It's dark and the only
light in the room comes from a sixty-watt bulb in a small lamp on
the nightstand that's pushed into the side of the bed. Shadows move
and flicker on the wall and Twist can barely make out the shape of
the Game Boy from the stairs slipping out of his shorts. The other
shadowy figure is curled on the bed. The body looks young and clean
in the light but the skin is taut and her breasts are hard and firm.
Almond colored skin and tangled, knotted hair that touches the girl's
shoulders only briefly before her fingers push it away.

She rolls her head to the side and in the light Twist sees the face of
the girl who went from Bone's bedroom to Dizzy at the Viper Club.

"Dizzy brought her back here a little while ago when he was done
with her," the kid at Twist's elbow is saying. "For all of us. Just to get
our G on, you know?"

She sees Twist and her eyes open wide.

"I'll do any of you," she says in a coarse whisper to the kid in the
shadows, "but not him."

"What're you talking about?"

"That one. I'll do all of you. Not him. There's something about
him."

"Shit," the kid spits back. There's none of the first Game Boy's
humor in his smile; his expression is serious and urgent, with no time
for talk until after he's done doing what he needs to do. "You ain't
got no choice, bitch. You get in the car, you go for the ride. No stops
along the way and no choice what road you want to take."

"Anybody but him," she says again, more adamant this time. She
sits up and draws the sheets under his chin. "I don't like him."

"What's with her?" the kid at the door asks Twist.

Twist shrugs.

"What she says don't matter," he says. "Not if you want some."

"It's okay," Twist says, turning away.

"Not tonight."

He and the girl are not really that different. He leaves the room
without another word.

◆ ◆ ◆

This time Twist knocks on the third floor bedroom door first
before entering.

"I ain't heard nothing in there for a long time," the skinny kid at the door hisses. He says it like a warning; fearful that some kind of danger lurks behind the door. "Not a fucking sound."

Twist doesn't respond.

The kid unlocks the bolts slowly, keeping the AR-15 pointed toward the door with his finger curled around the trigger, just in case. Twist feels the barrel nudging him in the back and turns slowly, angling the gun toward the floor with his hand.

"I'm not the one you should be pointing at with that thing," he says.

He knocks once more, and then the kid opens the door and takes a step back to let Twist pass. It's close to one and Twist feels he owes Valentine the courtesy of knocking first; it doesn't feel right walking into the room unannounced. It's like Michael Valentine has been in the room so long that it doesn't belong to the Skulls any longer but to him.

The bedroom light is on but it takes a moment for Twist's eyes to adjust to the shadows as well as the darkness. Valentine is on the floor with his feet locked beneath the bed frame, struggling to lift his shoulders off the floor as he strains to finish his sit-ups. His hair is pulled back tight in the ponytail again and his shirt is off; his back wet with sweat and the dust on the floor sticking to his skin. But his stare hasn't changed; it's hard and focused. He glances at Twist but doesn't stop. Instead he moves slowly forward, touching his elbows to his knees, and then eases backward to the floor before doing it again. Valentine's shirt and jacket are folded on the end of the bed and his shoes are to one side, like he expects to wear them again. Only his tie is still rolled up on the floor like it doesn't matter.

The skinny kid stands in the doorway, his stare moving between Valentine and Twist. Twist motions toward the open door and waits until the bolts lock in place before turning back to Valentine.

He carries an eight pack of Bud long necks in one hand and the radio from his apartment in the other as he sits down in the chair.

"Had a feeling you wouldn't be sleeping," Twist says.

"No idea what time it is," Valentine says, slowly spinning around until his back is against the bed and his legs are out in front. "Got no way of knowing that it's night without a clock."

"It's almost two. If you're wondering."

Valentine looks at the radio and the eight pack. "What's this? Late night entertainment? Kill a couple of beers, listen to some tunes, and stare at the prisoner?"

"Beats watching reruns downstairs with the other guys."

"Watching South Park would be a hell of a lot better than sitting here," Valentine says.

"You want one of these?" Twist asks, offering a Bud.

Valentine nods. Twist rolls the bottle slowly across the floor but it still sprays the wall when Valentine opens it. Valentine tips his head back and takes a long, hard swallow of beer and suds.

"You eat?" Twist asks, opening his own Bud and bringing it to his mouth. "Somebody bring you food?"

"One of your guys was up here earlier," Valentine says, gesturing at the empty bags and containers. "You know, I don't want to sound ungrateful or like I complain too much, but maybe you want to try something different next time? I'm tired of Quarter Pounders and fries. A little variety would be nice."

"See what I can do," Twist says with a shrug. "Maybe a sandwich?"

Valentine scrunches up his face. "Pizza would be better."

They stare at each other in silence, still feeling the ground between them as they sip their beers. Twist is unsure about the things ahead. He knows that the distance between them can be useful and work to his advantage, but he's not so certain he wants that kind of help.

Valentine swallows a mouthful of beer, wiping the back of a hand across his mouth. "What's with the radio?"

Twist pushes it across the floor.

"Thought maybe it would help. You know, give you a little music or some news to listen to," he says. "At least you'll be able to tell what time it is."

Valentine examines the radio between his hands. He frowns and looks at Twist. "The cassette door is broken."

"That matter?"

Valentine shrugs but still looks annoyed.

"You got some tapes you were planning to play?" Twist asks. "Something you're dying to hear?"

Valentine just smiles and shakes his head without answering. He turns the knobs and dials and the radio crackles with static as he speeds through the AM band. The noise is loud and the sounds echo inside the small room, loud enough that Twist is sure the guys downstairs banging the girl from Murray Street can hear it. But he doesn't care what they hear from this room.

"Be nice if I can find a score," Valentine says. "Find out how the Mets did."

"St. Louis beat them," Twist says emotionlessly. "Four to three in extra innings."

Valentine frowns. "Cardinals always play us tough. They got all those lefties on their pitching staff. I've never seen a team built like that," he says. "The way they keep bringing lefthanders out of the bull pen makes it tough to anything going.

"You see the game?" he asks. "Highlights? Know what happened?"

Twist shakes his head. He's got better ways to waste time than watching baseball games on TV.

"Wonder how they lost."

"Why's it matter? They lost and that's all that counts," Twist says. "Mets will be lucky to win eighty-five games this year."

"You got an opinion, huh? Think you know something about baseball?"

"Told you before, basketball's what matters to me," Twist says, smiling the kind of easy smile he usually shares with Eddie Dallas. "Baseball ain't nothing compared to hoops. It's like being out in the world versus being stuck in first grade."

"You keep talking," Valentine says, smiling as he shakes his head. "You're good at that."

That doesn't bother Twist. Not the same way it did when Cuba opened his mouth and said the same thing earlier.

◆ ◆ ◆

"You ever wonder why you're doing this?" Michael Valentine asks him.

Twist screws up his face and looks at him. "I do what I have to do."

"What's that mean?"

"It means what it means," Twist says sharply.

"You make it sound like you guys are on some kind of crusade. Like it's a holy mission from God or something."

Twist swallows his Bud without letting his expression give anything away. Sometimes it's hard explaining things and saying words the way he means them. Sometimes people don't understand, so most times he doesn't bother explaining.

"It's like I said," he says. "I do what I have to do. I don't think about it much."

"This what you see yourself doing the rest of your life?" Valentine asks, popping the cap on another bottle of Bud. "That your dream?"

"Man, I don't even know what the fuck I'll be doing tomorrow," Twist says, scowling. "How can I plan out my future or tell you what I'll be doing the rest of my life? I can't see nothing like that."

"You don't have dreams? Things you want?"

Twist shakes his head.

"Everybody has dreams," Valentine says with disapproval in his voice. "You can't tell me nobody walking around doesn't have some kind of dream that pushes them."

"Learned to take everything as it comes and just go with it," Twist says. "Maybe some days you change the things you can change, but you don't worry about nothing else. Most times you can't even see that far down the road."

Valentine's expression is one of disbelief.

"Everybody's got dreams."

"Maybe everybody you know," Twist says. "The people I know are different."

"If you don't have dreams, how you supposed to know when you're happy? How can you know you've got everything you want?" Valentine asks.

Twist doesn't say anything.

The light flickers and the shadows on the wall dip and dance. There's a talk show on the sports channel but it's just radio chatter; voices and conversation that don't mean anything to Twist.

"Maybe all I care about right now is seeing tomorrow," he says finally.

"At least you got that," Valentine says as his voice sinks.

The room gets still; it is a quiet broken by conversation on the radio and those words pass into the night. The distance between Twist and Valentine suddenly feels heavy again, like it did that first time in the room. Twist stares at Valentine, thinking he should say something else. He starts but nothing comes out right, and Twist chokes back the words and lets it go.

Valentine takes a deep breath and turns up the radio.

"What about you?" Twist finally manages in a voice that is so quiet it is almost lost in the noise of the radio. "Any dreams? Anything you want?"

Valentine shrugs.

"Nothing that matters in here," he says.

"The only dream I got right now is to make it through the next hour," Valentine adds. "And when I make it that far, I dream the same dream again. I just want to keep that dream alive as long as I can."

Michael Valentine pushes away the empty Bud bottle and draws his knees up close to his chest. He leans his head back into the bed and closes his eyes for a minute. "This is some life you got, huh, Twist?"

Twist looks up at him. "You think you got me figured out?"

Valentine nods. "Skulls and basketball. No dreams and no hope. Nothing else but Skulls and basketball," he says. "That's your life."

"Skulls, basketball, and getting laid," Twist corrects quietly.

Valentine opens his eyes, and when their stares meet they each break into smiles.

◆ ◆ ◆

Valentine is holding his third bottle of Bud with his eyes closed and his head resting on the bed. For a moment Twist thinks he's fallen asleep and it disappoints him. It feels like the first time all day he's found something worth a smile.

The little voice inside his head reminds him that this is only temporary and that it can't last. In less than twenty-four hours he'll be the one who has to put the gun to Michael Valentine's head and blow him away without a second of regret or hesitation. He'll have to do it without thinking and without questioning his actions.

He tries ignoring that voice but the words don't change.

"You know, we're not that different," Valentine says now with his eyes still closed. "All things considered."

"We're different. Don't matter what things you want to consider."

Valentine shakes his head slowly. "Not the way I see it."

"We're different," Twist says again, harder this time. "What's between us is different. All you got to do is look at us to know it."

"You're talking about the black-and-white thing."

"Yeah, that part of it."

"Sometimes you got to look past that," Valentine says now, opening his eyes again to stare at Twist. "Got to look at things you can't always see."

Twist takes out a pack of Camels and shakes a cigarette loose. Everything in his life and everything he knows has to do with color but it's not worth arguing the point. "Okay, ignore the color thing. We're still different," he says. "You and me, we're not the same. Just because you say it doesn't make it true."

Valentine shakes his head again, more persistent this time. There's a firmness in his voice, like he believes the words now more than ever before. "We're the same kind of guys."

"Both of us are caught in something we can't control and something we don't understand," Valentine says.

"I understand what's going on."

Michael Valentine just shakes his head.

Twist kicks at an empty bottle and sends it rolling to the wall. "You sitting there telling me you don't know what this is about?"

Valentine shrugs. "What I'm saying is that all we're doing is our jobs, you and me," he says. "We're the same kind of guys, doing what we got to do but doing it from different sides. Don't you see that?"

"It's more than that."

"No it's not. It's just a job. This is what we do. This is who we are."

Twist shakes his head. "More to it than that. Maybe you just can't see that."

"Maybe for you, but you're not like these other guys," Valentine says, taking another sip of beer. "Anybody can see you're not like that guy you call Cuba. If you ask him, he couldn't even tell you why he's into this or what it's all about."

"You think you know that much about Cuba?"

Valentine smirks and shakes his head. "Man, I know a dozen guys just like Cuba in my own neighborhood. I know how they operate and how they think. They're the kind of guys you offer a thousand dollars with no strings attached, and they can't believe there's nothing behind it. Always suspicious."

"Kind of thing they don't understand," Twist says.

Valentine nods. "They'd rather kill you for no reason cause there's something in doing it that way that makes them smile."

"The only difference between Cuba and Giaccolone is the clothes they wear, the houses they live in, and the whores they bang at night.

Cuba probably finds himself a different whore every time he's got a hard-on. Giaccolone's the same as him, except he's got an old lady he goes home to when he's done."

Twist takes a drag on the cigarette and leans back in the chair.

"What makes you think I'm not the same," he asks. "How much do you think you really know about me and who I am?"

Michael Valentine stares at Twist. He looks at him like he understands something that Twist hasn't yet figured out for himself. "I don't know what you're all about, Twist. Can't tell you nothing about your life, the same way you can't tell me nothing about mine except what we shared so far," he says slowly. "But you're not like Cuba. You said so yourself.

"Even if you didn't say it, I could see that myself."

"That doesn't make you and me the same," Twist says.

"Guys like Giaccolone and Cuba, they're different than us," Valentine says. "You and me aren't like them. You see that, too, right?"

Twist lets out the smoke and stares down at his Nikes.

"Maybe," he finally concedes.

"Maybe in another time and place, we might even be friends," Valentine tries, still looking at him. "If things were different."

Twist doesn't answer and he doesn't meet Valentine's stare. Maybe the lines aren't as clear and distinct as they should be, but it doesn't take a lot of work to figure out where everybody's place is, and where they all stand. Nothing about this has to do with friendship.

"Tough to say," he says to Valentine.

"Not that tough."

"It is for me."

"What're you afraid of?" Valentine asks, still staring at him. "That you and me aren't so different? Is there something so fucking wrong about that?"

Twist doesn't answer.

Valentine finishes the last drops in the bottle and takes a deep breath, letting it out slowly. "All I'm saying is that if you and me were somewhere else it wouldn't be like this," he says. "We could be friends."

Twist thinks about it. Maybe he might look at things differently if his world wasn't filled with guns and violence and hate and dead brothers and guys who get snatched off the street. But his world is different.

In his world, "might haves" and "could haves" don't matter.

◆ ◆ ◆

The beer is gone and they're tired of talking. It's late and morning will come too soon; Twist knows he should get back to his apartment to find a couple of hours for sleep. Valentine's eyes are sagging and the pauses in their conversations get longer as they run out of things to say.

Twist moves slowly out of the chair and says something about calling it a night.

Valentine's head is against the bed and his eyes stay closed. But he says, "You guys decide who's gonna do it?"

"Do what?"

"You know what I'm talking about."

"I don't know what you mean," Twist says, stopping and shaking his head.

Valentine smiles and opens his eyes. "Don't bullshit me, Twist."

"I don't know what the fuck you're saying," Twist says, harder this time. "How can I bullshit you if I don't know what you're talking about?"

"I know you guys are going to kill me," Valentine says. "No way anybody ever makes a trade, one guy for another. That's Hollywood bullshit. Things like that don't ever happen. Not in your world, and not with Giaccolone."

"I figure I got maybe another day," Valentine says, "before one of you guys comes up here and puts a bullet in my eye."

Twist tries something about how nothing has been decided and that nobody's made any decisions, but Valentine waves it off and shakes his head. When he speaks his voice isn't hard but slow and easy, like he's accepted what's coming and he's trying to prepare for it.

"All I want to know," he says now, "is who's gonna pull the trigger?"

The words stick inside Twist's head and he can't get rid of them on the way home.

CHAPTER NINE

The morning is rough and unforgiving.

Twist wakes up with a cold, hollow feeling he can't shake. It's the kind of empty feeling that lurks in the background, like a voice second guessing every decision and thought, and he knows it will last far into his day.

It never gives him a moment of peace.

His cell phone rings but there's no reason to answer. It's probably Eddie Dallas, calling to remind him about their eleven o'clock meeting, or somebody from Murray Street bothering him about something else. Either way it's too early and Twist doesn't have what it takes to answer the phone.

The ringing ends as abruptly as it started, and silence returns.

He lays back in bed and stares at the ceiling.

The bedroom is dark but Twist is done sleeping. In the early morning hours his past sometimes slams together with his present. Sometimes he can deal with everything that comes at him, no matter how old or far back the memories go but most mornings he can't. Each memory reopens another wound. This morning his head is filled with faces from his childhood, of men moving quickly out of his mother's bedroom before dawn; none of them ever noticing the pairs of eyes watching from the darkness of the apartment. Twist can still hear the questions he and his brothers asked and the silence they got as answers. It was all they had until they figured out on their own what was going on.

Twist takes the pack of Camels off the nightstand and shakes out the last cigarette, glancing once at the clock radio. He lights up and lays back down with his head on the pillow.

Minutes pass before the phone rings again. Twist tries ignoring it but the sound stays inside his head the same way the memories of those men cruising through his living room in the early morning hours do. He blows out a smoke ring and knows there's nothing anybody can say that he wants to hear.

It all comes down to one thing for him. Michael Valentine will be dead by the end of the day and there's no way to change that.

Nothing else matters.

The phone keeps ringing and even though Twist squeezes his eyes shut he can't block out the sound. It doesn't go away.

◆ ◆ ◆

Twist puts down the coffee cup and levels his sunglasses so he can better watch what's going on. The 9mm is in his lap beneath a paper napkin with the safety off and Twist moves his hand away from the table, resting the fingertips on his thigh, just in case. There are two kids at the door. One moves outside before Twist can get a look at him so it's the other one who draws his attention. He is tall and black, carrying an attitude and a nasty expression, and Twist doesn't like the way the kid's eyes wander around the diner. His stare is too calculating and measured. He takes in the old guys at the counter, then follows the waitress as she hurries into the kitchen holding an empty coffee pot. Twist knows that look. It's as if the kid is sizing up opponents, judging strengths and weaknesses, and he is suddenly tense as he leans into the table, feeling the tingling in his chest and the surge of adrenaline.

It's a familiar feeling, like the one that came over him in the airport parking lot with the Italians.

The kid throws Twist a look but there's nothing behind it.

He slaps his change down on the counter and takes his coffee but Twist doesn't ease his hand back onto the table until the kid has gone through the door.

It's only then that he puts the safety on again.

The diner is a small sit down in East Orange, just off Springfield Avenue, hidden in the shadows of the old Piels Beer plant at the end of the street. There's nothing special about it; once it might have been the kind of place that was busy all the time when the bottling plant was open, but that was at least ten years ago. There are no more around-the-clock work days broken into eight-hour shifts, and the procession of workers on the street at all hours of the day are only ghosts. Now it's the kind of place that may not be around in another week. There's a long Formica counter running the length of the diner and a handful of booths in the back by the kitchen doors. Faded, yellowed signs describing the daily specials are taped above the health certificates, and framed black-and-white pictures of former mayors and long-dead high school ball players are nailed to the wall. The stools and seats are faded green plastic, patched and repaired with tape that doesn't match the color. Small jukeboxes are spaced along the counter and the booths, and something that sounds like one of those early seventies groups like the Drifters or Spinners comes through the speakers.

A couple of plumbers sit at the counter in their overalls sipping coffee and trading sports highlights from last night's Mets and Yankees games. Other guys in their fifties do the same thing in groups or sit alone, buried in newspapers along the length of the counter. None of the faces have changed since Twist walked in and sat down in a booth. It looks like most of the diner's business is done through a sporadic stream of customers who come in quickly to order, then run back outside with coffees, rolls, and egg sandwiches.

It's the kind of place where Twist can quietly mind his business because nobody knows him, and nobody bothers him.

There are no guys in black BMWs leaning out windows with automatics or gangsters showing colors, looking to create their own legends for people on the street to remember. It is ten minutes away from Newark and an entirely different world.

He likes being anonymous.

Twist could feel eyes watching him when he parked on the street but nobody did anything except follow him with their stares. Nobody paid attention to him and the looks he got were born out of curiosity. There was nothing more to any of it. When those eyes were convinced there was nothing to him they quickly turned away. It was only those two guys by the door who drew his attention—red bandannas, jeans, and Ray-Bans, with their arms crossed tight across their chests, almost daring confrontation.

They watched Twist slide into the booth and he could feel their eyes on him.

If there is a problem, it's that he doesn't know the turf or the colors—none of it means anything to him. He doesn't know about disputes, rules, or how to read the stares so Twist watched them as cautiously they watched him. He couldn't know who they were or what they expected as he slipped the gun in his lap and flicked off the safety with his thumb. It was there, if he needed it.

But the guys didn't even look back at him once they got their coffees.

Twist drinks his coffee and pokes slowly through the eggs, soaking up the grease and yoke with a stub of toast. The queasy feeling in his stomach still lingers and the coffee and eggs don't make it any better. It's probably way too early for a shot of Jack Daniel's but he could use that more than the eggs and cigarettes. His cigarette smolders in the ashtray, untouched and forgotten. The smoke curls toward the ceiling as he takes another bite of toast and stares at his reflection in the window as he swallows.

Drawn, weary, and a little more haggard than Twist realized, it hasn't changed much in the past few hours.

He stares into his eyes, probing for something in the expression, and suddenly feels very alone. There have been plenty of times when he was lonely and by himself, and most times he chose that solitude. He likes time for himself and needs it. But this feeling goes deeper than that and Twist can't shake the despair it carries.

He thinks first about his brothers and how they are dead or as good as dead, and tries finding memories that bring back a smile. But nothing comes, no matter how hard he tries, and he realizes that it's worthless going any further. He can see his mother sometimes in those early morning thoughts, but there's nothing good about remembering her either.

Twist takes a drag on the cigarette and shakes the images from his head. The coffee in his cup is cold but Twist sips it anyway, thinking that with luck somebody will bring Michael Valentine more than coffee and an Egg McMuffin for breakfast. He mentioned that to one of the Game Boys before leaving last night, but there are no guarantees anybody did anything. He hopes he can remember to pick up the newspapers again and maybe another cup of coffee on the way back before meeting Eddie. Twist figures that Valentine will want to read about last night's Mets loss, although he still can't figure out why something like that matters so much.

Pieces from their conversation come back and words stick with Twist as he slowly pushes the food around his plate. Things were said that didn't seem important but are important enough now that he keeps coming back to them while sitting in the diner.

"You guys really think this is something you can win?" Valentine had asked somewhere between the beer and cigarettes, and before the conversation fell away. "Really believe that?"

"Depends," Twist said with a grunt, "on who you ask and how they look at it."

"What's that mean?"

"Means the answer you get from me ain't the same one you get from somebody like Cuba or Bone. Different guys believe different things."

Valentine shook his head. His smile was impatient. "Asking a simple question. Doesn't take a lot of thought or bullshit to give me an answer I can understand."

Twist took a long time. "When it all started getting heavy some of the guys were talking about setting up a meeting with Joey Dogs," he said, turning Valentine's head. "They thought maybe there was a way of getting together with him the same way you guys are getting together with the Bloods.

"Thought we'd have a better chance to win that way," he added.

Valentine kept his frown, slowly shaking his head. "What made you think that?"

"Didn't say it was me."

"Joey Dogs is a piece of shit. Nothing good about him."

Twist smiled. "You saying that because it's something you believe, or because Joey Dogs took a shot at Giaccolone a couple of months ago and now you guys want his blood in the street the same way you want to see ours?"

"Does it matter?"

"Matters," Twist said evenly. "It matters if the way you look at Joey Dogs is because of what he is, or it's because Giaccolone got a hard-on for him."

Valentine shuffled his feet and sat up a little straighter. "Let me tell you about Joey Dogs," he said. "The guy don't have no values and no honor. He don't care nothing about what anybody else has earned, and if Joey Dogs doesn't see anything in it for himself, Joey Dogs doesn't care about it."

"Yeah, but having Joey Dogs with us might have tipped the odds," Twist said. "Made it different."

"Wouldn't have been any different. Wouldn't have changed a fucking thing."

Twist sipped his Bud. "Some guys thought it might have helped."

"You still lose in the long run," Valentine said. "No matter how much of a hard-on Joey Dogs has for Giaccolone, a guy like him looks at you guys only one way. After everything is over, and him and his crew have helped you do what you want to do, you're still only colored guys who have something he wants. Then they're going to want it for themselves and they'll take it.

"Nobody gives two fucks about colored guys," he said, like it was something new Twist just learned.

"Hear that from everybody I meet," Twist said quietly. "Not just Joey Dogs."

"No offense."

"I know."

"I'm just saying that it wouldn't have mattered," Valentine said. "You wouldn't have been no better off with him and his crew."

Twist had kicked impatiently at the floor beneath his chair. "I'm not talking about what Joey Dogs could have done for us. I'm just trying to explain that maybe there are a lot of guys with ideas how to win this," he said. "But none of them really know anything about what it's going to take."

"Maybe it's something none of us can win," Valentine said quietly.

Those are the words that stick with Twist now.

"Want more coffee, honey?"

The voice comes out of nowhere and Twist looks up to see the waitress at his side, waving the coffee pot over his cup. She's a big woman, late forties, with too much lipstick and mascara, and her hair is tied up in a tight bun that's wrapped in the kind of white netting nurses wear. There's a disinterested stare in her expression, and she fills his cup without waiting for a response, dropping some containers of creamer on the table.

She is gone as quickly as she appeared.

The coffee burns the roof of his mouth. He pours in cream to kill some of the heat, moving the spoon slowly in small circles inside the cup. The waitress came up on him too quickly and he should have seen her coming but he missed it. Twist knows that if she had been an Italian or a Blood he'd be a corpse.

Somehow that doesn't bother him too much. Not like it used to.

He thinks about death and what it will be like after Valentine is dead but Ice and Malik are still missing. The pain in Valentine's expression is more noticeable whenever he talks about it; there are people in his life who will cry for him and miss him. Those are people who matter. Twist thinks about what would happen if it were the other way around, and Valentine was the one pulling the trigger on Twist. Who is left to cry for him?

Twist takes another sip of coffee and decides that it doesn't pay to think about it.

He turns back to the window. The day will be as hot as ever; it already has that kind of feel. It's a day ready to be filled with demands and plans and the anticipation about where the events will lead them, and what will happen by the time Twist walks into Valentine's bedroom one last time to pull the trigger.

Twist sighs and stares at the face in the reflection again. It has changed into the face of a stranger.

◆ ◆ ◆

"Been trying to get you," Raphael says. "You know getting phone time in here's a real bitch. Can't be doing this whenever the fuck I feel like it."

"Sorry," Twist mumbles.

"Don't have hours to be fucking with the pay phones."

"I said, I'm sorry," Twist says again, this time a little harder.

"Ain't trying to get in your shit, but I only got so many times they let me make a call then I lose the shot," he says. "After that it's back to the laundry detail. You feel me?"

Twist doesn't answer. He shifts the Pathfinder into drive and slides it into the street, angling the SUV behind a Suburban Transit bus crawling down the street at least ten miles an hour below the speed limit. There's a morning newspaper along with a copy of the latest *Sporting News* on the passenger's seat, and a Styrofoam coffee cup on the console between the seats.

"You feel me, right?'

Twist understands. It doesn't take a lot of imagination figuring out what his brother's life is like inside East Jersey State.

"Got those Camels you sent me," Raphael says. "Appreciate you making that happen."

"No big deal."

Raphael grunts. "Matters. Shit's better than cash. Maybe next week you get one of the young'uns to bring me some Marlboros too."

Twist holds the coffee cup between his legs before peeling open the lid and working it carefully to his mouth.

"Things okay?"

"Just day to day living," Raphael answers. "Got some Bloods getting in my face, but there's enough friendlies in here to keep things from going too far. They just punks. Young'uns doing their first times. Ain't done nothing to brag about and they just looking to cause some shit with me and make a name, you know?

"I got to take steps, I'll shank the motherfuckers in the shower and deal with the fallout when they find the bodies."

Twist takes a sip of coffee. It steams up his sunglasses as he brings the cup to his mouth and he holds it there.

"What you hear about Malik?"

"Ain't hearing nothing," Twist says. "Thinking that we just about out of time, no matter what we trying to do to get answers or force resolution."

Raphael is quiet for a moment. When the words finally come there's an edge to his voice. "Thinking maybe this strategy ain't working out the way it's supposed to. You sure you know what you're doing?"

"A little late to be questioning it now, don't you think?" Twist asks.

"Ain't offering nothing more than an observation," Raphael says. "I'm in here. Don't have a lot of pull no more if I'm not on the street. Just asking if maybe you bit off more than you thought. Thinking that maybe it might be going someplace you didn't think it would go. Now it's creating problems and situations none of you ever figured on facing."

Twist says nothing.

"Maybe you didn't think this through and consider everything the way you should."

Another fucking critic, Twist thinks. One more voice filled with criticism.

He takes another sip of coffee and draws a deep breath. "Think we thought this through when we laid it out," he says. "Maybe underestimated the willingness of the Guineas to talk and negotiate. But that was our only mistake."

"Thought you, out of everyone in that building, would have looked at all the angles and known how things work with them people," Raphael spits back. "You know they don't negotiate and don't do much talking. They got only one way of dealing with us.

"Thought you would have been smarter about that."

Twist lets his head drop back against the seat, and wonders again how hard it would be to disappear. He would have at least a couple of hours before anyone figured out he was gone, and even longer before they realized he hadn't been taken out by the Italians. Plenty of time to steer by Maria's to pick up her and Angel. They could get on the Turnpike and drive south until North Carolina or Georgia or Virginia, and he'd never have to go back to Murray Street again.

"Did what made the most sense," he tells his brother. "Kept you in the loop and didn't hear you telling us to do nothing different."

"Sounds like you got some real issues the way it's shaking out," Raphael says.

"We're taking steps. Trying to fix things."

"Think those steps gonna' bring back Malik?"

"I don't know."

"You ask me, you got only one thing you can do now. You feel me?"

"I know," Twist says in a quiet voice.

"You ain't getting answers. Don't waste no more time with that guy," Raphael says. "Cut your losses and do what you got to do.

"You know what I mean by that, right?"

Twist squeezes his eyes shut for a few seconds then opens them as he inches the SUV forward. "I know."

"Good," Raphael says. "And you got to be the one that's got to do it."

It's nothing Twist doesn't already know.

"Can't be nobody else. It's got to be you," Raphael says. "No good if somebody else does it."

"Bone's got a good reason too."

"Yeah, but it ain't Spider that's missing," Raphael shoots back. "You got to be the one."

"Cuba and Bone said the same thing," Twist says.

"Cuba and Bone got a point of view you got to respect," Raphael says. "May not be the same as yours, but you still got to listen to it and respect it."

Twist says nothing. His brother is no different than the others—telling him things he already knows or has figured out.

Twist wishes he could disappear just like Ice and Malik and never let himself be found.

◆ ◆ ◆

Twist takes the steps at 1117 Fairmount slowly and cautiously, almost expecting somebody with a semiautomatic to come out of the shadows.

The street is quiet at nine o'clock in the morning. There are only a few cars on the street and even fewer people passing on the sidewalk. There are men hurrying to jobs at gas stations, warehouses, and sweatshops downtown, and older ladies who work as domestic help in Short Hills and Bernardsville hurry to catch the 8:15 train from the Broad Street Station. There's no sign of the old Cuban who had been sitting on the steps the other night, drinking his beer and smoking cigarettes. Probably too early for him to crawl out of bed. Twist can hear voices and laughter on the street but it's still too early for most of the neighborhood kids to be outside—they're inside, glued to *Looney Tunes*, *Avatar*, and *SpongeBob* reruns.

The lobby door is unlocked and Twist enters without ringing the bell.

Maria doesn't work Thursdays and he figures it's too early for her to shuttle Angel to her mother's place so she can have the morning to herself. She does that sometimes, and before everything exploded with the Italians, Twist could count on a couple of hours every Thursday morning with no locked doors and no interruptions. It was a time when they could be together for more than sex. Those were the moments they could hold each other while sorting through their lives, and those moments had meaning to him. Maybe he can use this time to make things better between them.

Make it like it used to be, and make it meaningful.

Her words still resonate and Twist knows there is enough truth in what had been said to draw blood. With everything in his world falling down around him he knows it's been impossible to be there; at least not in the way she wants. She doesn't understand that there are priorities and that guys in the Skulls depend on him the same way she does—he's got responsibilities and obligations. Maybe by telling her about Valentine, Malik, Ice, and the Italians she'll understand. Maybe once she sees for herself the private hell he's been living, she'll see there was nothing else he could do and forgive him.

Of course, excuses are easy to find, he thinks glumly. Cuba and Bone find excuses that justify everything they do. Doesn't mean they are right or justified.

Twist is convinced that truth has to count for something.

While driving over to Fairmount he worked through a variety of apologies. He goes over the words again as he goes up the stairs. He wants to tell Maria that there is too much going on in his life and that maybe he lost sight of what is important. He has to tell her that she matters to him. Those are the words she wants to hear, and the kind of thing that will make everything better. Maybe when everything is finished between the Skulls and Italians he can really make things right again. Forever.

He owes her that.

Twist moves through the hall, nodding to the thirtysomething lady coming down the stairs with a kid in tow. He hugs the wall so she can pass, shaking loose a polite smile, but she doesn't acknowledge him.

There's a feeling inside, although it's tough sorting out exactly what it is—it could be hope or desire, or maybe even anticipation, and he can't be sure. Twist takes the stairs up to Maria's apartment two and three at a time.

It won't take long for that feeling to disappear, and he wants to hold it as long as possible.

Twist knocks on the door and waits. He can hear the sound of *Good Morning America* on the TV inside the apartment, loud enough to carry to the hall but not too loud that it drowns out his sound at the door. He waits and when nothing happens, knocks again. This time his knock is louder and longer.

There are footsteps shuffling across the carpeting and Maria's voice comes out muffled, telling Angel to turn down the television. There's no surprise in that, and he doesn't think much about it.

Her voice comes closer. "Who's there?"

"It's me," Twist says.

There's nothing from the other side of the door. No movement to unlock the door and no words to answer; just the sound of the TV. In that moment Twist realizes that he badly underestimated just how pissed off she is, and how much more work it will take to make it better.

He knocks again, adding, "Hey baby, I'm sorry. Open up."

"Your phone broke or something?"

There's something in her voice. It's a hard edge like the one he heard yesterday, but this time it's more than that. It's like there's something beyond the words and attitude that are coming at Twist.

"What are you talking about?"

"You can't pick up the goddamned phone and call first?" she says.

Twist frowns. "I thought I'd come by to surprise you."

"I don't like surprises, Twist. You know that."

"I'm sorry."

"Sorry don't cut it no more," she says. "I'm not in the mood for surprises. Not from you."

"What is this?" Twist shoots back, rapping again on the door, this time using a fist. "Open the fucking door! Stop playing games!"

"It don't work that way."

"God damnit! I said I'm sorry."

From down the hall he hears the sound of a door opening and he feels different sets of eyes watching every move. There's another sound, loud and sudden, of a chain sliding into it's bolt and stretching tight against a door. Twist doesn't have to turn to know he's probably being watched by everyone on the floor but he doesn't care.

He quickly tires of the routine at the door.

"Come on, Maria," he says, his voice lower and nastier. "Open the fucking door."

"Go away, Twist."

Twist bangs on the door again. "Either you open the door for me or I'll kick it off its hinges," he says. "I don't even need the key I got in my pocket."

There are voices again but this time there's a difference. They aren't hushed or muffled, nor directed at Angel, or have anything to do with turning down the TV. Twist hears those voices and understands the edge in Maria's voice.

That icy cold feeling returns.

The bolts and chains come off the door but it takes forever to open even a crack. It's the kind of long, slow pause that can give a shooter hidden behind the door enough time to load, aim, and squeeze off a clip full of shots from a semiautomatic. The door opens with a bang and Twist steps backward, letting his hands drop to his waist. His gun is in his pants, pressed against the small of his back and his mind is already racing, calculating how quickly he can get to it if he needs it. A tall, thin guy, light-skinned with dark wet hair that's cut short on the back and sides and high on top fills the doorway in that moment. He wears a white T-shirt and the kind of heavy navy blue pants Twist sees on the mechanics and bus drivers who work at Penn Station. He's early twenties, a hoop earring in his left ear lobe, with a thin moustache across his upper lip like most of the Puerto Ricans who live on Fairmount Avenue. On his right bicep there's a heart and blood tattoo and on his left forearm a knife and gun ringed by a blue and red circle, but there's nothing in his hands.

Twist looks at him. In that second he sees a picture of this guy doing Maria on the couch, with his face buried in her shoulder while she wraps her legs around his back. The image doesn't disappear because he knows it's true.

He can't see Maria any longer because the Puerto Rican takes up the space in the doorway.

"You got a fucking problem?" the guy says, taking a small step across the hall toward Twist. "You don't hear the lady? Can't understand the words?"

"Who the fuck are you?" Twist spits back.

The man says nothing.

Twist looks over the guy's shoulder and sees Maria. She's got on a short red T-shirt that barely covers her stomach and a pair of shorts that are cut high and tight. Bare feet, with her hair long, wet, and loose as it falls to her shoulders.

"Who the fuck is this?" Twist asks her.

"A friend," she says. "Somebody from the building."

"The lady don't want you around here," the guy says. "You understand that?"

Twist turns his stare back to the guy. "What makes you think I'm talking to you?" he says. "You got nothing to say that I want to hear."

The guy edges up on his toes, moving in close and dipping his shoulders lower. Looking for something.

"Hector," Maria says from behind him, putting a hand on his shoulder. Twist's stomach turns at the sight of her hand touching his shirt. "It's okay."

Hector's voice comes out low and hard anyway. "You hear what the lady is saying?"

Twist hears the challenge in those words and sees the threat in the way Hector positions himself in the doorway. He knows where it's going and what's going to happen if it stays this way—it's like a car careening down a hill with no brakes, picking up speed and losing control the closer it gets to the bottom. Twist stands in the hallway, feeling like he's stuck behind the wheel of that car with no way to turn out of the inevitable crash.

He looks past Hector's shoulder to Maria.

"Baby."

"Don't 'baby' me," she says.

"Is that what this is all about?" he asks. "You got something with him? You doing him all the times I can't be here?"

The guy steps forward until he's almost in Twist's face and jabs a finger hard in his chest. "Think it's time maybe you get the fuck out of here," he says. "Just take off and don't come back."

"Big words."

"Yeah, but you should be able to figure them out," Hector says.

Something turns inside as Twist stares at him. He knows nothing about Hector but hates everything he sees, and he wants to take away everything the guy owns. Right now, he puts Maria among Hector's possessions. He pushes the finger away and says, "Stay out of my face."

"I'm telling you one last time to get the fuck out of here," Hector says.

Twist's voice is paced but the control that comes through barely hides the rage building inside. "And I'm telling you again, this ain't about you," he says slowly. "This is between me and her. It don't have nothing to do with you."

"I'm here."

"I don't give a fuck where you are. This ain't about you."

"I'm here. That makes it something to do with me."

Twist hooks his stare into him for a minute, then looks over his shoulder again to Maria. "Hey baby…" he tries, but that's as far as he gets.

Hector is tough and bold, and Twist is a challenge he's not afraid to face. He comes forward again jabbing his finger at Twist's chest, like he wants to drive home the point. It's his way of letting Twist know what he's got but Twist figured that out the minute he heard their voices behind the door.

It is then that he snaps.

He shoves the hand away and when Hector takes a step toward him Twist shoves him backward with both hands. Hector catches himself. He takes a swing at Twist, leading with a clumsy left hand that has nothing behind it. The way he throws that punch tells Twist everything he needs to know about Hector's fighting abilities; it starts at his waist and takes a long, slow time to travel the distance. Twist slips beneath the fist and comes up fast with his hand open, slapping Hector across the cheek.

The sting straightens Hector.

"You motherfucker," he hisses. "You motherfucking nigger."

"No! Hector!" Maria cries, grabbing for him.

By then it's too late for Hector to stop or pull back.

He puts his head down and charges Twist like a ten-year-old on the blacktop in his very first fight. Anything he ever learned about fighting stays buried beneath the emotions and rage that lurch him forward. It's so easy for Twist that he doesn't think about what to do— it's reflex and reaction. He steps inside the charge and locks his arms around Hector's shoulders, using the Puerto Rican's momentum to carry them across the hall, driving hard into the wall. With his head tucked beneath Twist's arms, Hector absorbs the crash.

He slams hard into the wall with his head and neck, and most of the fight drains out of him in that instant.

Twist spins free as Hector struggles to find his balance and right himself. Twist comes up with a knee, burying it in a soft, fleshy spot between Hector's ribs and stomach, sucking the air out of his chest and stomach. Hector lets out a low, wet groan as he rasps for breath. Twist does it once, twice, then again for a third time until Hector loses his grip on the wall and falls to his knees. His mouth is open, sucking for breath, but no sound comes out.

Somewhere in his thoughts Twist can hear Maria's voice screaming at him to stop but he's lost that kind of control.

It's beyond him to stop now.

He takes Hector by the front of his shirt and lifts him to his feet, slamming him backward into the wall. Hector's head drops forward but Twist pumps a right to his face. He feels the skin splitting against his fist with the second punch, and the blood that comes is warm and wet on his hand. On the fifth punch he shatters Hector's nose, the cartilage cracking with a sickening pop. When he smashes Hector's front teeth next the sound isn't as loud, although Twist slices open his knuckles on the jagged, broken tips. He feels Maria's hands on his arms but that doesn't stop him, and he keeps punching until Hector's face is a bloody pulp of sagging, discolored flesh and bone.

When Twist finally lets go of his shirt Hector drops to the floor.

"Baby!" Maria screams, pushing past Twist and dropping to her knees at his side. Blood smears her shirt as she pulls him close, cradling his head in her arms and shielding him from Twist. "Oh, sweet Jesus..."

Twist doesn't know how it happens, but in an instant he has his 9mm in his hand with a finger on the trigger. The gun is there before he realizes it. He levels the gun at Hector and is surprised that there's none of the fear or hesitation he would expect.

There is no remorse and it comes to him how easy it would be to pull the trigger.

Hector can open only one eye to stare at Twist. The other is blue and already swelling shut. "Don't," he says. "Please. Don't do it."

Twist feels his breath hard and heavy as he stands there, inching his finger toward the safety. He's aware of the eyes everywhere around him, watching and waiting to see what he does next. But this time Twist doesn't feel the respect or fear in those stares; there's something different now in the eyes watching him. Twist turns slowly, looking from one side of the hall to the other.

It's when he turns back toward the apartment that he sees Angel in the doorway, Hobo hiding behind her ankles, clutching the battered purple dinosaur he bought her one Sunday when the three of them took a drive to the beach in Seaside Heights. There's a memory of the amusement park and the rides on the boardwalk, splashing in the ocean, and running on the beach, then a long drive home with her asleep in the back seat while he and Maria held hands in the front; those smiles last and stay with him.

She watches him now with the same kind of expression she uses for the cartoons on TV.

Twist lowers the gun.

He takes a step backward, and then another that puts distance between them.

"Get the fuck out of here!" Maria screams from her knees. "Get the fuck out of my life!"

Twist doesn't look back until he hits the bottom step.

♦ ♦ ♦

Twist sits in the Pathfinder staring at Maria's building. He shakes and shivers from the coldness sweeping through him. There's nothing different about the building; from the outside there are no signs of what just happened inside or how it has all just has crashed and burned. Nothing about his world remains. The gun is still in his hand; it feels like such an important part of him that Twist doesn't even know it's there.

CHAPTER TEN

Twist is in the car but he's lost track of time.

It could be five minutes or an hour; time is nothing that he can be sure about.

He's doing the twenty-five mile per hour speed limit on Martin Luther King Boulevard, squinting through the sun glare from behind cheap sunglasses and trying to pull himself back into the morning. The cup of coffee from the diner is still in the console, unopened and probably cold now. The cellular is on the passenger seat, beeping with voice mail messages and missed calls. Twist takes a drag off a Camel then lets the butt sit smoldering—untouched so long that it burns out in the ashtray. There's a Jimi Hendrix song on the radio but nothing about it sticks. It would be different if Eddie was in the car; Hendrix is serious business to him. Almost everyone has something they believe in passionately and with Eddie Dallas all it takes is criticism of Hendrix to provoke his rage. There is no room for joking about Hendrix, and sometimes Twist can ride that throughout the entire day if he wants to bust him.

But none of that matters now.

It's hard keeping anything straight. The only thing Twist can hold on to is that last image of Hector, bloody and beaten on the floor, and the voice inside tells him he should have put a bullet in the spic's head when the chance was there. It's a voice that sounds surprisingly like Cuba's. It would have been easy to tie up loose ends that way. Easy chances and golden opportunities don't come his way too often, the voice screams.

It's the same chance he had to do Bone.

He tells himself now that he's got to learn how to do what it takes when those moments come and worry about consequences later.

Twist is still stuck on that thought when the cell rings again, and he thinks that maybe he should have turned it off. Instead he reaches for the phone, clinging to the faint hope that it might be Maria calling to apologize. He can almost hear her saying how sorry she is—that Hector means nothing and that everything that happened was a mistake and a misunderstanding that she wants to go away.

Twist spits out a glob of phlegm that just clears the window and shakes his head. He knows the only real misunderstanding would be thinking that something like that could ever happen.

He looks at the number. It's a safe number so Twist answers the call.

The voice he hears is thick and raspy from cigarettes and Jack Daniel's.

"Where the fuck you at?" Cuba snaps. "Why the fuck don't you answer?"

Twist slows to a stop at a traffic light and squeezes his eyes shut. There's no way he wants any part of this conversation, and no way he's prepared to handle it the way it should be handled.

"Been around," he says. "Why do you want to know?"

"You don't answer your fucking phone? Been calling you since six."

"Don't answer it if I don't want to talk to nobody," he says evenly. "Or if I've got nothing to say. Or I'm doing something."

"I been leaving messages all morning."

Twist opens his eyes long enough to see that traffic isn't moving yet. "Haven't listened to them."

"You can't even pick up the phone to check in?" Cuba says. "You know what the fuck we got here! Don't it make sense that you should call in to see what's going on?"

Twist takes a breath and holds it. "What's up?"

There's a brief silence when all he hears is Cuba's heavy breathing on the other end of the phone, and Twist adds, "Me and Eddie are meeting with the guy from the Viper in a little while," he says. "Didn't figure I had to check in with you. Figured you'd remember."

"I been trying to call you all goddamned morning and nobody knows where the fuck to find you," Cuba says. "Ain't a guy around here who got the number of your bitch. Takes hours to track you down because you're too busy sticking it around the neighborhood to let anybody know where you are."

"Where I've been has nothing to do with you."

"It's got everything to do with me and everybody else if I need you and I can't find you!" Cuba yells.

"Didn't know I had to answer to you," Twist says in a slow, paced voice.

Cuba's voice is loud but Twist ignores it. He turns up the radio and loses most of Cuba's words in the last guitar chords of the Hendrix song, weighing out his options again. Right now the option that looks best is the one where he tells Cuba to go fuck himself and hangs up before the conversation gets any further and he has to listen to more bullshit about accounting for himself and his actions. He could do that and not have any second thoughts. There's still time to get on the Turnpike and steer the Pathfinder toward North Carolina.

Only this time he'd have to do it alone.

There's something on the other end of the line, like it's being taken away from Cuba and put in someone else's hands. Cuba's tirade ends in quick silence and Bone's voice comes through in Twist's ear.

"The last thing we got time for is the two of you arguing like a couple of bitches," he says. "You in your car?"

The light turns green and Twist pulls slowly into traffic. He mutters a "Yes," to Bone.

"Then drive your ass over here and don't stop for nothing," Bone says.

"Why?" Twist asks.

Bone's voice is tense and strained. "You got a question for everything you get asked to do? Know it ain't safe to talk on no cell. Good number or not."

Twist closes his eyes again. "Is it about Malik?"

"It's the Guineas," Bone says. "They ready to talk. Want to meet."

◆ ◆ ◆

The cell rings again five minutes later.

The morning traffic is slow on MLK Boulevard where it turns into Broad downtown. Twist has driven only a few blocks since hanging up, although he's not paying attention to details like that. The meeting changes the equation and affects what's going on with Valentine too, but Twist can't figure out how much worse this will make things and what it means to Valentine's fate. Most times he doesn't know all the answers but he's dead sure about this—nothing about this meeting makes sense if Ice and Malik are still alive. If they're dead, nothing about this meeting can do any good.

Twist picks up the cell on the second ring without looking at the number.

Cuba's voice is back. "Been a change in plans."

"What now?"

The words are sharp and hang there. Words with Cuba don't disappear. They settle and last.

"You got something going on with this attitude of yours that's getting inside my head and bugging the piss out of me," Cuba mutters, low and hard. "I'm telling you this now, so maybe you can do something about it before we get into it later."

There's a moment of heavy silence when Twist doesn't say anything else. The two of them share short, hard breaths and silence on the phone. He turns onto a side street without bothering to use a directional, jabbing a middle finger at the car horns and voices yelling at him. He checks the rear view mirror to make sure there's still nobody back there, no flashing cop lights, and waits out Cuba.

"Don't bother coming back here," Cuba finally says. "Ain't no reason. It's more important for you and Eddie to get with our guy like we planned."

"If that's what you and Bone want."

"Ain't what we want," Cuba corrects sharply. "It's what got to be done."

Twist doesn't say anything. He just steers the car back onto the street, rechecking the mirrors.

"Make sure what he's got is worth the cash we're laying out," Cuba says. "With all the shit going down we need everything he's got if it's good."

Twist's voice changes. "Maybe you want to do this instead of me," he says. "If it comes down to you and Bone not having enough trust in me, just say the word. You can get in your car and do it yourself."

"I don't have time," Cuba says. The way he says it makes it sound like an idea he's already considered but decided against. "I can't do everything myself."

Twist looks out the window at the rows of homes lining the street. Two small boys, no shirts and wearing only shorts and Nikes, are turning a wrench on one of the corner fire hydrants while another kid waits for the spray to start.

"Just get it done," Cuba says. "I already got one of my kids with Eddie, just in case you need more muscle."

Twist keeps his eyes on the street. The only reason Cuba has one of his kids with Eddie is to be a spy, but he doesn't say that. There are already too many words between them.

"I know what we need," Twist says. "I'll take care of it."

◆ ◆ ◆

Eddie Dallas is sitting on the porch in an old wicker chair when Twist pulls up to his house. It is a small two family with white vinyl siding, black trim around the windows, and a small plot of grass in the front that Eddie waters and mows at least twice a week. The grass turns green only a few days each summer and there are usually more weeds than grass, but Eddie tends to it religiously as if landscaping matters. His mother and two sisters live upstairs, sharing two bedrooms and a bathroom while Eddie keeps the downstairs bedroom for himself.

"It's safer that way," he once explained to Twist. "I don't got to bother them with my business and we stay out of each other's way."

Eddie's mother is a nurse at Beth Israel and his sisters split their time between part-time jobs downtown and classes at Rutgers night school. It's been a few years since Eddie bought the house in the Ironbound section but they are still the only black family in a neighborhood of blue collar, working class Portuguese families. Nobody has accepted them yet. Eddie knows about the eyes following him wherever he goes, watching everything he does. There are always police cruisers passing his house a little too slowly, and spot lights lingering on the house longer than they stick on other houses on the street. But Twist has never known Eddie to complain. If anything about it bothers him he doesn't let on.

Twist thinks he cares more about what it means to his mother and sisters to have a nice house in a decent neighborhood than the other ways it costs him.

There's a second floor porch that opens into one of the bedrooms upstairs and as Twist slowly climbs out of the Pathfinder he catches a glimpse of Eddie's younger sister. She's tall with long hair and sharp pretty features, and there's a trace of a pink blouse and a smile before she disappears inside. Their world is one that Eddie keeps separate from the one he shares with the Skulls; off limits to any of them.

Eddie is wearing a pair of Ray-Bans and drinking a bottle of Snapple as Twist gets out of the car. His feet are propped up on the porch railing and his Nikes move back and forth to the song on his IPod.

There is another figure on the porch. Cuba's kid stands uncomfortably with his hands in his pockets, staring down at his feet. He leans backward against the wall and eyes Twist as cautiously as he watches the street around him. Twist recognizes him from the Viper Club; another tough Game Boy ready to do whatever Cuba wants him to.

The kid might be thinking it's the best thing that could happen to him but he has no idea what he's in for with Cuba or where it will lead. Cuba rewards the people he takes under his wing, but when they screw up or he's finished with them they disappear just as fast. The kid has a lot to learn about the way things work.

Eddie comes off the porch to meet Twist. His expression is grim and humorless. He holds a pack of Marlboros in one hand and shakes out a smoke as he walks.

"Whassup?" he says.

Twist sucks one last pull off his own cigarette and flicks the butt to the street. "Not much," he says slowly. "Guess you know about the meeting, huh?"

Eddie nods. "Got Cuba's call first thing this morning. I'm in dreamland with JLo and a killer hard-on when he calls. Twenty minutes later I got this young'un at the door and he's been stuck up my ass ever since," he says, jerking a thumb toward the kid watching from the porch. The kid meets Twist's stare and waves a hand slowly. "Figure Cuba's giving him a little piece of the action as a reward to see what he can do."

Twist lights another Camel.

"Think they ready to trade?" Eddie asks.

Twist shrugs.

"It's what we've been waiting for, right?" Eddie says, brushing the braids out of his face. "Whole point of snatching the guy off the street was to get a face-to-face. Find out about Malik."

"Think I was wrong," Twist says quietly. "About negotiations getting us what we want."

Eddie stares at him but Twist can't see what's behind the sunglasses. He takes a drag on the cigarette and kicks at a stone on the sidewalk.

"Whassup with you?" Eddie asks, dropping his Ray-Bans. "You don't look so good."

Twist doesn't answer.

"Probably just getting on like everybody else," Eddie says. "No sleep, too much to drink, and no time for nothing else. The Italians, Ice, and Malik. You probably running on empty, man."

"Need a little rest to help you think clearly," he adds.

"Probably right," Twist says.

Eddie's stare stays with Twist, waiting for more but he doesn't answer. Finally Eddie steps around him and starts for the street and Twist follows a few steps behind. They cross the asphalt and go down two houses to a Dodge Caravan parked in front of a fire hydrant. It's brand new with a temporary license taped inside the back window, and when Twist slides open the door it still has that new car smell.

"Got it last night," Eddie says with a smile. "Took it out of a hotel parking lot up near Madison after I left the Viper Club."

"What the hell you doing up there?"

Eddie shrugs. "I figured we needed clean wheels today and there was too much risk letting one of the guys get it around here," he says. "Cost me train fare to get there but it was the easiest setup I ever seen. It's one in the morning when I hop off the train, walk twenty yards and I'm in the middle of the hotel parking lot.

"No valet parking and no security guards," he adds. "And a back entrance that's open all night with no gate. The van was screaming to be taken."

Twist nods, lowering his own shades to eye the van.

"I figure some old man is doing dinner and having a big night out on his old lady," Eddie says, grinning. "Guy's probably had a hard-on poking through his pants all week, just thinking about a night away from the kids. Sucker probably doesn't even know the van's gone. It's like I hear this van calling from the train, drawing me in like radar."

"Ain't no better than that," Twist agrees half-heartedly, looking around the inside of the van.

The van is clean and carpeted, with two bucket seats in front, a center console between them, and a small sun roof that Eddie has popped open to bring in air. The two bench seats in the back are gone so there is plenty of room to carry the guns and ammo from Cooper. And the temporary tag in the window cuts down the odds of getting stopped by cops.

"And get this," Eddie adds, looking in from the other side. "I didn't even have to wire it."

Twist stares at him and Eddie tosses him a set of keys.

"Had one of those magnetic key cases stuck underneath the dashboard," he says. "Figure they just asking for it to be lifted."

"Good for parts when we're done with it," Twist says.

"Already got it set up at the chop shop."

Twist goes back to the Pathfinder and pulls it into the driveway, angling as close to the house as possible so he doesn't block Eddie's mother's car. He takes his cell and sticks the 9mm beneath his shirt before moving back to the van. When he turns back to the house he catches another glimpse of the pink blouse on the second floor.

Eddie starts for the driver's door. He stops and looks back to the house where the kid is still on the porch, hands in his pockets, watching everything without moving.

"You gonna stand there all morning?" Eddie yells.

The kid comes off the porch like a shot. He goes in the side and slides the door shut, finding a comfortable spot near the back door.

"You want to be here, you got to keep up," Eddie says, getting behind the wheel. "We don't have time to be waiting for you. Nobody here to wipe your nose."

"Don't worry about me," the kid says, cocky and tough as he shows them his twenty-two. "I can take care of myself."

Twist turns, fixing his stare on the kid. "You want to make this easy," he says, "The best thing you can do is not say a fucking word. Don't open your mouth. Just pay attention and be quiet. Pretend you're Helen Keller."

"Who that?"

"Don't push it," Twist says.

The kid opens his mouth but something in Twist's expression shuts him up quickly.

"It's cool," he says softly.

Eddie steers away from the curb. Twist watches the street while the kid sits on the floor in back, quietly hugging his knees. Eddie pops a CD into the dashboard stereo and Twist grimaces when a Jimi Hendrix song blares out of the speakers.

"You know where we're going?" Twist asks.

Eddie nods. "Small rest stop off the Parkway, past the Driscoll Bridge" he says. "Supposed to meet Cooper there first, then he's gonna take us to the guns. He's got a place in Perth Amboy, near the water. In some old printing factory."

"You know anything about what he's got?"

Eddie shakes his head. "Don't know more than that. Rest is all to be discovered."

They are on the Parkway going toward the Shore. Eddie Dallas is in the driver's seat, focusing on the cars ahead while keeping the van's speed constant at fifty miles per hour. Twist rests his head back against the seat and stares at the road, but all he can see is Michael Valentine staring back at him from the end of the 9mm.

"What do you think about this thing with the Italians?" Twist asks. "About meeting them?"

"Got a bad feeling about it," Eddie says. "A bad feeling that don't go away."

"Having a bad feeling about a lot of things."

"Me too," Eddie says.

"But this is different," Twist adds.

Eddie looks at Twist, waiting.

"I think it means Ice and Malik are dead," Twist says in a quiet voice.

"Think so?"

Twist nods without speaking. He lights a Camel and takes a deep drag, letting the smoke fill his lungs and throat. "Ice is dead," he says. "No way they keep him alive after hacking off a finger and yanking out a tooth. Just a question of how badly they fucked with him. And if the body turns up."

"What about Malik?"

Twist looks away and stares at the trees along the side of the road. "Figure he's dead too," he finally says in the same quiet voice. "Only with him it ain't a question of 'if' the body turns up, but where. The

Italians got to make a statement. Same way we do. Figure they'll make it with him."

Eddie keeps his eyes on the road.

"So why we meeting if it's not to talk about exchanging that guy for Malik?"

Twist takes a deep breath.

"It's about letting us know they still call the shots," he says. "Forcing us into something we don't want to do."

"Surprised Cuba and Bone don't know that," Eddie says.

"I think Cuba and Bone already got that figured out," Twist says. "Think they want that confrontation."

Eddie doesn't say anything and stares straight ahead.

They go over the Driscoll Bridge through the Raritan tolls, veering left into the Parkway rest stop. Traffic is heavy in the northbound lanes but only spotty heading south and they move easily between lanes. Twist sits up straighter and his stare narrows. Eddie slows the van as they come off the ramp, passing the commuter parking lot entrance on the left. It is not large, holding only a few hundred cars, and a patrol car cop could survey the entire lot in seconds to figure out who belongs and who doesn't, but it doesn't look like the kind of place police patrol regularly. There are no guards and no gates to get in or out. Eddie takes it in so he can remember the details again. About two hundred yards past the rest stop is a Lukoil gas station and long lines of cars in both directions wait at ten service bays. Eddie steers around the pumps and follows signs for the rest stop parking lot.

There is a string of cars angled into parking slots in front of a small brick and aluminum-sided cottage housing bathrooms, Dunkin" Donuts, a Bob's Big Boy fast food sit-down, and a Nathan's. Cooper's bodyguard leans against the trunk of a new Lexus, dressed neatly in a pair of gray slacks and a black T-shirt that is tight against his chest and arms. Sunglasses wrap around his face. There's a PBA card pasted to the inside of the back window and a Fraternal Order of Police decal on the bumper. He smokes a cigarette and carefully eyes each approaching vehicle.

Eddie pulls the van into the first empty parking spot near the Lexus and kills the engine.

"Don't like doing this here," Twist says in a quiet voice. "Probably nothing to it, but it don't feel right."

"I don't like nothing about anything no more," Eddie answers, looking past Twist at the guy.

The bodyguard notices the van and fixes his stare on it, waiting for the first move.

Twist turns to the Game Boy in the back and says, "You stay here."

The kid has already started for the door and Twist's words drop him back to one knee. He wears a surprised expression. "Didn't think I was here to sit in the van," he says. "I thought I was here for action."

Eddie glares at him in the mirror. "Nobody asked what you thought you were here for," he says. "You do what you're told."

"Cover us," Twist says.

The kid doesn't answer as Eddie and Twist get out of the van.

The bodyguard turns slowly. Everything about his movement is paced and controlled, like he's so sure about himself that he doesn't have to work to impress anybody. There is a sense of power in the way he carries himself, and it is something Twist knows none of the Skulls will ever have, no matter how hard they try. What they have and what they show on the street comes from being able to take away things other people own.

What Cooper's bodyguard has is something he has earned.

There are no hand shakes or hellos—the bodyguard looks right through them. Twist returns the stare, waiting him out.

"You didn't come alone, did you?" the guy says finally.

Eddie shakes his head. "Got a kid in the van," he says. "Brought him along to help load the product."

"I'm not wearing a wire. And I ain't no cop. You don't have to speak in code with me," the guy says coolly. "Call it guns. Ammo. That's what it is."

"Got a kid in the van," Eddie replies sharply. "Brought him along to help load the guns and ammo."

"Where's Cooper?" Twist asks.

"Ain't here."

"Can see that. Where is he?"

"I'll take you to him," the guy says, moving his glare from Twist to Eddie, then back to Twist again. Nothing in its intensity changes. After a moment he says, "Follow me. Try to keep up without riding up my ass and attracting attention."

"Try my best," Eddie mutters. "Hope it ain't beyond my abilities."

When they're back in the van he looks to Twist and says, "Real charming guy, huh?"

They drive back across the Parkway to Route 9, then take a small two lane bridge north across the river into Perth Amboy. There are oil storage tanks along the bank of the river and a scattering of old warehouses and factories that look abandoned with broken windows and doors boarded shut, and FOR SALE or FOR LEASE signs hammered into the brick. None of it looks familiar but it could be a city just like Newark. There's nothing that different about it.

They follow the Lexus, snaking between buildings and skirting the river's edge, and it looks like just another street until Twist sees the concrete barrier at the end. The street is much like the others in the neighborhood. There are signs of life in the cars parked along the sides of the road and faces poke from doorways and through windows, but nobody gives them a second look. The Lexus slows and turns into a small alley, coasting carefully between two low brick buildings. Eddie follows, steering cautiously—Twist thinks that they probably couldn't even open the doors to get out; until the alley opens into a small brick courtyard. A rusted metal gate is pushed to the side, held open by a rotted two-by-four brace. There are weeds shooting up between cracks in the bricks and the doors facing out to the courtyard are padlocked shut. The windows in the buildings are broken or black with dirt—it's been a long time since any delivery trucks pulled up to the loading dock doors. The sign reads REO PRINTS but the paint is sun-bleached and the words have faded with time.

Cooper is waiting on the loading dock, dressed casually in tan chinos and a long sleeved white button down that is rolled up to his elbows. He wears a pair of mirrored sunglasses like cops wear and sips from a cup of Dunkin' Donuts, and as the car and van pull closer he waves.

Eddie parks behind the Lexus and turns off the engine. He and Twist eye the area, wary and cautious, looking into the shadows and recesses of the buildings. The space is too confined for Twist's liking—there's no room to move or maneuver. It is the perfect location for an ambush.

Trust is fleeting, and Twist knows everything has a price. There's history with Cooper but nothing solid enough that he's willing to let his guard down. The black bodyguard gets out of the Lexus and with a look toward the van, moves to Cooper.

Twist sits the Game Boy back down with his stare. "Don't go nowhere," he says. "We'll go out and see what the deal is. You watch the street. Stay by your cell and cover us."

The kid returns a stare.

"You feel me?" Twist asks.

"It's cool," the kid says, flashing his twenty-two again.

"Don't be no hero," Eddie says as he gets out of the van. "Don't have Cuba here watching your ass if you wave that gun at these guys."

The kid stares and doesn't say anything.

Cooper slides off the loading dock, taking one last sip from the cup before pouring the rest to the ground. It splashes and puddles on the asphalt and he drops the empty cup into the puddle without a backward look as he steps over it. He flashes a grin and says, "Should have had Arthur tell you to back the van in. Would have been easier to load."

"No problem doing it this way," Eddie says as they move forward. Eddie carries the Nike gym bag loaded with fifties and hundreds close to his body, guarded and cool. Twist is aware of his own 9mm pressed against his back.

"Brought company, huh?" Cooper says, nodding toward the van and the Game Boy's face behind the wheel.

"Just a kid to help load the guns," Twist says coolly. "How about you? Got anybody hidden in the shadows we need to worry about?"

Cooper laughs and shakes his head. He doesn't answer and that response bothers Twist. Cooper starts for the side of the building, motioning for Twist and Eddie to follow. Arthur trails a few steps behind Eddie.

They go around the corner, past an old green dumpster that is empty but still smells of rotted garbage, and Twist fights the urge to peer inside to make sure there are no familiar corpses in it. Cooper swings open an old door and steps inside. Twist and Eddie exchange uneven looks before following into the building.

It is hot and stuffy inside, and even though the building has been abandoned the thick smell of paint and chemicals remains the same way the smell of oil and grease hangs in the Murray Street garage—like time hasn't washed the life out of the building. They follow Cooper down a long, narrow corridor pockmarked with cracks and holes, up three metal steps, and into the huge open space that had once been the factory. The floor has a dirty, oily feeling underfoot, and the only light cutting the darkness comes through broken windows. There are bits and pieces of cinder block and rocks scattered among the glass shards on the floor—probably thrown through the windows by neighborhood kids with too much time on their hands, and except for five large crates in the center of the floor, the space is empty. Their footsteps echo as they walk.

It takes a moment to make out shapes in the darkness, but there are two other figures in the room. One is a kid, maybe twenty, but no older. Bony and thin, with shoulder length blond hair and acne scars that stand out in the bad light.

The other is a guy who moves in and out of the light across the room. Twist can't make out anything about him except the outline of the rifle cradled in his arm.

Twist feels a tightness in his chest and a lump in his throat. He and Eddie exchange brief glances and slow a step.

Cooper goes to the crates.

He nods and the blond kid pries the top off one of the boxes.

"Steyr AUGs," he says. "Sweet, huh?"

"Got this together as quick as I could," Cooper says, kneeling down and reaching inside the box. "A little more time, I might have got you better variety."

"Got a kind of sense of urgency to the situation," Twist says.

"Figured that," Cooper says.

Twist and Eddie move closer. Inside the box rows of rifles are laid out neatly side by side. Towels are rolled up and bunched between them, along with rags covering the guns. At the end of the crate magazines and ammo clips are stacked in neat piles.

Cooper takes out a long black and steel rifle, smacks a magazine into the gaping space at the bottom and holds it out for both of them to see. He hands it to Twist saying, "Check this out. Tell me what you think."

The gun is lighter than the AR-15s the Skulls use. Twist takes the rifle in his hands, bracing it against his shoulder and checking the sight lines in its scope. "Good piece," Cooper says as Twist raises it toward the far wall and imagines a target, swinging it along the sight lines to get a feel for the gun. "You got a forty-round magazine behind the trigger guard. There's not much of a kick to it and you can squeeze off the clip in a couple of seconds."

Twist hands it to Eddie Dallas. "Feel this."

Eddie balances it in his arm. "Nice heat," he says. "Got power?"

Cooper nods and points toward a dirty wall across the room. It's about fifty feet away, with a stack of plywood sheets leaning against old mattresses. "Give it a rip," he says.

Eddie lets a slight grin break his face. He takes a moment to get a feel for the rifle, then squeezes the trigger. The Steyr jerks up slightly, making a rapid pop-pop-pop when it fires. Hot shells fly out of the magazine and scatter on the floor, rolling beneath Twist's Nikes. He can see from Eddie's expression how much he likes the way it feels.

Cooper lays out another gun from the crate, and the blond kid follows his lead, pulling two smaller pistols and another rifle from the other crates. "I gave you those Steyrs and some Galils like I promised," Cooper says. "Mixed in a couple of Street Sweepers too."

Twist stares at the South African 12-gauge shotguns. Cooper explains that decades earlier white cops in South Africa used them to crush ghetto rebellions and demonstrations before the country's politics changed, and that they have been banned in America for at least fifteen years. The gun holds twelve rounds in a fully rotating chamber, and Cooper tells him that he can empty the chambers completely in no more than three seconds.

"Used for riot control," he says. "Takes longer to reload than empty the clip."

Eddie hands the Steyr to the blond kid and picks up the Street Sweeper.

The noise inside the warehouse is deafening, and when Eddie finally stops squeezing the trigger the sound echoes for a long time until fading. Across the room the plywood is splintered into pieces, and huge chunks of wood are blown out in spots from the Street Sweeper.

"Only thing I couldn't get were the grenades your friend wanted for the Steyr AUGs," Cooper says. "Have to give you a rain check on that."

"Probably just as well," Twist says.

Eddie holds a forty-four Magnum. He examines it carefully, moving it from hand to hand, feeling its weight as he squeezes the grip between his palm and fingers. It's heavier then the 9mms and

.22s they carry, and has a much harder kick when fired. It will take a strong, steady stance to keep the recoil from knocking the shooter down. But the range is good and the Magnum has the kind of stopping power that can bring down anyone, no matter what they're carrying or how fast they are moving.

"I might want this for myself," he says, looking at Twist.

"What do you think?" Cooper asks.

"It's all good," Twist says. He takes the Nike bag off the floor and rips open the zipper, putting it down in front of Cooper. Cooper kicks it open with the tip of his shoe and looks at the green inside.

"I'm sure I don't have to count it," he says with a smile. "Trust, right?"

Twist nods.

"You're involved in some serious shit," Cooper says, bending down to zip the bag shut. It's an observation more than it's a comment. "Guess shotguns and .22s aren't enough, huh?"

"Got beyond that a long time ago," Twist says.

He watches Eddie striding across the room, kicking past the shells on the floor to examine the bullet holes strafed into the plywood and mattress foam. The blond haired kid follows closely behind, still silent as he stays in step and matches Eddie's stride.

"My old man used to be a cop," Cooper says, watching Eddie the same way Twist does. "Some nights when I was a kid we'd be sitting in the backyard, just staring at the sky and he'd tell me all kinds of stories about what it was like being a cop. How it felt and how it was a good thing. He never had to pull his gun, and he never had somebody pull one on him. By the time I joined that changed. I had .38s and .22s pulled on me more times than I can remember. When I was a rookie a guy tried taking me out with a sawed-off shotgun one night when I pulled him over for speeding."

"It's a whole different world now," Twist says. "Everybody's looking for confrontation."

"Guess resolution comes with a price, huh?"

"Things change," Twist says. "We're just doing what it takes to survive and protect what's ours."

Cooper nods. "Who isn't?"

◆ ◆ ◆

Cuba and Bone look pleased.

"Money well spent," Cuba says. "Love this."

He has one of the Street Sweepers in his hands and from the way he strokes it, it's easy imagining him emptying the magazine into a crowd on a Belleville street with that same grin stretched across his face. The guns spark a brief attitude change as Game Boys jam inside the garage, tearing at the boxes to get their hands on the rifles and hand guns. They're aware of what the firepower means and it's given them hope, letting them think they have an edge that wasn't available before.

Twist is the only one who isn't sold on that concept.

These are the kind of weapons you don't just pick up and shoot. It takes time and practice to control them accurately—comfort goes a long way toward creating an advantage.

But there is no way that will happen. Cuba takes on every challenge headfirst, like a fullback going through a linebacker for a touchdown. Strategy and tactics aren't important; he doesn't care what it takes to win or how bloody it gets.

And this feels like it's heading that same way.

The garage is filled with guys on chairs and others stretched out on the floor, stuffing bullets in clips and jamming shells inside shotgun barrels. Cigarettes burn in ashtrays while fingers work on ammo clips, and the downstairs is thick and hazy with smoke. Rocco has one of the ARs in pieces on the coffee table, slowly snapping each section in place as he snorts scoops of white powder from a plastic teaspoon. He talks a steady stream of bullshit while he works; the way guys who don't know any better talk.

Like this is the kind of game where winning a battle means talking and bragging as well as you shoot.

Twist knows the Italians don't play that way.

He bumps fists with Dizzy and settles into the empty chair alongside T. Capone. He's taken his time returning to the kitchen, walking among the crew, watching them load and listening to their chatter. Twist pulls closer to the table and looks around, gauging expressions and seeing what has changed with them. The arrival of the guns created a brief spark of talk and excitement but the novelty quickly wears off. Each is absorbed in the new weapons, getting comfortable with the way they feel, practicing the movements necessary to slap magazines and ammo clips in and out of breaches. Everyone concentrates. Nobody speaks.

Bone doesn't look up from the Magnum in his hand. "Time we start talking about this meeting," he says to Twist.

Twist looks at him. "What time we supposed to meet?"

"Three."

Twist looks at the clock on the kitchen wall then shakes his head. "That doesn't give us a lot of time," he says.

Cuba glares from across the table. "Tell us something we don't already know."

"We need more time."

"Ain't gonna get it. The Guineas said to be on time," Dizzy says.

Twist sits back in the chair. He lets his head drop backward and closes his eyes.

When he finally opens his eyes again, he asks. "How could you agree to three o'clock? We need to plan."

The stare Cuba shoots him is hard and feels familiar. "Had more time this morning when they called and three o'clock wasn't staring us in the face," he says. "Didn't think you'd be so hard to find. Didn't think you'd be off whoring around instead of being a part of that conversation."

Twist avoids Cuba's stare and finds Bone instead. "Any ideas?"

"You the one who's got that job," Bone says, looking down again at the Magnum. "That's what we waiting for. You tell us."

"Where's this supposed to happen?" Twist asks.

Bone doesn't even look up. "Harrison. The old Spanish restaurant across from the PATH station," he says. "The place been closed for years. Ain't nobody never there. You know it, right?"

Twist frowns, nodding his head slowly.

"Got a big parking lot and plenty of empty space."

Twist shakes his head.

"Got a problem with it?" Cuba says, glaring across the table.

"I don't like it," Twist says.

Cuba cuts him with a stare. "I chose that place myself."

"So maybe you chose wrong," Twist shoots back.

The attitude in his voice freezes the talk but Twist blows through the silence. He's past the point of caring how anything looks or sounds to anyone else. He turns his stare back on Cuba and leaves it there. "Too many places to stick shooters around that parking lot," he says. "We'll be out in the open."

"Got guys there now," Cuba replies. "Watching."

"Just because we got guys there don't mean anything," Twist says. "Can't make ourselves invisible if the cops roll by."

He wonders how much anyone thought this through. What if it's a setup? What if the police show up? What if Malik is really dead, and none of this matters any more?

Twist takes a deep breath and holds it.

"We need to rethink this," he tries. "Find someplace where we got a close, confined space. No surprises."

"Too late for you to be second guessing," Cuba says. "What's done is done. Only surprise is why you ain't stepping up. Especially now. Especially because of Malik."

Twist slams his fist down on the table, bouncing bottles and sending bullets rolling in different directions. The suddenness is like an explosion that cracks through the room. Heads jerk and turn, bodies kick away from the table, and even Bone raises his head to stare at him. "Fuck you!"

Everyone stares at him but nobody moves.

Finally Bone says, "You need to chill. This is about Ice and Malik," he says. "We hear what they got to say and what they want to offer."

Dizzy nods. "Just doing the right thing."

"Too late for that," Twist mutters, staring into his hands. He's sure they can all see that too, but nobody don't want to say anything about it or has the balls to challenge Bone and Cuba. "I don't like it," he says again. "It's not safe."

"That's why we got you," Bone says.

"You in charge of planning. It's on you," Cuba comes back across the table. "You make sure nothing bad goes down.

"You the man who's responsible."

◆ ◆ ◆

Twist goes up the stairs slowly.

Time is running out and he feels it with every second. He can hear Cuba bitching downstairs, yelling that there are more important things to do than waste time on the third floor. He hears him going on about how Twist should be scouting the location and doing what it takes to make sure everything goes right. How he's wasting his time with Valentine. Talking to a dead man nobody cares about.

But Twist has unfinished business in that bedroom.

A kid named Boo is at the bedroom door, using the same stare on Twist that Cuba has perfected and passed on to his kids. It's cold and steely; one that says everybody he comes across is a threat to be measured first. They exchange looks but no words pass between them. By now the guys doing guard duty know to open the door without question, and Boo does it without prodding. He stands behind Twist, watching a few seconds longer than he should, before finally closing the door. It's like he's trying to figure out what's there, the same way Cuba tries every time Twist goes up the stairs.

None of them are able to put it together, no matter how much they try.

The room is still dark and stuffy, and there is the start of a stale, heavy odor that fills Twist's head when he steps inside. Michael Valentine is on the bed. The radio is turned down low but Twist can hear music from the classic rock radio station. Valentine's face is drained, tired, and streaked with sweat, and his eyes are swollen and puffy.

Twist nods a hello and tosses the newspapers at Valentine's feet. The copy of the *Sporting News* is mixed in among the papers and Twist pokes it to the top so Valentine can see it.

"Thought you'd want that," he says.

Valentine accepts it with what passes for a smile.

"How's it going?"

Valentine shrugs. "Hours just run together. It's hard going on like this, you know?" he says, turning his head and losing some of the words in his shoulder. "The radio and the papers help. Starting to wish the time would pass a little faster."

Twist wonders why he would want that. If his own time was limited, he'd want it to drag on forever. He would hang on to every second before it got taken away.

"You get breakfast okay?"

"Coffee and toast. Some eggs too. Wasn't McDonald's," Valentine says, opening his smile a little more. He sees Twist standing instead of sitting and asks, "You're not staying?"

"Can't," he says. "Got a meeting."

Valentine's smile quickly fades. "Who you meeting?"

Twist shrugs. "Can't say for sure. Probably the usual crew. I don't think they're going to change the welcoming committee at this point, do you?"

"You thinking something's going to happen if you meet with them?"

Twist shakes his head. "We're dancing. Guys are jabbing and throwing punches, but nothing's going on that'll do any damage. Just feeling out positions.

"Just talk. No action," he adds. "More negotiating."

Michael Valentine looks at him. There's something there; Twist can see that in his eyes and expression but it doesn't come out right away. Valentine wrestles with the words but can't find the ones he wants and there's nothing else between them except the song on the radio. They face each other, staring in strained silence, and then Twist hears Cuba's voice from the downstairs again. It's louder this time, still bitching about time and Twist and all the other things that aren't getting done.

Twist starts to the door with a sigh.

"Twist."

Valentine's voice is quiet but it turns him.

He looks at Twist and says, "You know guys like Giaccolone don't negotiate, right?"

Twist nods. He understands.

CHAPTER ELEVEN

"I don't like this," Twist says.

"Nothing to like," Eddie Dallas agrees quietly. "Not a fucking thing."

Twist rubs his eyes and shakes his head slowly. There are horns and shouts around them as cars inch past the double parked Pathfinder but he ignores the noise and stares straight ahead. "We do this here," he says, "and we're dead."

"A good chance somebody gets killed, no matter where we do it."

"Anyplace else it's only a chance," Twist says. "The odds change here."

Eddie slowly nods his agreement. "Got that right."

The restaurant is a yellow stucco building with a red roof that's missing tiles in spots and has plywood boards covering the windows and doors. A chain stretches across the parking lot entrance but it sags in the middle and dips close to the ground. The asphalt is cracked and split and weeds pop up in those spots. Broken glass and trash litters the sidewalk by the entrance and one of the plywood boards has been pried off a window where somebody tried getting inside. The Route 280 overpass loops around train tracks and trestles and juts over the restaurant parking lot, low enough that somebody with a running start can grab a finger hold and pull himself up on the roadway. There's a chain link fence at the back of the lot bordering the river's edge, but it is rusted with age and pitched to one side; nothing there to stop anybody from getting in, or keep anyone out.

Eddie takes another drag on his Camel.

Twist sips a warm Pepsi and takes it all in.

It's wrong. There's too much open space and too much traffic passing on the street as well as the overpass. It's too close to the PATH train station, and Twist knows how easy it would be for a cop to come along and fuck up everything without even trying. No matter how much you plan, you can't anticipate the unexpected. Twist squints at the building across the street. It is a tall turn of the century building and there are too many open windows where a shooter with a scope can do a Lee Harvey Oswald and pick off the Skulls one by one. There are too many places to hide and not enough time to find them.

"That feeling I got about this ain't getting no better the longer we sit here," Eddie says.

"We going to be sitting out here, inviting anybody with a gun and a reason to take a shot at us," Twist mutters.

"Be just like fucking target practice."

Twist takes another swig of Pepsi. "Can't trust the Guineas to honor rules about this meeting," he says. "When it comes to something like this, they'll have guys all over the place, pulling triggers if they see any advantage."

Eddie Dallas flicks his cigarette butt out the window. "True dat."

A few minutes pass in silence. The only sounds are those that come from the cars passing the SUV while drivers curse at them.

"You know, if anything happens to you, I'm the shooter," Eddie says, lighting up another cigarette. He closes his eyes and leans back in the seat. "I get to do Valentine if you can't."

Twist looks at him and Eddie can sense his stare, even without turning or opening his eyes. He shrugs and turns back to Twist, saying, "Makes sense if you're Cuba and Bone because this way they stay clean. If it ever comes around and we put this thing back together with the Guineas, they got one of us to offer as the triggerman."

"A sacrifice."

"That's if they want a body to show for doing Valentine."

Twist shakes his head.

"Guess Cuba and Bone think it gives them options," Eddie adds.

Twist finishes the Pepsi and thinks about that as he stares down the street. They sit in the car watching the restaurant but nothing changes no matter how long they stare.

Twist finally shifts the Pathfinder into drive and pulls out into traffic.

Eddie stares at him, thinking for a moment before asking, "Where would you want to do this if we could change it?"

"Kind of late for that, don't you think?"

Eddie just shrugs.

"If I had my way," Twist says, "I'd do it some place where we control who comes in and what goes on around us. Some place that's tight and confined, where you don't got shooters on rooftops all around you."

"And where's that?"

"Maybe in one of those Route 1 motels near the airport. Be close. It's public," he says. "Risk the same for both sides."

Eddie nods but doesn't say anything. He keeps looking out the window, and after they drive a block he points toward a 7-Eleven store on a side street. "Pull in up there."

"What for?"

"Had a thought."

"You need to go to 7-Eleven to think?"

"Got to get some coins."

Twist pulls into the parking lot and nudges the car slowly and easily over the speed bumps. "What about that Budget Royale Motel across from the airport? We've been there before," Eddie says. "Layout's pretty good, right?"

Twist looks at him in silence.

Eddie can feel Twist's stare again, even without turning his head and he offers a shrug. "Said yourself it's too risky trying to make this happen at the restaurant."

Twist pulls the car to a stop and closes his eyes.

"The way I see it," Eddie says, "we got no other option left.

"I still know a few Guineas who will talk to me. Thinking maybe I can reach out and make something happen."

Twist hands him some dollar bills and watches him go. He makes one call, does what he needs to do, then cuts the connection and dials Maria.

The phone rings but no one answers. There's no surprise in that; it could go on that way for hours and Twist knows nothing will happen and nothing will change.

If there was any hope Maria would pick up the phone, it is gone, and Twist realizes that the sound of a phone ringing unanswered might be the loneliest thing to hear, especially when you're desperate.

He finally ends the transmission and turns off the phone, stuffing it in the center console before leaning back in his seat to wait.

"You on the phone again?" Eddie asks when he returns, rattling a handful of quarters from the 7-Eleven. He tosses a pack of Camels on the front seat and hands Twist another can of Pepsi. "You got us rooms?"

Twist hands Eddie Dallas a piece of paper ripped from a spiral notebook. There are two numbers written on it.

Eddie takes the paper and stares at Twist. "Call your lady again?"

Twist nods.

"What's going on with you and her?"

Twist can only shrug; it's hard finding what he wants to say, and most times the words that come don't go far enough to offer explanations. He wants to tell Eddie about that image he has in his head of Hector doing Maria on the couch. Or the way Maria looked to Hector to protect her and keep her safe. None of it makes sense and Twist can't figure out where it slipped away or when he lost control of what he had.

Eddie looks at him. "Maybe sometimes you just got to let it go if it ain't right. Just walk away and don't look back, huh?"

Twist doesn't answer and Eddie walks across the sidewalk to the pay phone.

◆ ◆ ◆

"Been a change," Eddie says again into the phone. "Plans have changed."

The words are familiar. He has repeated them to a variety of voices, pumping handfuls of quarters into the pay phone to keep the connection alive while bouncing through a succession of people, trying to find one who can do something before he runs out of change. Twist watches from the car. Eddie's expression is detached and he stands quietly at the phone outside the 7-Eleven, until finally a voice on the other end of the receiver engages in the conversation. He listens then replies, "The place they told you ain't gonna work."

Something is said and Eddie says, "You want to meet, it ain't happening there."

Twist sits in the car, scanning the parking lot for trouble. Two kids sit at the curb sharing an orange soda and a pack of Twinkies. A couple of guys come out of the 7-Eleven bouncing a basketball back and forth and sipping Slurpees, and an older lady, pushing seventy and wearing a floral print house dress and nursing withdrawal pains, shuffles through the other door, muttering something as she walks. Twist turns to the street and sees the black-and-white cop car on McCarter turning into the parking lot.

He instinctively squares himself behind the wheel.

"I know it sounds like a fucking setup," Eddie says with his back turned to the street. "But you go down to the restaurant and you be sitting by yourself. We won't be there."

The cop car rumbles across the speed bumps fast enough that the muffler scraps and drags as the body bounces up and down on its chassis. There are two figures inside, and although it's tough making out faces, Twist can see their heads following the guys cutting back toward the street with their basketball. The guys don't give the cops a second look but Twist stays frozen behind the wheel, waiting.

"I'm done explaining," Eddie says sharply. "You want to meet us, you be at the Budget Royale on Route 1 South. It's down the road from the airport. You know the place."

The voice tries telling Eddie that they don't know where the motel is and Eddie slams a hand on the wall. "Bullshit! We got together there last year," he snaps. "You go ask somebody and they tell you that."

He turns toward Twist and for the first time sees the approaching cop car. There's nothing in his face to show concern but Eddie's voice drops as he turns his back to the Pathfinder to face the 7-Eleven again.

"Everything else stays the same," he says into the receiver. "This the only thing that changes."

The cop car inches alongside the SUV then stops as the two sets of eyes inside take in everything about Eddie at the pay phone, the Pathfinder, and Twist behind the wheel. Eddie finishes his conversation with his back still turned to the car. Twist feels the edginess in his own hands, the knot in his stomach, and the weight of the 9mm pressed hard against his back. But he stays perfectly still and holds his breath, aware of the looks he is getting from the cops. Eddie slams down the phone and turns back to the car, keeping his chin up as he saunters nonchalantly across the sidewalk.

"Move the car," a white cop face behind the wheel says. "See the sign? It's a no parking zone. Can't park here."

Eddie smiles. "Sorry. Just making a call."

Twist keeps his face expressionless and his stare straight ahead. It never changes.

"Don't really give a shit what you're doing," a black cop face in the passenger seat says. "Said you got to move."

"Move it," the first cop says again, firmer. "Now."

Eddie nods and gets inside, taking his time to carefully buckle the seat belt then lock the door. The cops watch. Twist shifts into drive and pulls away slowly, keeping an eye turned toward the rear view mirror to see that they don't follow. He doesn't let his breath out until he's back in traffic on McCarter.

"It's changed," Eddie Dallas tells him.

◆ ◆ ◆

"It's changed," Eddie says to Cuba and Bone.

The two of them consider Eddie's statement. Cuba has his hands flat on the table, the fingers pressing down so hard that the tips lose color while Bone sits alone on the other side of the table, edgy and drawn. Bone takes long, deep drags on his cigarette, holding in the smoke until his eyes water and redden before finally letting it out. He looks older and tired. Some of that is from no sleep, but most of it is from the cycle of coke highs and lows that have kept him functioning for weeks. There are cracks in his cool and the strain of the situation shows.

There are others at the table who watch Eddie and Twist, then turn to look at Bone, waiting for a reaction before they form one of their own.

"It was wrong," Twist adds. "Didn't make sense."

"What was so wrong about it?" Cuba wants to know. "You saying the location was wrong or the fact that I was the one who picked it that was wrong?"

"I'm saying that everything about it was wrong," Twist says, letting Cuba read into that statement anything he wants. "We do it there and we wind up bloody. Or dead."

"I changed it," Eddie says in a composed voice. "Called one of the Guineas I know and changed it."

Bone weighs those words, measuring what they mean. He holds one of the Magnums in his hand and drops it below the table to his lap. The rest of the house is quiet and the Game Boys across the room move tentatively, waiting to see what follows. Cuba looks to Bone for an answer, wearing his usual look of anger and rage, but with Cuba that look is constant and there is no surprise in it. He needs Bone to shape his direction with something like this.

"It takes balls doing something like that," Bone finally says.

"I did what I had to do," Eddie says nonchalantly with a shrug.

"We saw what we would be facing and made a choice," Twist adds quickly. "Wasn't any way to pull this off at that restaurant. We want to do this right, we got to go someplace where we got an advantage. Or at least some place where they got no edge. Someplace where we not looking over our shoulders."

"You got a better place?" Cuba asks across the table. "Better than the restaurant?"

"Budget Royale Motel," Twist says. "The motel on Route 1 South."

"What makes you think that a better place?"

Twist waits while that settles. "We been there and we got history," he says. "It's a place where most of us know the layout and know what's around. There ain't no surprises."

Cuba stares at him, letting his agitation grow and build speed. But then something changes and he lets it go, choosing silence instead. Twist focuses on Bone, blocking out everyone else and distancing himself; finding a place where it's just him and Bone doing this.

"I know a guy works the front desk. Got us two rooms on the second floor, back of the motel," Twist goes on. "We set up in one of the rooms, put guys outside the door, and park a couple of shooters around the perimeter where nobody can see them. Control the situation. You won't be standing out there where some Guinea with a rifle can take you out long distance."

"Telling me you did this for me?" Bone says, smiling the way he always does when he hears something he doesn't believe. "You telling me that you give a fuck about me getting shot?

"You give a fuck about me?"

There is something in those words that Twist is expected to answer but he looks past them. He studies Bone's face the way he studied the restaurant half an hour earlier. "I think if you want to do this right, you stay home and let us do it," he says slowly. "Last place you need to

177

be is at the motel where the Italians can take you down and fuck up everything we got.

"We're just supposed to be talking, right?"

"Listen to this," Bone says to Cuba, smiling. "I got this nigger telling me how to do things now. All of a sudden, everybody around here got balls."

"It's like everybody thinks they in charge," Cuba sneers.

And that is the last advice Twist offers. He knows that the best thing for everyone would be for Bone to get taken out, but only if the next bullet gets Cuba.

Bone turns to look at him.

"Okay. We try it your way," he finally says. "At your place."

"Let me tell you one thing," Cuba puts in. Although his stare is linked to Eddie's and he points a finger across the table at him, Twist knows where the words are aimed. "This one belongs to you two fucks. If it goes down wrong, it's on you."

◆ ◆ ◆

The Budget Royale is a no-frills motel that caters to out of state truckers, welfare families, and one night stands from the nearby go-go bar needing a bed for a couple of hours. Not much more than a bed and bathroom in each room. It's the kind of place with no room service or honor bar, and where the maid doesn't bother leaving a mint chocolate on the pillow after making up the room. Most times they don't even change the sheets or linens. The motel is L-shaped with parking slots angling along both sides of the building and a driveway curving behind it before coming back onto Route 1. Room 213 is the last room at the back of the second floor, at the top of the stairs leading down to the parking lot. The door faces out toward the Budweiser bottling plant and two Skulls with .22s tucked inside their shirts stand on the walkway, leaning over the metal railing watching the traffic.

Inside the room a single bed takes up most of the space along with a small walnut veneer nightstand bolted into the floor. The carpeting is old and dark brown, with cigarette burns and stains, and the framed pictures are covered by Plexiglas and nailed to the wall. There's an Essex County phone book and a torn copy of the Gideon Bible on the nightstand, and the last person who used the room shoved a copy of the *Daily News* in a drawer where the cleaning lady left it. A small color television is bracketed to the dresser but the sound is bad and hard to hear. The sign outside advertises cable TV and free HBO but the only channel Twist can tune in to is the public television station. Bone keeps walking over, flicking the TV on and off, waiting for something different to happen. An open doorway leads into the five-by-six bathroom that has only a sink, toilet, and shower stall. The air conditioning is cranked as high as it can go, and every time the thermostat kicks on it makes a rattling sound that drowns out conversation but doesn't cool the room.

A door to the adjoining room is open, and inside Room 211 Cuba paces back and forth holding one of the Magnums. He wears a shoulder holster over his T-shirt with the butt of a .45 exposed. There's a Street Sweeper on the bed and a stack of magazines on the nightstand, and Keyshawn sits nervously on the bed fingering the lines and grooves on the shotgun. He waits in silence like everyone else. The TV in that room is low but nobody pays any attention to it. The door to the bathroom is closed; Dizzy is inside on the toilet, humming a DMX rap as he goes about his business.

Bone paces the floor while Twist holds his position at the window, standing behind the heavy drapes and peering outside. The motel's layout works to their advantage. The rooms are isolated and Twist's friend at the front desk told them no one else was registered in any nearby rooms. They have space and solitude. It's early enough and most of the motel's customers will start drifting in after dusk, and only a few of the rooms look occupied now. Twist doesn't want to take any unnecessary chances; it's one less thing to worry about.

At least that much is good.

He kicks at a rip in the carpeting with his Nikes and then watches the trucks rumbling past on the highway, looking over the shoulder of a guy named Mookie positioned outside the door. The uneasy feeling lingers. He thinks about trying again to convince Bone to call off this meeting or at least go back to Murray Street but he knows Bone never listens when Cuba is around. Alone he might have a chance, but with Cuba there Bone is too far into it to hear what Twist might say. Getting the meeting moved was enough of an accomplishment, and there's no way to do more than that. From the looks that passed between Cuba and Bone Twist saw that their minds were made up, each of them thinking they know more than Twist really does.

Twist made another attempt on the way to the motel. They were in a beige Honda stolen from the long-term airport parking lot, and Twist was behind the wheel with Cuba and Bone in the back seat, while the guns bought from Cooper were wrapped in blankets in the trunk. Twist kept the speed under fifty and watched his mirrors while Eddie Dallas sat in the front, looking through a pack of Virginia Slims he found on the dash board and checking the glove compartment for loose change.

"This might be a mistake," Twist tried.

Only Cuba would meet his stare. Everyone else in the car wore blank expressions and silent frowns, waiting for the words to pass.

"Getting so you sounding like one of the neighborhood whores who can't decide who to fuck first, the way you keep changing your mind," Cuba said from the back.

Twist shook his head. "Maybe if you'd been paying attention you would have heard me saying I don't think this meeting feels right," he said. "Been saying that forever."

"Been hearing you the whole time," Cuba answered. "But your words stopped meaning shit a long time ago."

Bone turned his head.

"Now you trying to say we should cancel this meeting?"

Eddie Dallas nodded but Cuba didn't wait for a response. "How we supposed to do that?" he said with his voice getting higher and then lower. "Can't call them up again and say something else came up. Not if we want a shot at finding Malik and Ice."

Twist didn't bother with the comment about Malik and Ice. Instead, he said simply, "Just don't show."

Eddie looked at him. "You mean let them get here and wait around until they figure out we not coming?" he asked and Twist nodded.

"It would give us time to rethink this whole thing," he said. "Plan it better."

"You a cold motherfucker," Bone told him, but he didn't mean it as a compliment like he does when he says it to Cuba. There was more to it than that. "Do that and you handing out a death sentence to Malik and Ice."

"That what you want?"

"That's how you see it."

"Ain't no other way to see it. Reason we doing it in this motel is so you can make this meeting work to our advantage. Get us information," Cuba said, leaning forward in his seat. "Two of you the ones who insisted that the restaurant was wrong and that doing it here makes it real, right? You wanted this."

Bone shook his head. "Too late for this conversation now."

"Never too late for nothing," Eddie Dallas said, tossing the Virginia Slims pack out the window and searching his pockets for a Marlboro. "Always got options."

"Fuck you and your options!" Cuba yelled and Twist knew there was nothing more to say. He let it go, even though Eddie tried carrying it further until Cuba leaned across the front seat and jabbed a long, thin finger into Eddie's shoulder. Even though the finger poked Eddie, his words were once again meant for both of them.

"You got to make sure nothing bad happens. Do this right so we got nothing to worry about."

It should be that fucking easy, Twist thinks now.

Dizzy comes out of the bathroom in 211 with a nod to Cuba and heads back outside to the walkway, going through the door in 213. They have been careful to avoid using the door in 211—anyone watching would only see the traffic in 213 and this way they keep their presence in 211 a surprise. Bone paces back and forth between the rooms, talking on his cell to somebody outside and carrying on a half-assed conversation with Cuba about one of the girls he picked up at the Viper Club. Keyshawn watches Cuba, waiting to be told what to do next. Nothing is happening outside but Twist stays at the window, checking out planes on their low approach to the airport, dropping toward the runway before disappearing from view. It is too noisy and he knows he could probably never get used to a night in here, even if other people could. His mother used to tell him that a person could get used to anything, no matter how bad it was, but that never worked for Twist.

He frowns and keeps staring outside.

Mookie turns to hear something Dizzy says, blocking Twist's view of the parking lot until he moves back into position at the door. Six-eight and lanky, with barely enough muscle strength to lift himself up the stairs to the second floor, he's maybe sixteen but no older. Mookie's a kid who can play center on the basketball courts but who gets knocked down every time he tries for a rebound if the other guy has positioning and elbows. He has size but nothing else. Mookie has a twenty-two stuffed under his T-shirt but he's just another body Twist wants at the door to provide hands and extra cover if needed.

The way Bone sees Mookie, he's somebody who can stop one of the bullets meant for him.

Twist stares out the window. Two Skulls are watching from a car parked downstairs in the lot, there's another guy at the front desk with Twist's friend, and Eddie Dallas is positioned on the roof of the Ramada next door, leaning into one of the Steyr AUGs while waiting to see what develops. There are guys in cars up and down Route 1, holding guns and cells. Rasheed and LJ will be on the walkway when the Italians show, wearing blue cleaning uniforms they took from the supply closet with rifles stuffed inside their cleaning carts and .22s hidden under their shirts. The only question is whether Twist needs another body at the door with Dizzy and Mookie to frisk the Italians.

He knows that one way or another he'll learn that answer too late.

Cuba and Keyshawn will be in the next room, ready with the Street Sweeper and Magnums if it doesn't go well. You always need a "just in case" option.

"First sign of trouble, you get in here," Twist told them.

"Don't hesitate. Just do it," Bone added in a voice that gets lower and scratchier the further he gets into his day. "Better you overreact and do something like that than leave the two of us standing here holding our dicks. If you wrong, we can fucking apologize later."

"If you come in shooting," Twist said, "just don't miss."

Keyshawn nods his understanding.

The plan is simple. They will let the Italians bring in their own muscle to search the room and frisk him and Bone, and once they are convinced it is clean, their muscle can go out on the walkway with Dizzy and Mookie and wait. Having the firepower outside eliminates risk right away so they can talk; if talk and negotiation is really what everyone wants. The door between the rooms will be locked in case the Italians check it, but once they sit down Cuba will quietly unlatch it and wait. If something bad starts there are cells in both rooms, and he and Keyshawn can be inside the room in seconds.

"It's important for you and me to keep our backs to the window. Let the Guineas come all the way inside," Twist says again to Bone. "They'll think they got some kind of advantage if they facing us and the door. Be thinking they can see everything going on."

"Wish I could hold a gun in here," Bone mutters. "Don't feel right doing this without carrying."

Twist shakes his head. "You want this to go down right, the last thing you need is a piece."

But he doesn't say anything about the 9mm he has stuck inside the drapes with duct tape.

Cuba looks at him and shakes his head, and Twist knows that there is still unfinished business between them. Bone doesn't say anything; instead he looks to Cuba and smiles. Twist ignores whatever is in that smile and eyes the parking lot.

There's a dumpster pushed up against the fence, old and green, with rust holes so big in spots you can stick a fist through them. One of the wheels is broken and it sticks out at an odd angle, and the garbage men who emptied it earlier that afternoon left the trash, garbage, and cardboard boxes scattered on the ground around it. Twist checked it when they first pulled into the lot. Since then no one has been near it, and it is in the same place where the garbage men left it. Twist stares at the dumpster now, taking in everything about it.

He thinks about sending somebody down to check it again but decides there isn't enough time.

He taps on the window to get Mookie's attention and says, "Be awake."

Mookie nods and turns back to the parking lot.

There are no signs of the Italians, although Twist is certain they are around. The beauty in changing the meeting's location is that it has taken away any advantage the Italians might have had to control the location. He's sure they have already staked out their own positions but he feels good about minimizing some of that risk.

The only person in the parking lot now is a drunk old black man dressed in tattered khakis, a flannel shirt, and without shoes, passed out in his own puke near the entrance to the motel. He's been slumped against the fence since they pulled in. He's the only one who isn't a threat, although Twist made certain they checked him out before taking positions. At least he is out of the way so he won't be a factor in anything that happens.

Bone comes and stands at the window.

"You still don't have to go through with this," Twist says to him.

Bone doesn't turn his head. "Ain't got no other choice."

Twist runs a hand through his hair. "You don't see Giaccolone doing this, do you? Don't think he'd put himself out here where somebody can take a shot at him."

Bone shrugs and smiles a grin that bears all his teeth. "I can't help it if the old Guinea's fat and lazy and scared. He don't got no more balls. What kind of man sends other people to do something he should be doing himself?"

A smart one who wants to live a long time, Twist thinks.

"Just gonna listen to what they got to say," he says. "If they wanna' talk it don't hurt none to listen. But there ain't no deals with them until we settle what's between us. Nothing until they take care of this situation with Ice and Malik," he adds before moving away.

Twist shakes his head at the size and scope of his misunderstanding.

CHAPTER TWELVE

Mookie stands quietly outside the motel room window. He's not like other first-timers who get involved in something like this and can't shut up. From the time they got in the cars at Murray Street until he took up his position outside the door, Mookie has been a stone, looking for shooters and watching traffic while soaking up every word in the conversations around him. Twist tries to see whether it's fear or adrenaline hidden in his expression and wonders which will come out when Mookie is needed to do more than watch.

He picks up his cell and dials Eddie on the Ramada rooftop.

"Seen a black Ford Explorer slowing down in front of the motel once or twice but it ain't stopped," Eddie tells him.

"Look like anybody?"

"Can't see faces. Tough to see that kind of detail up here."

Twist repeats that to Bone who takes it in quietly.

"Be ready," Twist says. "Shit happens, right?"

"Ain't just sitting up here watching women and catching a breeze," Eddie answers.

There's nothing for at least fifteen minutes. The time rolls along slowly and Twist is aware of every sound and movement; from the pounding in his chest to the tingling in his fingertips to the way his stomach rises and falls with each breath.

He lights another cigarette and waits.

Something in the parking lot gets his attention.

He moves quickly through the door to the walkway between Dizzy and Mookie who hold their positions like they've been instructed and don't move. The afternoon is filled with noise—traffic on Route l races past, jet engines whine on the airport runways, and a jack hammer splits concrete and asphalt at a construction site nearby. A motel room door on the first floor is open and the sound of an afternoon cartoon show on television carries. Twist leans over the railing to see two boys, no older than seven or eight, playing tag between cars in the parking slots close to the rooms. Both are bare foot and shirtless, and one kid has a long, jagged scar on his back that starts at his shoulders and curves down into his pants. Their black skin is wet with sweat as they chase each other around the cars. If either has noticed the Skulls positioned around the motel they've paid no attention—they are too busy to care.

"Shit," Twist mutters.

Bone's head snaps up. "What's wrong?"

"A couple of kids down in the lot," he says over a shoulder. There is something about the way they laugh and play that is part of Twist's memory, familiar enough to hold on to, but inches out of reach and gone before he can get it for himself.

Bone frowns. "Who gives a shit?"

"They're just kids."

"So what?"

"They're gonna get in the middle of this," Twist says.

Bone says something else but Twist has flipped his cigarette to the ground and started toward the stairs. Mookie and Dizzy turn to watch, and he hears Bone's voice getting louder as he moves. Bone's words sail away in the afternoon noise. Dizzy takes a step to follow but Twist shoots a look that stops him where he stands.

"Be right back," he says. "Ain't nothing I can't handle."

He catches a glimpse of Bone coming through the door and hears him yelling, "Where the fuck he going?"

But Twist doesn't stop.

He takes the stairs two at a time and jumps the last three, landing on his toes and pivoting toward the lot. He moves fast, hurrying to make up distance quickly. He's aware of the eyes watching him; he looks toward the Ramada but can only assume that Eddie will be able to know his intentions. There's an open door five rooms away where the television plays, but nobody inside when he passes. There is more movement at the end of the parking lot but it's only an old white lady moving from her car to one of the rooms, struggling to carry a plastic laundry basket while digging her room key out of a purse. She doesn't give Twist a second look.

He approaches the two boys.

"Hey," he says evenly.

They stop and turn in the middle of the lot. He can see them trying to figure out who he is and how much authority he has, and why they need to listen to him. They keep their distance and instinctively draw closer to each other.

There's a familiarity in that, and Twist recognizes it from his past.

"Got a second?"

Neither answers.

Twist nods slowly and moves forward again. "Just want to talk."

He's always been comfortable dealing with kids, and he thinks that these guys are no different than Angel. Eight-year-olds are easy.

One of them curls up his lip and sneers. "What the hell you want, man?"

Great. Eight-year-olds with attitudes.

He comes within five feet of them and stops. He looks down at their feet and notices them both bouncing uncomfortably in place on the hot asphalt, moving quickly from foot to foot. But their stares remain tough and defiant, and filled with attitude. "Your mom around?" he asks in an easy voice. "Maybe I can talk to her?"

"About what?"

"Just want to talk."

The kid who sneered steps forward with his hands on his hips. "She ain't here right now."

"Didn't think so," Twist says with a smile. "Don't need no baby sitter, huh?"

"What you want?" the second one demands.

Twist lets a grin roll onto his face. The three of them stare back and forth, nobody moving, until Twist reaches into his pocket. When Twist lifts it out he is holding two fifty dollar bills between his fingers. Both kids' eyes open wider and the first one takes another step closer, peering at the bills to make sure they are real.

"What you doing with that money?"

Twist keeps his grin. "Maybe I'm trying to figure out how smart you are," he says. "I'm thinking that this can be yours real easy, but I'm wondering whether you got what it takes to earn it. A lot of guys see something good, they get suspicious and think it's too good to be true. Miss a lot of opportunities that way."

"What you mean by earn it?"

"Means it's yours if you do something for me."

The first kid looks at the other kid then back at Twist. "What you want us to do?"

"It's simple," Twist shrugs. "I'll give you this money and all you got to do is get back inside your room, close the door, and don't come outside again until your mother comes home. No matter what, you keep the door closed and stay inside the room."

"What for?"

"Don't matter what for. I'm just paying you to stay inside and don't come out."

"That's it?" the first one says with a frown.

"She ain't coming back for a long time," the second kid says, looking at the other one. "Remember?"

"Yeah."

"Gonna be hours."

"It's a long time to stay inside," the first kid agrees, "just cause you say so."

Twist nods. "I hear you," he says, looking like he understands everything. "But you got to ask yourself what's more important right now. Playing outside like you do every day, or putting fifty a piece in your pocket. And you don't have to give it to no one. Don't have to tell nobody neither.

"That's the kind of money ain't nobody else gonna give you for doing nothing.

"Your choice."

"That all?"

Twist smiles. "That's all."

The two kids exchange stares, weighing his offer. They have been taught that something this good usually has strings attached, and they stand there looking behind the offer to see what else is there. While they debate the seconds drag along and Twist feels his own edge returning, and he keeps glancing at the motel entrance, expecting to see the Italians driving into the lot. He can feel everyone else watching too, and the knot in his throat tightens while his stomach flips and churns. Twist doesn't see the kid's hand reaching out to grab the money but he lets it go easily when it's yanked from his fingers.

The two kids run back to their room, slamming the door behind them and leaving Twist alone in the lot.

He smiles and takes a deep breath.

Twist turns and walks back toward the stairs.

"You one fucking crazy nigger," Bone sneers from the railing above. "I can't figure out nothing going through your head no more."

"Nothing to figure out."

"Shit," Bone says. "Got serious issues I don't even think you understand."

Twist doesn't answer as he climbs the stairs.

◆ ◆ ◆

When the Italians finally show it's almost twenty minutes past four—at least an hour past the original meeting time. The waiting is part of the process; either the Italians want to cover all exposed angles around the motel and eliminate risk, or they plan to use the time to swing control back in their favor. Tension and waiting are just a part of the game. A dark green Town Car pulls into the lot with its directional blinking, and the turn signal stays on even after the driver steers toward the back of the motel. The Town Car stops beneath the walkway. A guy, short and late twenties in dark sunglasses, gray slacks, and a jacket, gets out and hurries to the drunk slumped against the fence. He glances back over his shoulder but doesn't stop. He nudges a foot into the drunk's ribs, then again a second time, and when the drunk doesn't move he leans down for a closer look before nodding to the driver. The Town Car sits parked with the door open, but the guy stays in the lot, eyeing the walkway and hugging the fence as he guards the perimeter.

His stare holds on Dizzy and Mookie at the door to Room 213.

Minutes pass slowly.

Twist is on the phone with Eddie, backing off the walkway and edging into the room with an eye on the car. Behind him Cuba and Keyshawn slip carefully inside Room 211, closing the door gently and locking the door. There are words between Bone and Cuba but Twist can't hear what passes. "You see him?" he asks Eddie.

"He's the first one I drop," Eddie says. "If it comes to that."

The cell in Bone's hand rings. He puts it to his ear and listens to the guy at the front desk. "Got another car coming in," Bone says to

Twist, breaking the connection and nearing the window to survey the lot.

Twist pushes aside the curtains.

A black Cadillac Escalade does the same kind of slow loop around the parking lot and pulls alongside the dumpster. The driver stops twenty feet from the side of the other car and rolls down one of the windows. The cars are close but it's impossible to see anyone inside either car.

Twist feels the lump in his throat hardening with each swallow.

He taps lightly on the window. "Watch that other car," he tells Dizzy through the glass. "Eddie's got the Town Car."

"Got it," Dizzy says.

Bone is up on his toes, moving quickly around the room to close drawers and doors and hide all traces of suspicion. Twist turns to him.

"You ready for this?" he asks.

"I want to look these motherfuckers in the eye and hear what they got to say," Bone says, shaking his head with a sneer. "Want to see them piss their pants when I tell them I know they offed my brother. Then see their expressions when Cuba and Keyshawn bust in here blazing. Let's see how cool they are when that happens."

Twist can only stare at him.

In that moment he understands that there was never any intention to negotiate.

He shoves the cell in a pocket, backing away from the window and door, measuring the distances between each. He's slow and deliberate, quietly counting the steps although he doesn't know why, and aware of every sound and movement outside the door. The phone feels heavy in Twist's pocket but it has a purpose and he wants it there.

"I hear my phone ring once the Italians are in the room and I'm gonna kiss the ground and wait for the shooting to stop," he said back on Murray Street. "If the phone rings it better be because there are six Guineas pointing heavy artillery at us, and not because somebody needs to know who's buying pizza tonight. You feel me?"

Bone moves back to the bed and waits, clearly uncomfortable without a gun in his hand; unable to strike the kind of pose he wants the Italians to see when they open the door. Twist goes back to the window, again counting the seven steps it takes. The doors on the Town Car are open but nobody makes a move yet. There's a whining noise coming out of the Cadillac, like the sound an electric window makes when it's rolled down as far as it can go but the person doesn't let up on the button. Twist figures that whoever is calling the shots is doing it from that car.

Anything important starts there.

Two guys in windbreakers and dark slacks get out of the Town Car and start slowly toward the stairs. Another guy fans out across the parking lot with the guy who kicked the drunk, watching the fringe. Another slides out of the Cadillac and leans across the hood.

"It's happening," he says to Bone.

Bone grunts and folds his arms across his chest.

"You cool with this?"

Bone shoots him an icy stare. "Don't think it's your place to be asking me something like that."

There's somebody else behind the wheel of the Town Car but Twist can't see anything about him. He hopes one of the Skulls has a clear shot.

And that they'll take if it's there.

He hears noise on the stairs and moves away from the window as the two windbreakers cross the walkway toward the room. Figures move in front of the window and Twist and Bone exchange looks. There are muffled voices outside the door. Words are thrown back and forth before there's a quick rap at the door. Dizzy steps inside, his voice is directed at Bone and Twist but his body is turned toward the men on the walkway. There's a dark shape over his shoulder that tries looking past him for a glimpse of the room.

Dizzy keeps the shotgun close to his hip. "Explained the conditions," he says.

Bone nods. "They got a problem with it?"

Dizzy's eyes dart inside. There's a look of uneasiness in his stare and he quickly turns his head back outside.

"Ain't happy about it," he says, "but they'll go along with it."

Bone nods. "Let's get it on."

The two windbreakers pass Dizzy and enter. One takes up a position in the corner of the room by the window, his shoulder touching the drape where Twist taped the gun. He's fifties, probably close to Valentine's age, with a short crew cut hiding a receding hair line and a dark scowl that never leaves his face. He points a sawed-off shotgun at Bone and Twist, watching the other guy picking carefully through the room. Dizzy stands behind him with his own shotgun angled and ready. The other guy is younger and beefier, but wears the same pissed-off-at-the-world expression as he goes through drawers and searches under the bed. He tries the door to Room 211 and finds it locked from the other side. He puts an ear to the door and listens for a moment, then exchanges looks with the other Italian as he flips the dead bolt and locks it from his side. When he's satisfied, he stands toe to toe with Twist. Twist stretches his hands toward the ceiling and lets the Italian pat him down. His touch is rough but the guy is thorough. When he's finished he moves to Bone, starting at his ankles the same way he did with Twist and working upward. Twist keeps his hands pointed to the ceiling, moving his stare from the guy in the corner to Dizzy and Mookie on the walkway. There's a suit standing close but Twist can't see who it is or what he's doing.

Dizzy keeps his shotgun pointed in the room while Mookie holds his piece on the Italian. Twist is certain that the Italian has his own gun pointed at somebody; he just can't see who.

The guy patting down Bone stands up and nods to the suit at the door. "They're clean."

One uncomfortable minute passes into the next, with Twist keeping his eyes on the door, watching Dizzy's expression for changes, and waiting to see if something different comes across his face.

Sally is the first one to pass the window. He's wearing a dark suit, white shirt, and a red tie, and his hair is slicked back. There's another guy named Vito who follows a couple of steps behind. He's bulky, with shoulders that are broad and thick, squeezed into a dark gray pinstriped suit. He smooths out the wrinkles and creases, straightening the jacket as he moves next to Sally and looks through the window. Twist knows him but never found a reason to exchange words with him.

Dizzy looks in from the walkway while Mookie finishes patting them down.

He nods to Bone and Twist.

The two windbreakers back out the door and Sally and Vito enter slowly. They move toward the bed, taking in everything about the room while sizing up the two Skulls. Dizzy looks over their shoulders for direction and Twist nods. When he closes the door they stand six feet apart—the Italians just inside the door and Bone and Twist at the foot of the bed. Sally lets a slow grin slide onto his face as they square off.

"Didn't enjoy getting felt up by your man outside," he says.

Bone stares. "Wasn't no fun with your boy grabbing me neither."

Twist says nothing as he moves across the room and takes up his position close to the drapes. Bone stays where he is with his arms folded across his chest.

Sally is all business and there's nothing warm or sincere about the smile. "You ever wonder how it is, that after all this time we're standing here like strangers in some motel room like we don't have history between us?"

"Past the point of thinking about that," Bone says in an even voice. "We need to deal with the here and now."

Sally goes toward the bathroom, running a hand across the TV set as he passes Bone. He looks at the dust on his fingertips and wipes it on the bed spread, shaking his head. Vito takes two steps into the room.

"Maybe things can change," Sally says.

"Ain't no 'maybes,'" Twist says.

"Maybe you can't change what's already been done, but I got to think there's still time to make things different," Sally says, walking around the bed to face Bone.

They stand close, no more than a couple of feet apart. They hold each other's stare before Sally turns and backs up to the wall, eyeing both Bone and Twist together. "Still got a chance to change directions here before it gets worse.

"Came here to tell you that."

Twist keeps his eyes on Vito while Sally talks, staring at the hands hanging close to his sides and the bulge under his left arm that pushes out his jacket. There's an empty holster there but he wonders if Mookie was as thorough in his search as he could have been. Vito has yet to crack a smile; instead he moves his stare back and forth, wearing an expression that says discussion is his least favorite option for settling this dispute.

Just like Cuba.

Twist wishes he could feel the 9mm tucked inside his pants, pressing against his skin. Knowing that it is behind the drapes doesn't offer the comfort he thought it would—he needs it closer. He shuffles his feet and glances at the drapes, going through the possibilities and figuring that if anything turns bad he has to take out Vito first.

Like it's something easy.

"We're all reasonable guys, right?" Sally says.

"You know what this is all about. You know what we're looking for," Bone says, sticking a toothpick between his teeth and letting it roll to the corner of his mouth. "Ain't nothing to talk about until we clear the air on that."

"Don't see Ice out there. Or the young'un. Maybe you ain't ready to talk about where they at, but nothing gets done until we get that on the table," Bone adds.

Sally shakes his head. "Think maybe you got your priorities confused."

There's something in Bone's expression that says he doesn't really give a fuck anymore and that the purpose of this meeting is different than what was intended. All of a sudden the look he has worn for days has changed.

"Ain't nothing to be confused about," Bone says as his voice drops lower. "It's pretty simple. At least the way I see it."

It's not the words but the way he says them that tells Twist it was never about Ice or Malik. There was never any intention hearing what the Italians wanted or what they had to say. It has nothing to do with negotiations; and everything to do with staring into their eyes and looking for the shooter who pulled the trigger on his brother. And for Bone, finding the guy who gave the order is just as important as finding the shooter.

An eye for an eye; blood spilled for blood spilled.

Twist has heard it said and understands what it means.

Everything always comes down to revenge.

He hears Bone's voice and the knot tightens its grip on his insides.

"The way I see it, you guys made a big mistake thinking you can play the game this way," Sally says, looking first to Bone and then Twist for understanding. He shakes his head as if he can't even believe it himself. "That ain't good for none of us."

Bone smiles an ugly grin that's filled with equal parts hate and pain. He could be mouthing those same words back at Sally.

"You the ones who gone too far," he says. "Ice in the game. We get that. But the young'uns? That's a different story."

Sally's face doesn't change.

"Guys wear your colors, they understand the risks," he says.

"And the one who ain't wearing the colors?" Twist asks.

Sally shrugs. "What's it matter? Just part of what happens."

"So, this guy? The one we got right now," Bone says. "You standing there telling us it don't matter when he turns up dead?"

"Just part of what happens?" Twist asks.

Sally's smile melts while Bone's opens wider.

"You in something too fucking deep to be taking that kind of risk," Sally says as his expression hardens and his voice drops to a whisper. "It ain't gonna come out the way you think it will."

"You can tell that already?" Twist puts in.

Sally turns his stare toward him. "I'm telling you how it is. It didn't have to be this way.

"Trying to make you see that nothing's gonna get any better," he adds.

"This is as good as it gets?"

Vito nods his head up and down. "You can't win something like this."

Bone lets out a laugh and walks across the room toward Twist. Vito edges away, like he doesn't want to be anywhere close to him, and joins Sally on the other side of the bed.

The conversation dissolves into tense silence.

Twist glances at Bone. He stands defiantly, his arms still crossed over his chest and his stare fixated into Sally's chest. Nothing about it has changed, although nothing about Sally's expression has changed either. His glare is just as hard and angry. Twist can see Mookie outside the room, watching the Italians in their windbreakers with his eyes wide and his expression frozen. He can't see faces, only the backs of their jackets stretched across their shoulders. There's not much of Dizzy to be seen, just the barrel of his shotgun angled toward one of the windbreakers. Dizzy seems cool about everything, but from the way Mookie watches the walkway he looks distanced, like he's not a part of what's going on.

That bothers Twist.

"So where do we go from here?" Sally asks.

"You got a lot of answers," Bone says as Twist turns back from the window. "Maybe you got one that explains what's supposed to happen here today between us."

There is no smile on Sally's face.

"Because if you didn't come here to talk about what happened to my crew, why you even here?" Bone asks. "Why show up? Could've called us on the phone to tell us that."

Twist looks back outside the window, past the guys on the walkway, to the parking lot.

"This ain't getting us nowhere," Bone says.

He hears Sally say, "Tell me something I don't already fucking know."

Twist sees it all fall apart as he glances out the window. It comes in bits and pieces but he can see everything unfold; and when it happens, there is no surprise.

He always knew it would turn out this way.

Two more guys in dark suits get out of the Cadillac with their shoulders dipped low and their heads down. They move quickly across the parking lot, fast enough to draw Mookie's attention. Eddie Dallas would have a clear shot from the Ramada roof, and Rasheed and LJ should be able to follow their movement if they are paying attention. Sally is still talking to Bone, going on about why the guy who doesn't matter really matters to them as Twist angles for a better look. The phone in his pocket stays silent.

Suddenly everything explodes around him.

The guy who was leaning over the Cadillac reaches inside the car. When he swings around there is a gun in his hands, and although it's only for a second, Twist will swear later that it's a Steyr Aug, just like the ones they're carrying. The Guineas in the parking lot are crouched in positions, and as he turns, Twist sees one of the windbreakers at the door pulling a gun from inside his jacket.

In an instant there are shooters everywhere.

"Get down!" he yells.

Bone is frozen in place.

Twist shoves him to the floor. Bullets shatter the window and glass rains down on Twist as he pushes Bone to the side. There are screams and gun fire from the walkway but through all the noise and chaos Twist's phone remains silent. The window explodes above him as Twist covers Bone with his own body, then rolls across the floor. He crawls toward the drapes, lurching through broken glass that rips and digs into his hands and knees.

Bone is screaming for Cuba as he crawls across the room.

"Stay down!" Twist yells again.

He looks up to see the shotgun blast that blows away the side of Mookie's face.

The kid is dead before he drops to the ground.

Twist wraps his hands around the curtains and pulls hard, yanking the drapes, rod, and brackets to the floor. There are more gunshots and out of the corner of his eye he sees one of the windbreakers falling to the walkway with a chunk of his skull missing. Dizzy and another windbreaker are locked in a violent struggle for position with their arms wrapped around each other. They bang and bounce off the wall, twisting and turning on the walkway.

Twist digs deeper in the curtains but can't find the gun.

Across the room Vito charges for the door and Twist knows he's got no way to stop him from escaping. Even with his gun there's no chance to bring him down.

But just then Cuba crashes through the door. Wood splinters as he knocks the door loose from its frame and bursts inside, hitting Vito with his head down and his shoulder tucked low. The noise is like a head on collision between two trucks on the highway. They each bounce backward a step but both of them stay on their feet. Vito grabs for the Street Sweeper with one hand and pushes it out of the way, locking his other hand on Cuba's throat and squeezing tight. Keyshawn comes in behind them, swinging his sawed-off. Cuba holds both hands on the Street Sweeper, trying to jerk it free as he and Vito bang into the wall, then crash into the open door and smash what is left of it off its hinges. Neither will let go. Cuba tries pulling the gun loose as they roll across the room but the gun smashes into the TV, breaking the plastic casing and knocking it loose from its mounting bracket on the dresser.

Keyshawn takes another step forward and points the gun toward the back of the room. Sally dives for cover behind the bed as Keyshawn pulls hard on both triggers. The blasts spray the room with pellets that shatter lamps, pictures, and mirrors, and blow two huge holes in the plaster.

"Fuck!" he yells.

Sally jumps to his feet and barrels into Keyshawn, knocking him backward. He runs through the busted door into Room 211 while Keyshawn jams two more shells into the breech. He squeezes off another shot but Sally has already run through the door to the walkway, and Twist catches a glimpse of him dodging bullets and racing past the window above him.

Twist gets to his knees, still trying to find his 9mm buried inside the fabric.

Cuba holds his grip on the Street Sweeper as he and Vito roll across the dresser. The TV crashes to the floor and the screen explodes with a loud pop and a flash of flame and smoke. Blue smoke curls out of the hole where the picture tube had been. Cuba turns a shoulder into the Italian as Vito gets a hand free and pounds a fist into Cuba's mouth. The blow moves him backward a step but doesn't shake his grip free, even after he does it a second time.

Keyshawn steps toward them, gripping the shotgun by the barrel like he's stepping into the batting cages with a baseball bat. He takes a hard, level swing and nails Vito on the side of the head with the stock of the gun. Vito's body sags and his hold on the Street Sweeper weakens. It's not much but it's enough to give Cuba an advantage. He yanks the gun free and buries the muzzle in the Italian's stomach.

Vito's expression freezes in horror.

Cuba squeezes the trigger and Vito is jerked backward. The front of his white shirt bursts open and blood sprays from a huge hole where his stomach and intestines had been. Vito tries gathering his balance but can't get his legs beneath him, and he lurches and stumbles toward the wall. He looks from the hole in his body to Cuba and then back at the hole, trying to push the pieces of his stomach back inside his shirt.

Cuba takes a quick step forward and shoves the gun into his chest.

"Do the motherfucker," Bone says from his knees. "Do it now."

Cuba looks back to Bone and grins.

"Look at me," he says to Vito. "Open your fucking eyes and look at me."

Vito's head lifts.

Cuba pulls the trigger and the gun jerks upward. Dark blood splatters Cuba's pants and shirt as he squeezes off another shot that blows Vito's body backward on the bed. He stares at him a moment before spitting a glob of phlegm on his corpse.

Keyshawn grins.

"You got him good," he says. "Got that piece of shit just like he deserved."

Keyshawn pumps the shotgun once and obliterates Vito's face.

Twist's fingers touch the metal of his 9mm and he yanks it free from the fabric, coming out of his crouch and firing outside.

The first shot is random and blind but it hits the windbreaker on the walkway in the back of his knee. The guy screams as his hands drop off Dizzy, grabbing for the leg and lurching toward the railing. Dizzy jams the barrel of his forty five into the Italian's throat and squeezes the trigger. Blood and flesh spurt from his neck and the momentum of the blast topples his body over the top of the railing.

Bone gets to his feet by the bed and looks at Vito's corpse.

Twist turns as the room continues exploding around him. There are staccato pops of semi-automatics in the parking lot and bullets chew out chunks of plaster in the wall above his head. The remaining pieces of glass from the window crash to the floor. He struggles to his feet and looks outside to see the shooter by the Cadillac getting cut down by bullets from different shooters in the back and front. A bullet zings past and takes out a piece of molding by his head and Twist drops again, feeling the glass tearing through his jeans and the warm sensation of blood oozing from the cuts in his skin. Outside Mookie's corpse is faceless, slumped against the wall; his features blown away by the shot gun blast. The body of the Italian is face down next to him, blood streaming into a pool on the concrete beneath his body.

There are more gunshots as well as screams of pain and terror in the parking lot, but Twist can't see anything. He can't get a handle on who is doing the shooting.

Dizzy crashes through the door to the room and rolls to the floor, digging into the carpeting and pulling himself to safety on his knees and elbows. Gun shots pepper the frame around the door.

Cuba looks to Bone but there is no satisfaction and nothing about Bone's expression is any different. He struggles to his feet. His pants are torn and bloody and he hugs the wall as he steadies himself. He wipes a hand across his face and takes a step.

In the parking lot another Italian starts for the fence. Twist comes out of his crouch and hits him with half a dozen shots at the same time Eddie nails him from behind with a burst from the Steyr Aug. The guy tumbles into the chain link and crumples to the asphalt.

"Come on," Cuba says, pulling Bone toward Room 211. Keyshawn scrambles to follow as Dizzy checks the clip in his gun and huddles in the space between the door and window. Downstairs shooters are positioned between the Town Car and the Cadillac, firing at the rooms as well as any Skulls they see. Twist peeks outside but can't see their faces; all he hears is the mixture of bullets and voices.

It is bedlam, and Twist has a hard time holding his focus through the chaos.

What comes to mind is that it's been five minutes since the shooting started and his phone never rang.

Dizzy looks over at Twist. "What we do?"

"We get the fuck out of here," Twist says. "Same as them."

"How?"

Twist checks the clip in his 9mm. He leans into the wall and says, "Go through the next room. Out that door to the other end of the walkway, then down to the car."

"Where you think Rasheed and LJ are? Down there?"

Twist swallows. He knows what the feeling in his gut means but says nothing.

He nods at Dizzy.

Dizzy eases away from the wall and starts for 211 as Cuba bursts through the door to the walkway. Twist goes through the window in a crouch, kicking past the remaining shards of glass and leaning over the railing with his nine. He and Cuba fire at the cars below and windows pop and shatter from the bullets. Twist empties his clip into the Cadillac and the car horn suddenly blares and doesn't stop. Twist drops his clip and reloads.

The Italians scramble inside the Town Car, ducking low as Cuba drills more holes into the cars metal and fiberglass.

"Come on!" he screams.

Twist braces himself against the railing and squeezes the trigger. He hits metal and glass and keeps firing until there are no more bullets in the clip. The engine in the Town Car starts and the driver bangs it into reverse. The car peels backward out of the lot, tires smoking and squealing, and Cuba runs down the walkway and around the corner, firing the Street Sweeper at it. Cars on Route 1 swerve out of the way or stop in their lanes as the shots spray the cars. Cuba doesn't stop to consider where the bullets are going or who he might hit. He just keeps shooting until there's nothing left in the ammo clips.

The Town Car fishtails into the street and races south, disappearing in seconds down Route 1.

"Come on!" Cuba keeps yelling, still squeezing the trigger from the stairs. "Come on, you motherfuckers!"

"Let's go!" Twist hollers over a shoulder. "Get to the car!"

Bone and Dizzy stagger out of 211 and hurry down the walkway toward the stairs. Keyshawn follows, pumping the shotgun but there is no one left standing to shoot at. Twist looks down to the other end of the walkway and sees the service carts overturned. The fabric on the sides is shredded and the windows in the adjacent rooms have been blown out. Nothing moves except one of the wheels on the bottom of the cart; it spins slowly until it comes to a stop. Rasheed is slumped against the railing. His expression is frozen and his hands hold the hole where his chest had been, and the service uniform he had been wearing is in tatters. Twist can't see LJ; only a pair of legs that jut out from beneath the cart. Another figure is slumped over the cart but he's white and Italian, and at the moment nothing about him matters to Twist.

Twist drags himself off the railing and lurches down the stairs toward the Honda. He can hear the sound of sirens somewhere in the distance and the roar of an engine turns his head. The car with two other Skulls peels out of the driveway, with the guy from the front desk scrambling through a back window.

Cuba pushes the driver's body out of the seat in the Cadillac and slides behind the wheel.

Twist throws himself into the back seat of the Honda, bloody and hurting. Bone and Dizzy are with him while Keyshawn is in the front, shifting the car into gear. Blood streams down Bone's face from a huge gash across the center of his forehead and his T-shirt is dirty and specked with blood. Dizzy leans back and closes his eyes. Bone leans over the front seat and takes the shotgun from Keyshawn, pointing it out the window toward one of the white corpses on the asphalt.

He empties both barrels into the body.

"Damn Guineas," he says. "Fuck 'em all to hell."

Keyshawn steps down hard on the gas pedal, screeching tires and burning rubber as he accelerates out of the lot into the street. The Italian who had poked at the wino is face down on the sidewalk now, and another guy is ten feet past him, sprawled out spread eagle on the hood of a parked car. It's tough figuring out whether it's another shooter, or just somebody in the wrong place when everything went to hell.

Twist doesn't even bother trying.

The last thing he remembers when he looks back is Mookie's body on the walkway, blood splattered on the wall around what is left of his head.

Twist knows that any chance Michael Valentine might have had is gone.

CHAPTER THIRTEEN

Malik and Ice are dead. The motel shootout only confirms what Twist has feared all along.

He knows Malik is dead even before they find his body.

His burner finally rings but he lets it go unanswered. Keyshawn has the Honda pushing seventy down Route 21, weaving around a cloverleaf and cutting past cars. The engine strains to squeeze out extra speed and the valves clatter and shake. He looks over a shoulder and checks the mirrors. Inside the car it is quiet; nothing but silence as the day comes unhinged. Twist bends forward with his elbows resting on his knees and his chin in his hands, leaning into the door as Keyshawn speeds up to make a traffic light.

Twist watches Keyshawn's expression. It's one of determination; focused and straight ahead, and Twist realizes that Keyshawn is the only one who isn't worried that nothing they have will remain the same. Maybe there's something in that; something about being so focused on only one task that nothing else matters. Right now the most important thing is getting away. Later they can worry about fingerprints and clues left at the motel, the bodies left scattered on the asphalt and what the cops can put together, and dump the cars on Jersey City side streets with their original plates and the keys in the ignitions. All that matters is getting back to Murray Street.

Getting back and picking up the pieces.

"Slow down," Bone growls.

Keyshawn glances back. "Got to put distance between us and the Budget. Got to get us far enough away that the cops don't catch us."

"We far enough away," Bone says. "Just blend in with the traffic and don't do nothing that gonna have the law on our tail. Don't feel like answering no cop questions right now."

The phone rings again.

Twist opens it and grunts a hello. One of the kids from the house is on the phone, nervous and edgy as he gives the news that Twist has known would be coming sooner or later. A cold feeling washes over him.

Knowing what to expect doesn't lessen the impact.

"That Cuba?" Dizzy asks. "What's going on? Where is he?"

"Who the fuck you talking to?" Bone wants to know, reaching for the phone.

Twist cuts off the conversation and shuts the phone without a goodbye, keeping it out of reach of Bone's fingertips. He drops it to the floor and kicks it under the front seat, pushing it far out of sight. With his head back on the seat he closes his eyes and takes a deep breath. He tries clearing his head but can't shut out the rest of the world.

Twist can't focus. There is too much left in pieces.

"You got something for me," Bone says, "don't hold it inside."

Keyshawn takes another corner hard and the three guys in the back seat slam into Twist in a pile of bodies, elbows, and knees. His head and face smack into the glass and Twist feels a sharp pain shooting up and down his shoulder and neck. Somebody takes an elbow out of his ribs and an arm off his shoulder. He lets his head roll backward again as Bone straightens, and then pops a hard fist into the back of Keyshawn's seat.

"I said, slow down," he snarls, smacking the fist into the seat one more time. "Don't need no cop pulling us over because you can't drive worth shit."

Keyshawn eases his foot off the accelerator and falls behind a truck.

Bone looks to Twist. "What's going on?"

Twist takes a deep breath.

"Found Malik," Twist says in a soft voice, opening his eyes to stare out the window. The buildings and cars they pass are a distant blur and there are no images to hold as they move past. "Dumped the body about a half an hour ago."

Bone stares straight ahead and says nothing. There is no news in it for him.

"Where'd they find him?" Dizzy asks.

"Body was rolled inside a plastic sheet with two bullets behind the ear," Twist says evenly. "The guy back at the house tells me it looks like the he's been dead at least a couple of days."

"Like one of them kids can tell the difference between a real corpse and those stiffs they see on Xbox," Dizzy says with a sneer.

The words don't change anything in Bone's expression. He stares straight ahead and watches the road.

Twist takes a moment before adding, "Found him on the corner of Broad and Commerce. A couple of blocks away from the garage," he says. "Close enough so we would find him quick."

Bone turns his head. "Close enough that it's supposed to mean something."

Twist nods. But he knows how little Malik's corpse really means to any of the Skulls now.

◆ ◆ ◆

Everything back at the garage is in chaos. The Game Boy had been in the middle of telling Twist just how badly things had got when Twist cut off the call, and now he expects the worst as they approach.

Keyshawn stops at the corner to let them out. Twist can see the flashing blue lights of the cop cars and ambulance a few blocks away, and the area is alive with activity. He knows that Malik's body is probably still on the sidewalk, covered with a sheet and the area cordoned off with yellow crime scene tape, while a crowd of onlookers stare intently from the sidewalk. He could go there but seeing him dead won't change a thing.

And it will just attract attention from the cops.

It's only a matter of time before the cops show up at the garage. Somebody will put two and two together and come up with the Skulls, and when they do Murray Street will be crawling with uniforms and detectives trying to piece together everything they know. There's not much time to figure out next steps.

The three of them stagger from the car, reloading and checking ammo clips before shoving guns in pockets and hiding them in pant legs. Bone leans into Dizzy for support. His knees are bloodied and he struggles to find his balance, and Dizzy keeps a hand under his shoulder to guide him toward the house. Twist stares a neighborhood kid back into his house and watches Keyshawn speed away.

All he feels is an emptiness sticking inside his chest, squeezing the breath from his lungs.

Twist wonders if Ice and Malik were alive long enough to know what was happening; if either could figure out they were really dead before the Italians killed them.

Things like that stay with Twist as they walk through the garage doors at 38 Murray.

There are two kids by the door holding AR-15s while Rocco patrols outside, looking to the rooftops for snipers. Twist is the only one to acknowledge them as they walk up the sidewalk. Rocco gives a nervous smile in return but says nothing.

Inside the voices are loud, back and forth across rooms in anger and confusion. There is nobody to take charge and no one to bring order to the chaos. Nobody to explain whether what happened was good or bad, and all the Game Boys can do is assume the worst. The gunmen and lookouts from the Budget Royale are back and each has their own horror story, although nobody knows the complete picture. Each of them try to explain what happened, filling in details they remember, but their voices only create more confusion and questions that cannot be answered. Twist sees the confusion in the expressions of the kids and hears the panic in their questions, and the explanations about how it went wrong don't ease the fears.

None of them see it the same way.

Nobody is sure when it first went bad; all they see is that everything is coming apart and nobody knows which way it will go.

Dizzy comes through the front door first, banging it open and pushing past the soldier standing guard without saying a word. Conversations stop and heads turn; eyes shoot worried stares and one of the Game Boys jumps to his feet but Dizzy shoves him backward with a hand to his chest. No one else moves. He helps Bone negotiate the path through the legs and bodies in the front room, and then goes to the kitchen to find him a chair at the table. When Bone falls into the seat Dizzy turns to the refrigerator for a couple of Bud. He reaches for another and looks to Twist, but Twist is standing at the window with a quiet stare, blinking away the sweat dripping off his forehead. Dizzy returns the bottle.

T. Capone sits at the table smoking a cigarette. He waits until Dizzy is in his own chair, then spreads out his elbows out on the table and leans forward. "Heard it didn't go down good."

Bone opens his eyes slowly. He fumbles in a pocket for a Marlboro and draws it to his mouth, cupping his hands to light the cigarette. For a second there's the slightest trace of a tremble in his fingers as he tries steadying the match. Then it is gone.

He leans back in the chair in silence.

"Everything got all fucked up," Dizzy says. "Shit turned real bad."

Twist hears them retell the story but doesn't listen. He stares out the window in silence.

It is only when the Cadillac pulls up to the bay doors that he steps away from the window and draws his nine.

Cuba gets out of the Escalade.

His stare is calm and composed, like everything that just happened went down exactly the way he figured it would. He's got a .45 Magnum stuck inside his waist band and he pulls his shirt over the gun to hide it as he walks around the Cadillac. Twist hears him yelling something to the Game Boys on the sidewalk, and when they hurry to the car he opens a door, jerking a thumb toward the back seat. Hands reach inside and pull out LJ. His head rolls lifelessly from side to side, and his face is pale and colorless. He opens his mouth to speak but no words come out; only a stream of vomit and blood that splatters the front of his shirt as it spills to the sidewalk. The Game Boys lift him toward the door and Twist sees that both legs are red with blood that has soaked his pants from his thighs all the way down to his Reeboks. There's a bloody yellow bandanna wrapped tight around one shattered kneecap but it doesn't slow the blood seeping from other holes in his legs. Twist can see the bodies of two other Skulls in the back seat.

LJ moans softly. When he moves his head Twist can see the traces of tears that have streaked his face.

"Jesus Christ," Dizzy whistles. "That's some messed-up shit."

The door opens with a bang and the two Game Boys struggle to drag LJ into the garage. If the building is staked out already there's no way the cops will miss them carrying him inside. Just another clue that links them to what happened at the Budget Royale. They move him quickly upstairs to one of the bedrooms, leaving a trail of blood across the linoleum. Bone watches as the kids disappear up the stairs, and T. Capone gets up from the table and follows to see what needs to be done.

Cuba comes in a minute later. Dizzy pops open another Bud and hands it to him. He knocks back a swallow and finds a thank you for Dizzy.

"Rasheed's dead," he tells them. "Went back after you guys got out but there wasn't nothing I could do for him. Found LJ moaning his ass off next to him, alongside one of the Guinea gunmen. Finished off the Guinea. Didn't want to be no ambulance but I got Rasheed and Mookie's bodies. Bought us a little time but you know the cops gonna figure it out sooner or later."

Bone nods. "Found Malik a little while ago," he tells him in a hoarse voice. He fingers the label on his bottle and wipes away the beads of condensation forming on the glass, staring at the streaks they leave. "Been dead at least a couple of days."

Cuba's expression doesn't change. "Didn't expect no different," he says. "Anything about Ice?"

Bone shakes his head.

Cuba looks around the kitchen. Nobody moves and none of their expressions change. Back in the front room the Game Boys and lookouts return to the windows and doors, taking guns and pointing them toward the street.

"Don't see no Eddie Dallas," Cuba says. "Where the fuck he at?"

"Eddie's on his way," Dizzy reports. "Called a couple of minutes ago. Just dumping the car."

"Everybody else get back okay from the motel?"

Bone nods his head.

Cuba stands in the doorway across the kitchen from Twist. His mouth is open to say something but he doesn't get the words out before sobs from LJ start from the bedroom, low, hard, and loud enough that they cut off Cuba's words. Twist knows there's nothing any of them can do for him. He needs more than what the garage can give him.

"Cops closing in and you went back for him," Dizzy repeats, shaking his head. "Takes a lot of balls."

Cuba nods slowly with a look that says he didn't really think about it. It was just something he did; nothing more to it than that. His stare holds on Twist like he expects something else but Twist turns away and looks out the window again.

"Got something out in the car I want to show you," Cuba finally says.

He gestures toward the door and starts outside, and the guys in the kitchen get up to follow, with Twist bringing up the rear. A couple of the Game Boys trail behind, unsure and tentative. Cuba looks up and down the street first, then walks to the trunk and stops as the others gather around him. Twist runs a finger along the bullet holes in the metal, feeling the sharp ends of the holes jabbing his skin but he doesn't pull back the fingertips.

Cuba stands at the trunk with his arms folded across his chest, smiling a broad ear to ear grin.

He pops open the trunk. It rises slowly, the hinges creaking until stopping halfway up, and Cuba has to force the trunk the rest of the way to get it fully opened. Everyone crowds forward a step. Twist moves closer and feels the bile burning as it rises from his gut. Inside, duct tape tied around his ankles and wrists and with a dirty rag stuffed inside his mouth, is Sally. His shoulder is red with blood and his face is a pale, sickly white that stands out in marked contrast to the blackness of the trunk. His white shirt is ripped and torn and a crumpled jacket is rolled into a ball that props up his head, keeping space between him and the spare tire. He doesn't say anything and his eyes are shut, but he is still alive. Twist can see his chest rising and falling beneath the bloody shirt. His breathing is hard and forced, and each breath makes his body shake and quiver.

Bone smiles.

"They left him behind," Cuba says with his own grin. "Guess all that talk about honor they be talking about is bullshit when bullets start flying, huh?"

Twist shakes his head but Bone cuts him off before he has time to find his voice. "How'd you get him?"

Cuba shrugs. "Found him hunched over the wheel in the front seat, crying like a little bitch," he says.

"He hurt bad?"

"Took one in the shoulder," Cuba says. "Got cuts from the glass but didn't see nothing else when I shoved him back here."

"We can't keep him here," Twist tries. "It's only a matter of time before the cops start banging on the door."

"Don't need a lot of time to do what I got to do to him," Cuba replies.

"Gonna enjoy watching that," Bone says.

He gets some of the Game Boys to pull Sally out of the Escalade and drag him inside the building before anyone on the street can see what is happening. They carry him across the asphalt and disappear inside the garage.

Cuba forces down the trunk and tosses the key ring to another one of the kids, telling him to drop the bodies of Mookie and Rasheed and then make the car disappear.

"I don't like this," Twist says, shaking his head.

"No surprise in that," Bone says with a sneer.

Cuba shoots him a look. "There ain't nothing to like no more. This ain't no different from what you got going on with the Guinea up on the third floor. You the one who was telling us it was an eye for an eye," he says. "This ain't no different than that."

It's totally different, Twist thinks. What Cuba will do to Sally and why he'll do it aren't the same reasons they took Valentine off the street. Cuba wants something more. Twist imagines a picture of Cuba standing over the guy, twisting a switchblade inside his ear and laughing about it.

Bone starts back to the building. He clamps a hand on Cuba's shoulder and gives him a squeeze. "This changes things," Bone says with a grim smile.

"Giving them the kind of war they didn't expect," Cuba says.

◆ ◆ ◆

LJ's sobs carry from the bedroom. They are louder now and each one of them sitting at the kitchen table can feel the pain in his voice. Twist lights a Camel and drops the match inside one of the empty Bud bottles, waiting again for the quiet between cries.

"Somebody shut that fucking guy's mouth!" Cuba yells. "He's bawling like a goddamn bitch. Give him something so he shuts the fuck up!"

T. Capone comes back into the room with one of the Game Boys a step behind. Twist knows the kid. He's about eleven or twelve; one of the quieter ones who's there to get cigarettes or pick up pizzas when they can't get Dominos to deliver to the neighborhood. He's somebody's brother.

T. Capone slides into a chair. "Gave him some vodka and a little coke. Nothing else we got here's gonna work on making him feel better."

Another sob from the bedroom wails through the garage and even Twist looks up from the table.

"I'm going in there and putting a fucking bullet in his head myself if he don't shut up," Cuba bitches. "Listened to him all the way over here in the car. Now I got to listen to this shit again when I'm trying to sit here for five minutes and get my head together."

" We got to do something," somebody says from the living room.

"Like what?"

"Got to get him to the hospital," the kid says, looking at the guys around the table. His eyes are wide, filled with terror and fear. "Get him a doctor

"He needs help."

Twist shakes his head slowly. They've already got the two Skulls who were with Ice handcuffed to beds in Beth Israel, and there are two more corpses wearing Skull in the back seat of the Cadillac. They have left too many bodies, and the last thing they need to do is bring someone else to the hospital; it's the kind of trail that anybody with a badge can follow back to the garage. The cops are going to show up soon enough; they will need to vacate the garage and cover their tracks before that happens.

"No way," he says simply. "Can't be done."

"He gonna die if you don't!"

"You want to see a doctor then you put him in one of the cars outside and get down to that hospital in Perth Amboy," Twist snaps. "Take Route 1 and do the speed limit all the way there. Don't do nothing to draw attention from anybody on the road. Tell any doctors in the ER who ask that it was a drive-by."

"Tell them you think it was a bunch of spics," Cuba says.

"Say he was minding his own business, standing on the street, and somebody drove by and gunned him down, but you didn't see nothing."

"It's forty minutes," the kid says. "Beth Israel's maybe five to ten across town with traffic."

"Take him there and you'll have cops up your ass before you even get past the emergency room doors," Twist tells him. "Do it in Perth Amboy and nobody will figure out it happened here."

"Not right away," Bone says. "Buys us more time."

Twist nods. "By that time you're out of there and on your way home. Won't have to worry about no cops knocking on the door with questions we ain't got time to answer."

The kid looks at Twist. Fear and panic are still written in his face, and he's frozen in place. "It's gonna take a long time."

Bone shoots him a look. "So you better leave now, huh?"

◆ ◆ ◆

They are sitting around the table or slumped in spots throughout the kitchen and it's quiet again. What's there between them now has nothing to do with toughness or cool and everyone knows it. Dizzy chain smokes Camels as he holds his head off the table with his hands and pops open Buds, handing them to whoever wants one. T. Capone rocks back and forth in his chair and lets his stare go from one guy to another. He's the only one who has nothing to say and offers no opinion about the next steps they should take. Twist slips on a pair of Ray-Bans and lets his eyes close slowly, blocking out everything around him. Cuba is on his feet, tearing through the cabinets on a seek-and-destroy mission to find the last bottle of Jack Daniel's that he swears is stashed somewhere. He slams open another cabinet door, reaching inside and knocking a glass off the counter as he leans forward. It shatters on the floor but Cuba ignores it as he grabs the bottle hidden in the back of the cabinet.

Bone is solemn and quiet. He's had nothing to say since they came inside from the Cadillac. He drinks his Bud and takes in everything. His quiet has nothing to do with a search for words and thoughts hidden deep in places nobody else can get to; it's the quiet that says he is somehow happy about the way everything has worked out.

Twist reaches for his cigarette pack but finds it empty. The last one hangs from Dizzy's mouth. He gets up and goes across the room for another pack from the counter.

The door opens with a bang and Eddie Dallas walks in slowly. He looks tired, his eyes are red, and his shoulders sag as he walks. There's no animation in his movements; no groove in the way he carries himself, and no bounce in his step. Heads turn as he goes straight to the refrigerator, with a slow, silent nod toward the guys sitting at the table. Nobody speaks as he takes a Bud but all eyes are fixed on him.

He turns.

"Everything okay?" Twist asks, tipping down his shades. "How you doing?"

Eddie flips off the bottle cap with his thumb and draws in a deep breath. "Good as can be expected," he mutters. "Considering the shit that just went down."

"Wasn't pretty," Dizzy says, picking at the label on his bottle with a thumbnail.

"Fucking bloody is what it was," Eddie says. "Shit's fucked up."

"It was bad," somebody else says.

"Couldn't have been much worse," Eddie says.

"You know this is your fault," Cuba says with a sneer from across the room. He holds the bottle of Jack Daniel's in his hands but his stare goes right to Eddie and stays there. "You figured that out, right?"

Twist glares at him.

Eddie turns a shoulder and walks back to the counter, taking a fresh pack of Camels and a book of matches. He unwraps the cellophane on the pack and breaks the foil seal but doesn't draw out a cigarette. He taps the pack against the counter then sticks it in a pocket. Cuba follows with the Jack Daniel's in hand, staying right with him.

"You hear me?" he says. "You fucked up. Both of you."

Eddie turns to look at him. "I heard you," he says evenly. "Didn't think you whispered."

"You fucked up," Cuba says again.

"You fucked up," Twist says, pointing a finger at Cuba. "You're the one who wanted this. You had to do it face-to-face like this, and now we got guys dead."

"There wouldn't be nobody dead if you had listened and called this thing off the first time you got the idea," Eddie adds. "You wanted this."

"Lucky there aren't more corpses," Twist says.

"Did it the way you first put it together," Eddie says, "none of us would be here."

Twist nods. "Lucky we aren't all dead."

The words have no effect. "You didn't do your fucking jobs. Now we got bodies that don't need to be dead and cops gonna be asking questions about them Guineas scattered all around that motel parking lot," Cuba shoots back, putting the bottle down. "That's because of you. Both of you."

"Your opinion," Twist says, "doesn't mean shit just because you say so."

Cuba glares at him, the anger and agitation in his expression showing. His forehead is wet with sweat and the veins in his neck stand out against his skin. He starts to say something else but stops himself before he can get out the words.

Twist waits while it settles with him.

Eddie takes a swig of beer and leans back against the counter.

The room is quiet and Twist can feel the edge that hangs on each word. That feeling comes again, like the one that came at Maria's apartment with Hector. It starts low inside, tightening in his crotch and rushing upward fast and furiously, leaving him light-headed and dizzy with a rush of adrenaline and speed. When it washes over him everything becomes so clear that he is suddenly aware of how badly his world has turned. How nothing that has been lost will ever come back.

He hears Cuba saying, "You fucking feel me?," but the voice is distant. Twist stands up and walks toward the other room, but then turns around and comes back again. It's like he is considering the steps he needs to take to walk away, but cannot decide whether he wants to take them. He turns and goes back to the kitchen table.

Twist keeps his back to Cuba while ripping at the foil on his pack of Camels. The whole time he thinks, "Fuck you, Cuba."

"Whole thing was a stupid idea," Eddie says. "Didn't see the point of meeting these guys this way. Wasn't the way to negotiate."

Twist tosses the cellophane on the counter and slowly draws out a cigarette. He shakes his head and looks to Eddie. "Malik's body turned up," he says evenly. "Haven't found Ice but you know he's dead too."

"Nobody knows that for sure," T. Capone tries from his seat at the table.

Even Bone shakes his head.

Eddie slams his Bud bottle on the counter. The beer foams from the top, dripping down the sides and spilling over his fingers before pouring to the floor. Eddie glances at it but doesn't move to clean it up. His eyes hold on Twist instead, looking beyond his words and examining the expression on his face.

Then Eddie turns to face Cuba.

"What you got to say about that?" he asks.

"That's your fault too," Cuba says simply with a shrug. "Guy was probably alive until this whole thing went bad."

Eddie's braids fly back and forth as he shakes his head.

"You fucked up," Cuba says again, harder now.

Eddie shakes a little, and although there's nothing more to it than adrenaline, the movement brings a smile to Cuba's face. He takes that as a turning point. An advantage in what is going on between them. Twist turns and sees how much Eddie's stare has suddenly narrowed.

Eddie takes a short step closer to Cuba and faces him directly.

Nothing is said but the challenge is there.

"Don't get in my face, nigger."

Eddie doesn't move.

Cuba plants a hand in Eddie's chest and shoves him backward a step. "You the one who fucked up. How often I got to say it before you fucking understand that?"

There is no backing off. Eddie holds his stance and pushes Cuba's hand away from his chest with one hand, and pokes a finger in his face. "Only person around here who fucked up is you," he says. "You just too fucking stupid to figure that out."

Cuba laughs but there's a hollowness to it. "Fuck you, Eddie."

Eddie shakes his head. "Fuck you, bitch."

Twist waits for the words to pass but they don't.

He sees that neither will back off. What is there inches quickly into something different. As he takes off his Ray-Bans and tosses them to the table, Twist rises and starts toward them just as Eddie's open hand crosses quickly toward Cuba. The slap is hard and it turns Cuba's face around, the same way Ice's hand turned Sally's head in the Marriott parking lot. It hangs there and the room turns, changing before the sound of Eddie's hand against Cuba's skin has even stopped echoing.

Twist stops.

Everything that happens is slow and dreamlike but there is no pause in the action. Nothing stops once Eddie has put it into motion and Twist can't change it in time. Cuba's hand is quick. He reaches for the butt of the Magnum in his waistband and pulls it free, leveling it at Eddie's head in one quick motion. There is nothing different about Cuba's expression and no change in his eyes as he straightens his elbow and aims.

The gun barrel is the last thing Eddie Dallas sees before Cuba pulls the trigger.

For a moment there is nothing but the explosion.

The sound fills the room.

A small dot appears on Eddie's forehead, growing larger as dark red blood spurts out of the hole in a thick stream. In an instant it becomes a gaping hole that gets wider with each breath. Eddie staggers backward, hands reaching out toward Cuba and the gun but his legs can't hold him upright any longer. His eyes are open but there is nothing by the time he hits the linoleum.

The noise fills the room and takes a long time to disappear, and the kitchen is filled with the sharp, heavy smell of cordite. Cuba's expression doesn't change as his arm drops to his side.

Twist takes a step toward Eddie and stops.

"Jesus," Dizzy whispers. "The fuck did you do?"

No one else moves.

"He fucked up," Cuba says. "Ain't no difference between him being dead at the motel because he fucked up, or dead here for the same reason."

Twist's mouth goes dry and a numbness spreads quickly over him as he stares at Eddie's body. Blood flows from his wound and pools on the floor, but Eddie's heart has already stopped beating and soon the blood will slow to a trickle. Twist feels his own breath, shallow and hard. He feels distanced, unsure of his own thoughts and movements.

There is no time to consider anything else. There is a sudden surge of emotion and a reaction without any thought to the consequences.

Twist lunges for Cuba.

The suddenness of his attack catches Cuba off guard. Twist gets his hand on the gun and yanks it out of Cuba's fingers, flinging it across the room where it slides on the floor and gets wedged beneath the stove. Twist drives him backward through the kitchen and slams him hard into the refrigerator with a shoulder pressed into Cuba's chest. The refrigerator rocks and lifts, and inside the bottles and cans shift and fall on the shelves as Cuba and Twist wrestle and punch. Twist presses a forearm hard against Cuba's throat and tries driving it through his neck, using his other hand to slam Cuba's head against the refrigerator door. He can feel fingers raking his face and smell Cuba's hot breath on his own but he doesn't stop. He rams his palm into Cuba's mouth and then brings his forehead hard into Cuba's nose. He can feel the blood and bone against his skin and pain as his skin splits open, but he keeps Cuba pinned against the refrigerator and brings a knee solidly into his balls.

The shot to the nose already has him disoriented and Twist's grip on his throat leaves him sucking for air. The blow to the balls staggers him.

For just a second the fight drains out of Cuba. His body softens and a tear comes to his eye. His breathing turns shallow and rapid and he chokes back a breath, although nothing else changes in his expression as he fights to regain his cool. But the three or four seconds he loses in that moment are all that Twist needs.

By the time Cuba has sucked up his courage again Twist has his 9mm out of his pants and jammed into the flesh underneath Cuba's jaw.

"You're out of control," he says. "You're a fucking asshole."

He can feel himself shaking as he presses his forearm against Cuba's throat. The look in Cuba's eyes is different than it was before; it isn't the same way he watched Eddie Dallas tremble or how he stared down the Italians in the motel room. It is a look of unbridled rage that Twist has never seen before.

"You cocksucker," Cuba coughs, his eyes watering. "Who the fuck you think you are, pulling a gun on me?"

"Don't!" Bone shouts. "Don't do it!"

"Who the fuck you think you are?" Cuba repeats.

"I'm the same man I always been," Twist says.

"And who the fuck is that?"

"The man who gonna jack a bullet in your throat."

There's no give in Cuba's stance, even with the gun in his chin. He sucks in a breath. "Fuck you, Twist!"

Twist pushes the gun a little deeper into his throat. "Who says you got the right to pull the trigger on Eddie?

"You're the one who wanted this meeting," Twist says. "You fucked up. Not me. Not Eddie. You're the one who should be fucking dead on the floor right now."

"You motherfucker," Cuba says, low and even. He takes a step forward but Twist jams the nose of the gun into his throat and stops him. "You're a dead man."

Twist shakes his head. "I'm the one holding the gun."

"Ain't gonna have that gun in your hands forever!"

"Don't need it forever. Just need it long enough to put a bullet through your neck."

Somebody gets a hand on Twist's wrist but he manages to keep the 9mm stuck under Cuba's chin. There are voices in his ear but he can't make out words. Guys pull at him and try angling between them but they can't move Twist. He thinks about taking advantage of the opportunity. The chance came and went with Bone. He realizes now that nothing should keep him from doing what he knows is the right thing.

"I'm gonna kill you, motherfucker," Cuba says. As more hands and bodies get between them his rage grows. "You're dead, nigger!"

"Be living longer than you bitch."

"You be dead like your bitch friend on the floor."

"Ain't the time," Bone hollers. Twist can feel his breath on his face and his arms tight around his shoulders, pulling him away from Cuba, trying to get him back across the room. Bone moves him back a foot and puts himself between the two of them. "Got to chill the fuck out."

"You don't want to do it," Dizzy says. "This ain't what we should be doing!"

Cuba strains and struggles to get at Twist. The anger carries him now and the gun doesn't worry him. "You better pull the trigger while you got the chance," he says. "Better make sure you kill me now!"

"Gonna do to me what you did to Eddie, you limp dick pussy?" Twist says. "That make you a man?"

Cuba roars with anger. He tries breaking free to get after Twist again but there are too many hands holding him back. He bucks and kicks but can't get closer, no matter how hard he struggles. Twist feels the 9mm being turned away from Cuba's chin, pushed toward the ceiling, and with all the hands on his arm he can't hold the aim any longer.

"Ain't solving nothing this way," Bone yells. "You got to chill out!"

Slowly Twist feels the fight draining from him and the uselessness of everything sets in. The struggle loses its value, and he lets the gun be pulled away. Without the gun in his hand the pushing and shoving slows, and the bodies relax, easing off the fight. The guys who separate them maintain the distance, and nobody walks away.

Cuba stares at Twist through the crowd.

"You and me ain't done," he says. "This ain't over."

"I'm here," Twist returns, staring back at him. "You want a piece of me, you know where to find me."

Cuba nods. "Count on it. Be looking for you—"

Bone gets between them, pushing them in opposite directions like a referee sending two heavyweights back to their corners. He shoots Cuba a stare until some of the fire burns out of his expression and he drops his head. "Enough of this bullshit," Bone says. "This ain't the time. Not now."

Dizzy's grip relaxes and he lets go of Twist's shirt and shoulders. Twist eases the 9mm out of somebody's grip and slips it back in his pants, turning a shoulder to the crowd and moving away. Across the kitchen Cuba pushes off the hands holding him and turns to the cabinet, grabbing the Jack Daniel's bottle off the counter and filling a drinking glass. He downs it in one swallow without saying anything to the guys whispering in his ears.

Eddie's body lays lifeless on the floor.

"Too much got to be done now to waste it killing each other," Bone says, harder this time. When Cuba turns to face him he stays with that stare for a long time until he sees what he's looking for in Cuba's expression. "Later, you got a score to settle, you got plenty of time to do it," he says. "When this is done you two can deal with your shit."

Cuba nods slowly.

Bone turns for Twist but Twist ignores him. The numbness sweeping over him is complete, and whatever thoughts and feelings he has are disjointed and fragmented. He goes back to the table and sits down, lighting another Camel and blowing away the smoke without a word. He figures that Bone sees killing Eddie Dallas as part of a bad afternoon and nothing more. No attachment and no emotion. A couple of kids carry Eddie's body from the room and Twist watches, silently mourning his friend while thinking about how much he has lost this day. He wonders what they will do with his body and which one of them is going to be the one to break the news to Eddie's mother and sisters.

Slowly the others drift back to their places. Only Cuba stands, his back against the counter, filling his glass again with Jack Daniel's.

"What's next?" T. Capone asks, looking around from face-to-face. "Where do we go from here?"

"We got them good now," Dizzy says in a voice looking for reassurance. He says it like taking out a couple of the Italians at the motel and then grabbing Sally is a momentum changer, like making a free throw after the other team on the court has run off twenty straight points. "Makes things different, right?"

"This takes it to the next level," Bone says as he slides into his chair. He leans into the table. "Changes things."

Dizzy looks up. "What you talking about, the next level?"

"We gonna give them something else to remember," he says.

"How we do that?"

"First things first," Bone says.

He turns to Twist. "You gonna do that Guinea upstairs. Do it right now. That's the first thing we do."

He says it like that, with no emotion and nothing else in his voice. Just another fact. Something else that has to be done.

Twist takes another drag on the Camel. He looks up to see a grin breaking onto Cuba's face.

"Time to show we mean business," Bone says. He turns to each of them for understanding but comes back to Twist. "Eye for an eye. For Malik."

"Do it and get him the fuck out of here," Cuba says, forcing a grin. "Then I get to play with my hostage.

"Ain't gonna be bringing him no newspapers and coffee," he adds.

Bone looks at Twist. "You got a problem with that?"

Twist takes a deep breath and holds the smoke inside. He looks at the clock. It's close to six, and although it's only been a few hours since his day blew to pieces, it feels like the day has lasted forever. Twist thinks about Michael Valentine in the upstairs bedroom and feels the weight of all those minutes that he's lived while Malik and Ice have been dead. He sees Eddie Dallas dead on the floor when he closes his eyes, and wonders how he could have prevented anything that just happened. Is taking Valentine's life an even exchange, he wonders, that will really change anything?

If only things had been different. If only he was stronger.

If only he could have walked away with Maria before it got to this.

Bone is saying something else to him but Twist shakes head. There is nothing more to say, and nothing he wants to hear.

"You got a problem pulling the trigger, you let me know," Cuba says, pouring himself more Jack Daniel's. "I got no problem doing it if you can't find it in you."

"I don't need nothing from you," Twist says quietly, standing up.

"Good," Bone says, looking again at Cuba instead of Twist. "That'll send those fucking Guineas a message they ain't gonna forget."

CHAPTER FOURTEEN

Twist stands in the second floor bedroom, taking a slow drag on the Camel and watching the street below. Somebody from a different neighborhood would think it is just another boring afternoon on Murray Street. Nothing is happening and that inactivity hides an undercurrent of tension. The sidewalks are empty. None of the neighborhood regulars are around; it's as if they know what's going on and don't want to be there if the cops arrive. Or worse, when the Guineas show up and bullets strafe the houses and street. Guys are hidden in shadows, watching cars, looking for shooters. It could be Dodge City with everyone waiting for the bad guys to come riding into town for a final showdown.

Rocco stands in the doorway behind him.

"Takes balls to do what you did," he says. What's in his voice sounds like respect.

"Standing up to Cuba like that, especially after what he did to Eddie. Ain't too many guys can do that."

Twist says nothing.

That's what happens with guys like Cuba, Twist thinks. All his life too many people let Cuba get away with things that made him believe he was something special. Cuba has heard it so many times he believes it. Cuba thinks he has the kind of power that lets him walk through bullets and do things nobody can stop him from doing; never feeling consequences or the remorse that tears others apart.

When you think you have that, you can go on forever. Twist knows that guys like Cuba don't worry about what happens five minutes into the future.

"You really gonna pull the trigger if it comes to that?" Rocco asks.

"He didn't have a problem pulling the trigger on Eddie," Twist says.

Rocco stares at him. "Yeah, but doing Cuba just like that? You get the chance, you really gonna do it?"

Twist doesn't answer. He stays at the window, taking long drags on the cigarette. Rocco stares quietly, waiting for an answer. Twist doesn't know why it's so important to him or what it will do for him to know the answer.

When nothing comes Rocco finally turns and goes up the stairs to relieve the guard at the third-floor bedroom.

Twist welcomes the solitude and quiet. It is hard enough figuring out the things he's supposed to do and feel without wading through conversations.

He wants time to be alone.

But he can't even have that.

There's a reflection in the glass. It haunts him, like he's supposed to recognize the face of the stranger he sees. He stares at his nine and wonders why the gun finds its way into his hand every time there's trouble. It has gotten too easy, whether outside Maria's apartment or downstairs in the kitchen. It is too convenient and too quick of a solution, like the kind Cuba finds every chance he gets. There's a faint smell of cordite and gun powder, and the memory of the gun's kick when he squeezed the trigger hours earlier is strong—Twist can still see the expressions the Italians wore when the bullets ripped into them and no matter how long he squeezes his eyes shut that stays with him. Each of their faces is stuck inside his memory, and those corpses belong to him. It's the same way he remembers Eddie Dallas and his last expression.

He wonders if it will happen the same way for Michael Valentine.

Twist takes another drag on the Camel and stares at the stranger's reflection in the window.

◆ ◆ ◆

Twist takes the steps slowly, one at a time.

If he could move any slower just to delay what he has to do, Twist would find some way to do it. He still has no idea how he will pull the trigger on Valentine, and he can't even be certain what his final words should be. All he is sure of is what needs to be done. Cuba's voice is behind him as he walks the stairs to the third floor, bitching loudly that he wants it done before they run out of time and Twist knows he is right about that. Time is short.

The trip up the stairs is familiar, but it is different now.

Every other time Twist had gone up and down there was always another trip in his future. He knew he'd see Valentine again, and just knowing that made the trips different. But the next times are gone.

Rocco nods again as Twist motions to the door.

He enters the room slowly, moving cautiously and carrying an eight pack of Bud bottles. Michael Valentine is on the bed with his back to the wall. His hair hangs long and loose, falling in front of his face when he looks up. He has a short smile. There's not much warmth left to it; the same way Twist figures his own smile has started to drift and fade away. For him it's too tough faking anything any longer.

Twist doesn't wait for the door to close and lock behind him. He goes to the chair and slides it closer to the bed before sitting. Valentine stays on the bed, quiet and cool—measuring Twist's movements and watching everything with that careful stare.

Twist hands him one of the Buds without asking. When he sits back in the chair Twist can feel the 9mm jabbing into his back. He knows that if he wants, he can take it quickly in his hand, steady his arm, and squeeze off two or three shots and finish this. If that's what he wants to do.

He wonders again if Valentine has any sense that everything is about to end.

"Hey," he says.

"How'd it go?"

"Bad," Twist says in a voice that comes out strained. "It went bad."

Valentine's expression is beaten and worn out from endless hours alone and this news doesn't do anything for him. Twist stares at Valentine and thinks for a second that he could be looking in a mirror. There's nothing in Valentine's face that he can't find in his own.

"Heard all the noise and yelling," Valentine says evenly, popping off the cap on the bottle with his thumb. "Didn't take much to figure that out."

Twist stares at the floor. "Got that right."

"Bad?"

"It was quick and bloody," Twist says, finally looking up. "And it left a lot of bodies on both sides."

"Heard a shot downstairs too..."

Twist just stares back without answering.

Valentine doesn't say anything but in that stare Twist sees that whatever hope he had is gone now too. There are no more dreams and nothing left except the job that Twist is there to finish. He realizes time has run out.

He takes a heavy swallow from the bottle and says nothing.

"Was it anybody I've seen coming in here?" Valentine asks without raising his head.

Twist shakes his head. None of the Skull names mean anything to Valentine; the same way none of the Guinea names have meaning to Twist. He thinks that if he bothered spending time describing Rasheed or Eddie Dallas or even Mookie there might be a link for Valentine, but he knows that they don't really matter. They barely held a passing connection to Valentine's world and none of them are anyone he would give a second thought to if he weren't locked in the bedroom.

"You probably don't know too many of the guys around here anyway, huh?"

"Just faces. No names. At least nothing that sticks," Valentine mumbles, sipping his beer. "Not like anybody took the time to make formal introductions."

Twist lights up a cigarette and leans back in the chair, watching Valentine's expression while trying to figure out the thoughts going through his head. He's still aware of the nine, conscious of how it feels, and wonders if Valentine can see that in his own expression.

Valentine lets the moment pass before asking, "How much time we got?"

Twist hesitates. He thinks about his answer and decides instead that he won't lie to Valentine if he doesn't have to. It's not worth the effort trying to keep that lie alive any longer. He owes Valentine at least that much.

"Later," he says, looking away. "You got time."

"Just not enough time," Valentine says. "Not the kind of time I need, you know?"

Twist nods, thinking that he wouldn't mind having back the time he's lost either.

"I'm glad it's you," Valentine says in a quiet voice. "Glad you're the one pulling the trigger and not one of the other guys. There's something right about you being the one to do it."

"Says who?" Twist asks. Valentine doesn't answer and Twist lets it go. The truth won't gonna change nothing, he thinks grimly. Valentine knowing what Twist has to do won't make the job any harder, or change things between them.

It's something that has to be done and there's no way around that. Some things can't be stopped once they're started.

"I had one of your guys get me some paper and a pencil," Valentine says, reaching into the stack of newspapers on the corner of the bed. "I wanted to write down some stuff, you know? Maybe leave something meaningful for Angelina and the baby. Something that will last. Kind of tell them to hang in there and be strong after I'm gone."

Twist understands.

"What I'm thinking is that you can get it to them for me," he says. "After everything, you know?"

Twist shakes his head quickly. "That ain't gonna happen."

"Why not?"

"Ain't gonna happen."

"All I want you to do is get it to her. I'm not asking for anything else. You don't have to stay for coffee or talk about the fucking weather."

"Why can't I mail it?"

"Need to know it gets to her."

"How am I supposed to do it?" Twist asks. "Hop in the car and drive over there? You think I get five minutes if somebody in your neighborhood sees me standing on your doorstep, ringing the bell? They'll find me six weeks later stuffed in some oil drum locked away in Giaccolone's garage, or chopped up in pieces up on South Mountain.

"Or the same way they found Malik."

"It won't be like that," Valentine says. "I'll give you the phone number. You can call first."

"So she can save all the guys in your neighborhood the trouble of running down the street to get me?" Twist asks. "You figure she'll even give me more than ten seconds on the phone?"

"You explain who you are and what you have. She'll listen."

Twist imagines that conversation with Valentine's daughter. Explaining to her that it was his idea to take her father off the street, then telling her that he was also the one who got to put the bullet in his head. But that it was okay because her father felt comfortable and trusted him to get her the letter.

"Can't do it."

"You got to."

"I can't."

"It's important to me," Valentine says in that quiet voice again, looking hard at Twist. "There's nobody else I can trust. Nobody I can depend on. You got to do it for me, Twist.

"You owe me that much, right?"

He holds out the papers to Twist. There are only a couple of loose leaf notebook pages, covered with writing on both sides of each sheet; and he keeps them in Twist's face, waiting for a decision. There's determination in his face; a persistence that doesn't leave.

Twist finally reaches for them, wondering if the Italians gave Malik a chance to write his own farewell notes.

"You got to promise me she'll get this," Valentine says, staring hard into Twist's eyes as he holds his grip on the papers. "You make that promise."

"I'll do it," Twist says. "Got my word."

"It's important."

"I said I'd do it."

Michael Valentine lets go of the papers but keeps his eyes on Twist.

The silence again swallows the room as they retreat into their thoughts. Twist folds the papers neatly in half and puts them on the floor beneath his chair, still wondering how he can keep that promise. He's thinking about what he could say to Valentine's daughter. Just one more obligation, he thinks; something else he's got to do. He lights another Camel while Valentine drains the last drops of Bud from his bottle.

After a while, Valentine says, "You know, dying ain't gonna be the hardest thing.

"I can handle the bullets and the pain," he says. "What's been tough is thinking how I won't be around for the kid. Leaving him and Angelina alone. Knowing that is hard, you know?"

Twist is silent. There's a lot he can add to it, most of it firsthand experience about losing people you care about. He still hasn't learned all the ins and outs of Valentine's world, but Twist thinks he can tell him a little bit more about going through life alone and what it feels like. He knows about scars and the things he never had; the father who left, the dead brothers who are now only memories, and the mother who was never around for him; losing people in your family and not being able to stop it from happening again and again. Thinking that you're one of the good guys but realizing after a while that you're not. That is like a knife stuck between his ribs that never disappears.

He knows how bad it can fuck up your head if you keep it inside and never let it go.

But he keeps those thoughts to himself and says nothing.

Twist looks at his watch and gets that tense, edgy feeling again. It comes often; so much now that it feels like it has never left. There are voices talking to him as he sits there. They call out to him, reminding him how he can change lives and make things different, if that's what he wants. The same way he can put that 9mm to Valentine's head and change each of their worlds, he can just as easily go downstairs and take out Cuba and Bone and create a different kind of change. The only unknown is whether that makes it better or worse. Twist knows that no matter what he decides, nothing is ever going to be the same, at least not like it was. And the same way he can put himself in somebody else's life and change everything they have, everything he owns will be different too.

It will all keep changing somehow, no matter what he does.

He starts to say something about that to Michael Valentine, like he has to explain the things he sees and how it affects his point of view, but nothing comes out. The words get stuck and Twist just lets them fall away.

It doesn't matter.

Valentine looks at him and forces a smile.

"So?"

Twist looks up.

"So? What's next?" Valentine asks, popping off another bottle cap. "What do you do after today?"

Twist shrugs. "Haven't thought about it much."

"See yourself staying around here much longer?"

Who the fuck knows.

"I don't know," he answers. "Nothing left for me here no more."

"So what do you do?"

"Maybe I just get in the car and keep driving until I can't go no further."

"Think someplace else is gonna be better?"

Can't be worse.

"You got family?"

Twist just shakes his head without an answer.

"What about your lady?"

Twist's grin comes out forced and sad. "She's not a part of what I got no more. At least not the way I want her to be," he says, taking a deep breath and then another drag on the cigarette. "Guess I should have done a better job of holding on to all the things that mattered. Paid attention to the things that were mine, you know?"

"You got a chance to fix it? Make it better?"

Twist knows that chances like that are gone forever.

He shakes his head. "It's too late."

"Too bad you can't go back and make it better," Valentine offers.

Twist says simply, "Lost that opportunity a long time ago. Nothing left to make better no more. I just want to break even."

"What about the Skulls?"

Twist looks down at his sneakers. Runs a hand through his hair. "There's nothing there no more either."

Michael Valentine stares at him through the cigarette smoke. There's a little more to his expression than the words give away. "So why are you still in it? If that's the way it is, why don't you get out?"

Twist laughs and sips his beer.

"What's the matter?"

"Think it's that easy? Nothing happens like that," Twist says, snapping his fingers. "You think if you decided to call it quits a guy like Giaccolone's gonna let you go, no matter what you mean to him or what you say? You think you'd get that kind of chance? You in for life. Ain't nothing changing that except death or jail."

"It's different for me."

"Ain't no different," Twist says. "Same for you and me."

"At least you got the chance to do something," Valentine says. "I ran out of chances when you guys took me off the street and put me in this room."

Twist lets it go quietly. He crushes the butt under a Nike and reaches for another. He shuts his eyes for a second and thinks that if he concentrates hard enough he can hear Cuba's voice downstairs, bitching and complaining and he focuses on that instead of thinking about what Valentine is saying. Valentine sits in quiet thought; if he can hear Cuba he doesn't let on. He sips his beer and then runs his hands through his hair, smoothing it back and retying the ponytail with a rubber band. Twist thinks he does that the same way other people bite their nails or pull their hair.

When Valentine speaks again his voice is so quiet that Twist can barely hear him. "Maybe you and me need the same thing."

"What's that?" Twist asks.

"Maybe what you need is to get out of here the same way I need to get out," Valentine says, choosing his words carefully. "You and me need to find a way out of this building. A way to get out for good. Start over, you know?"

Twist looks at him. "What are you talking about?"

"I'm talking about you and me getting the fuck out of here. Out of this room and out of this building," he says.

"What?"

"Getting free."

"What the fuck is that going to do?" Twist shoots back.

"It gets us new lives. Gives us a shot to start over."

Valentine looks at him with an expression that says what he's talking about is so obvious Twist should have it figured out on his own. A look that says he can see it all so clearly that it surprises him Twist misses it. "I'm saying that we take out the next guy who comes through the door. Use his rifle to clear us a path downstairs and out the door," he says. "We do it fast then we disappear so nobody can ever find us."

Twist shakes his head and says, "You're fucking crazy."

"You're the one who's crazy if you can't see that it's our best chance."

"All I see is a dead man looking for hope."

"Don't you see? It's your only shot," Valentine says. "Mine too."

"No way," Twist says, hard and flat. "If you think you can shoot your way out of here like it's some kind of cowboy and Indian movie, you're fucking nuts. It ain't gonna happen because things like that don't happen in the real world. You try it and you get dead real quick.

"It ain't gonna happen."

"It can happen," Valentine says, edging forward on the bed until his feet touch the floor. He looks to Twist for some sign of understanding. "You take out the first guy fast and all of a sudden we got a gun. That"s all we need.

"There's nobody downstairs who's gonna be ready for something like that," he says. "And that's enough to get us through the front door."

The more Valentine talks the more he believes it; working himself into the idea and convincing himself that it makes sense. Twist wonders if Valentine is too far into his explanation to see how fucked up it sounds. It's the kind of dream you come up with when there are no more chances left and no more hope. It's one of desperation.

Twist keeps shaking his head but Valentine pulls him back in.

"Nobody will expect it. It's perfect."

"And what the fuck are we going to do when we get downstairs? What do we do after shooting up the room and taking out all the guys down there?" Twist says. "Go out on the street and keep shooting?"

"Then we get help," Valentine says. "Call some people…"

Twist stares. "No fucking way, Michael."

"Why not?"

"Who are we supposed to call? Who's going to help us?"

Valentine shrugs. "We got my people."

"Ain't no way I can do that. Your buddy Sally and I were already face-to-face today," he says, without mentioning that Sally is now tied up someplace else in the garage. "Even if this idea you got works and we get out on the street, the last thing I'm doing is turning myself over to your people to help me. When they get done cutting and chopping they'll find parts of me mixed together with all the bits and pieces of Ice they never got around to mailing yet."

Valentine shakes his head. "No way that happens."

"What makes you think it's even something I want to do?" Twist says. "What's in it for me?"

"You can get out of here," Valentine says. "Get in your car and just keep driving. Never come back."

"You're fucking crazy! It'll never work."

"It's a shot. Your only shot, and mine too," Valentine says. "You don't take it now there's no way you'll ever get that same kind of chance again.

"It's the only shot you got."

Twist takes a sip from the bottle, slowly shaking his head as Valentine talks. He crosses his arms across his chest and sits back straight in the chair. "It's not gonna happen."

"Why not?"

"Because it ain't, that's why."

"What's so important about staying here with these guys?" Valentine asks with a piercing stare. "You don't get out of here, you'll be dead too. Maybe it won't be a bullet that does it. Maybe it's a cop or a jealous boyfriend or some punk in a drive-by. Maybe it don't even matter how it happens. But it happens.

"The way I see it, the only shot you and me have is through that door together."

Twist just shrugs. "That's the way you see it."

"That's the way it is."

Valentine goes on about what they can do once they get past the guy at the door. How they can go out a second floor window or pick off the Skulls one at a time as they come up the stairs. He's full of possibilities and gaining enthusiasm—the more he talks, the more the plan excites him. Twist hears the words but there's no weight to them, nothing that means anything. He stares into Valentine's eyes, looking for something in his expression that will give him away and make it all bullshit.

He's not sure what he expects, but Twist figures that something has to be there and it has to show.

But there is nothing. Michael Valentine keeps talking like his plan is real, trying to convince Twist to buy into it.

Twist hears it in his voice and there is enough passion in his words to be convincing. There are possibilities. There is curiosity. He knows what Valentine is talking about, and knows all about the same kind of dreams. Sometimes late at night he would lie in bed with Maria, holding her tight, and talk about what it would be like to get away and start his life all over again. They would talk about second chances and new beginnings. The way Valentine goes on about it triggers those conversations and brings back the memories.

He knows it could never happen, but there's something in Valentine's voice that offers hope.

"You're fucking crazy," Twist says again.

Valentine shakes his head. "It's not that crazy that it can't be done."

"You're dreaming about something that won't ever work," Twist says. "Not the way you got it figured."

"You got a better way?"

"It's a million to one. What kind of odds are those?"

"It's a chance," he answers. "The only one you and me got left."

A chance, Twist says again to himself.

It is then that he hears Cuba and everything turns. His voice is loud and clear and Twist knows he will be coming up the stairs; ready to finish Twist's obligation if it hasn't been done, so he can go on to the next hostage. All the opportunities Twist has ever had and lost come back at him in that moment.

There's a finality in that realization.

Valentine is off the bed and on his feet. His voice is a hoarse whisper, urgent but strong. "We got to do it now."

Twist looks at him without moving.

"It can't wait," Valentine says, hurried and forced.

"Twist!" Cuba's voice calls from downstairs.

"You take him out as soon as he walks in the door," Valentine says. There's a purpose now in his movement; Twist hasn't seen that kind of spark since they wrestled him into the SUV. "He comes two steps inside and you put a bullet in his head. I'll go for the other guy as soon as you drop this one. It's over before they know it."

Twist still doesn't move.

"Goddamn it!' Valentine hisses. "It's all you fucking got!"

"Don't even got that," Twist says.

"What the fuck are you talking about?"

Twist reaches into his back pocket and pulls out a slim leather wallet. Slowly and carefully he opens the billfold and picks out a picture from between the plastic sleeves, twenties, and fifties folded inside. He puts the wallet back in his pocket but holds onto the picture. He stares at it for a moment, smoothing a wrinkled corner, then takes two small steps toward Valentine and pushes it at him.

"Take a look at this," Twist says.

Cuba's voice carries upstairs and they hear him snapping an order at one of the Game Boys in the hallway. But Twist goes on, paying no attention to the voice coming closer.

"That guy Malik," Twist says, looking at the picture, "He's the one you nabbed off the street. The guy at the liquor store, remember?"

Valentine looks back at him. "This ain't the time for it, Twist! No time for show and tell games!"

"I want to know if this guy in the picture is the guy you pulled out of the liquor store parking lot," Twist says.

"How the fuck should I remember?"

Twist stares at him. The gun is suddenly in his hand and he steadies it on Valentine. "You telling me you don't remember him? Or you telling me that one dead nigger looks just like the next one?"

Valentine hears Cuba's voice as it carries up the stairs and he turns back to Twist with a jerk. He takes the picture from Twist's hand.

"That the guy?" Twist asks again. "Is that Malik?"

"Didn't know his name."

"Is that him?"

"Yeah, so what if it is," Valentine says with a quick glance at the photo. "What difference does it make? You and me both know what he looks like. The only difference is that I didn't know his name when we took him out of the lot."

Twist doesn't answer. He takes back the picture.

"So what? What's the big deal?"

"That was my brother," Twist says.

The color drains out of Valentine's face. His mouth drops and his stare widens, but no words come out. The silence between them is heavy.

"Jesus Christ," he finally whispers. "This isn't about the Skulls, is it?"

"Never was," Twist says matter-of-factly. "The minute Malik turned up missing everything changed."

"But—"

Twist shrugs and forces a smile. "I'm sorry about all the guys who got offed. Things like that happen, you know? It's part of the game. There is something important going on there that's got to be resolved, but this got personal for me," he says. "And when that happened none of that other stuff mattered. Malik was all I had left. The only thing that meant something to me."

He has the 9mm in his hand, checking the clip and turning it over in his hand before raising it in Valentine's face. Valentine stares at the gun, lost and afraid now. For the first time it comes to him that he has run out of chances.

"You're really going to kill me, aren't you?" he asks in a quiet voice.

Twist doesn't answer. All he can think about is Malik's body dumped on the street like garbage. That stays with him as he stares at Valentine.

"I don't want to die," Valentine says softly.

"It happens that way sometimes."

"I'm sorry about your brother, Twist, but you know how things like that happen. You said so yourself," Valentine tries slowly, stammering to get out the words. "We're both in the middle of a goddamned war and you know there's gonna be casualties and people getting hurt and there's nothing you or me can do to change that.

"It shouldn't have to be this way between us."

Valentine stares at Twist, desperately looking for understanding. "Everything's got a price. That's nothing you and me don't know."

Twist stares straight ahead without saying anything and Valentine goes on, saying, "You and me, Twist, we're the same kind of guys. All we're trying to do is get ahead in our own way. We're the guys who are supposed to push ahead and live with that kind of shit. It don't make it any easier or any better, but you got to understand that better than anybody else. You're living it and breathing it every day, the same way I am.

"What happened with your brother has nothing to do with you and me. It's nothing personal. It's just one of those things," Valentine tells him. "A couple of hours ago you took out our guys the same way we took out your brother and that's the way it goes. In a fucking war people get hurt. Things happen, lives change, and nothing is ever the same.

"You and me are the same," Valentine says. "Nothing is that different between you and me. In another place, you and me could be friends."

"You want me to believe that?" Twist asks abruptly.

Valentine has backed up, edging closer to the wall but keeping his eyes locked on Twist. "It's the truth."

"Being friends ain't gonna happen," Twist says in a flat voice.

Valentine shakes his head, hurrying his explanation. The footsteps on the stairs are louder now and he turns his head toward the sound. "I'm not talking friendship like that. What I'm talking about is you and me staying alive. Doing for each other. It's all about choices!"

"This is about Malik. And doing what's right," Twist says. "Nothing else matters."

"What matters is getting out of here," Valentine tries desperately. "All we got to do is get out of here and we can start over. We still got that chance."

"There ain't no more chances," Twist says. "No more stories to tell."

The bolts on the door unlock and they both hear Cuba outside.

"Twist!" Cuba yells. "What the fuck's going on?"

Valentine looks to Twist.

"Talk to me, Twist," he pleads. "Please."

The door opens and Cuba steps inside the room. When he does Twist sees his options unfold.

With the gun steady in both hands Twist has the shot if he wants to take it. Valentine is right about that. Cuba pulls up short and there is a flash of fear and surprise in his eyes in that second when their eyes meet—it is the same look he wore briefly in the kitchen. There's a look from Rocco over Cuba's shoulder as he tries figuring out what is happening in front of him. And in that instant something passes between Cuba and Twist before Cuba says, "What is this shit?"

"Fuck you," Twist says.

He squeezes the trigger.

There is no recoil or kick to the gun. Twist holds it steady and level; there is no way to miss. He keeps his aim and fires a second time.

Valentine's chest explodes.

Blood spurts in arcs as Valentine's body slams backward against the wall before lurching and staggering forward a step. There is something new in his face. It might be pain or it could be surprise, it's tough for Twist to know what is there but he doesn't really care. All those things Valentine could be feeling don't matter. Cuba turns toward Valentine, fumbling for his own gun while Valentine's bloody body staggers a few more steps, and Rocco pushes forward into the room with his AR. But by then Michael Valentine is clawing desperately at his shirt, trying to get at the bullets burning through his chest.

There is nothing Cuba or Rocco can do but watch.

Twist has stopped looking. He doesn't want to see Valentine's stare or look into his eyes. He can see it all clearly as he steadies the gun, closes his eyes, and pulls the trigger again.

The third shot blows Valentine backward into the wall.

The blood from his chest sprays in all directions. Valentine stays there for a moment, hung against the plaster, sucking for each breath. His eyes are open but Twist turns his own head away and closes his eyes. There's a short, deep groan that comes out of Valentine's gut, and when he opens his mouth to speak he spits out a stream of dark, thick blood. He turns to look first at Cuba, then Rocco, and finally tries for Twist again. His shoulders sag and his body slides slowly to the floor, leaving a long red smear of blood streaking the wall.

Valentine's corpse drops to the floor and rolls on its side, his eyes still open and his head turned toward Twist. Twist doesn't open his eyes. There's nothing to see.

Cuba and Rocco watch in silence, looking first to Michael Valentine's body and then back to Twist.

Cuba pockets his .45. He stands in the doorway with his hands on his hips, shaking his head and smiling at the corpse. He kicks a Nike into his leg, poking the body with his toe. "This guy don't look like nothing more than a pile of dog shit now, huh?"

That gets a chortle from Rocco.

Twist turns. With his eyes still closed he lifts the 9mm toward the door in one swift, easy motion. Cuba's stare is only a few feet away from the end of the gun and his cool, defiant glare melts. The gun is level; comfortable now in Twist's grip. He squeezes the trigger once. Then again.

The first shot sends Cuba and Rocco flying face first to the floor.

Twist keeps his arms locked and keeps pulling the trigger. There's a jolt with each squeeze of his finger and the sound of the bullets echoes inside his head. The bullets splinter the frame, tear holes in the door, and frag out chunks of plaster from the walls. The empty shell casings pop into the air as Twist empties the clip. He keeps squeezing the trigger but the only sound left is the click in the empty chamber.

Cuba is on the floor, his eyes open wide. Slowly he draws himself to his knees and pulls the .45 out of his waistband.

Twist opens his eyes and stops pulling the trigger.

"It's over," he says.

He steps over Valentine's body and walks slowly between Cuba and Rocco without a word. He never bothers looking down at Valentine's body.

"Nigger," Cuba says in a low voice behind him. "Now I know you're fucked in the head."

Twist goes down the stairs alone, still holding the gun in both hands.

EPILOGUE

Twist is standing at the window on the second floor. The 9mm is still in his hand as he smokes the last Camel in the pack and looks down on Murray Street. The sun is low in the west and the street is quiet, although that peacefulness won't last. Sooner or later the cops will show up. Cars pass and voices carry from open windows and a few kids at the end of the block are pitching and hitting an old baseball, oblivious to the garage and everything inside it. Other kids skip rope and clap hands and dance on the sidewalk. Below the window the world goes on again like always. There is nothing different about this early evening. None of the people know anything about the quiet figure watching from the second floor and none of them would care if they did.

That voice Twist listens to still tells him that he can change his world, but it's not worth it anymore.

Twist holds Valentine's letter to his daughter and the photo of his brother as he looks out the window. There's a face in the glass that comes back at Twist. It's the stranger's face again. He knows that face and has seen it many times, and he recognizes everything about it. It's the same one that comes every time he turns, haunting his dreams and twisting them into nightmares. The expression he sees in the reflection is filled with fear and terror and he knows that the stranger has always been him. There was never any doubt about that.

He crumples the letter in his fist and lets it drop to the floor.

Twist stares at Malik's photo and holds it for a moment, then drops that to the floor with Valentine's letter.

ABOUT THE AUTHOR

Kevin Michaels is the author of the critically acclaimed debut novel *Lost Exit*, as well as two entries in the *Fight Card* book series: *Hard Road* and *Can't Miss Contender*. He also released a collection of short stories entitled *Nine In The Morning*. His short stories and flash fiction have also appeared in a number of magazines and indie zines, and in 2011 he was nominated for two separate Pushcart Prize awards for his short stories. Other shorts have been included in the anthologies for *Six Sentences* (volumes II and III) and *Action: Pulse Pounding Tales* (2).

He has also published a number non-fiction articles and stories in print publications ranging from the NYTimes.com and the Life/Style section of *The Boston Globe* to *The Bergen News and Press Journal* and raged in print at places like the *TriCity News, NY Daily News,* and *The Press.*

He is the Founder and Creative Director of Story Tellers which is a community-based organization that develops and promotes literacy through writing. Story Tellers provides under-served teenagers, young adults, and women from distressed situations the opportunity to discover the strength and power of their own voices (self-empowerment through self-expression).

Originally from New Jersey, he carries the attitude, edginess, and love of all things Bruce Springsteen common in his home state, although he left the Garden State to live and work in the foothills of the Appalachians (Georgia) with his wife, Helen and an assortment of children and pets.

http://kevinmichaelsfiction.com

APR 2 6 2018

~~ROTOR~~ 4/19

CPSIA information can be obtained
at www.ICGtesting.com
Printed in the USA
FSHW04n0756150418
47005FS